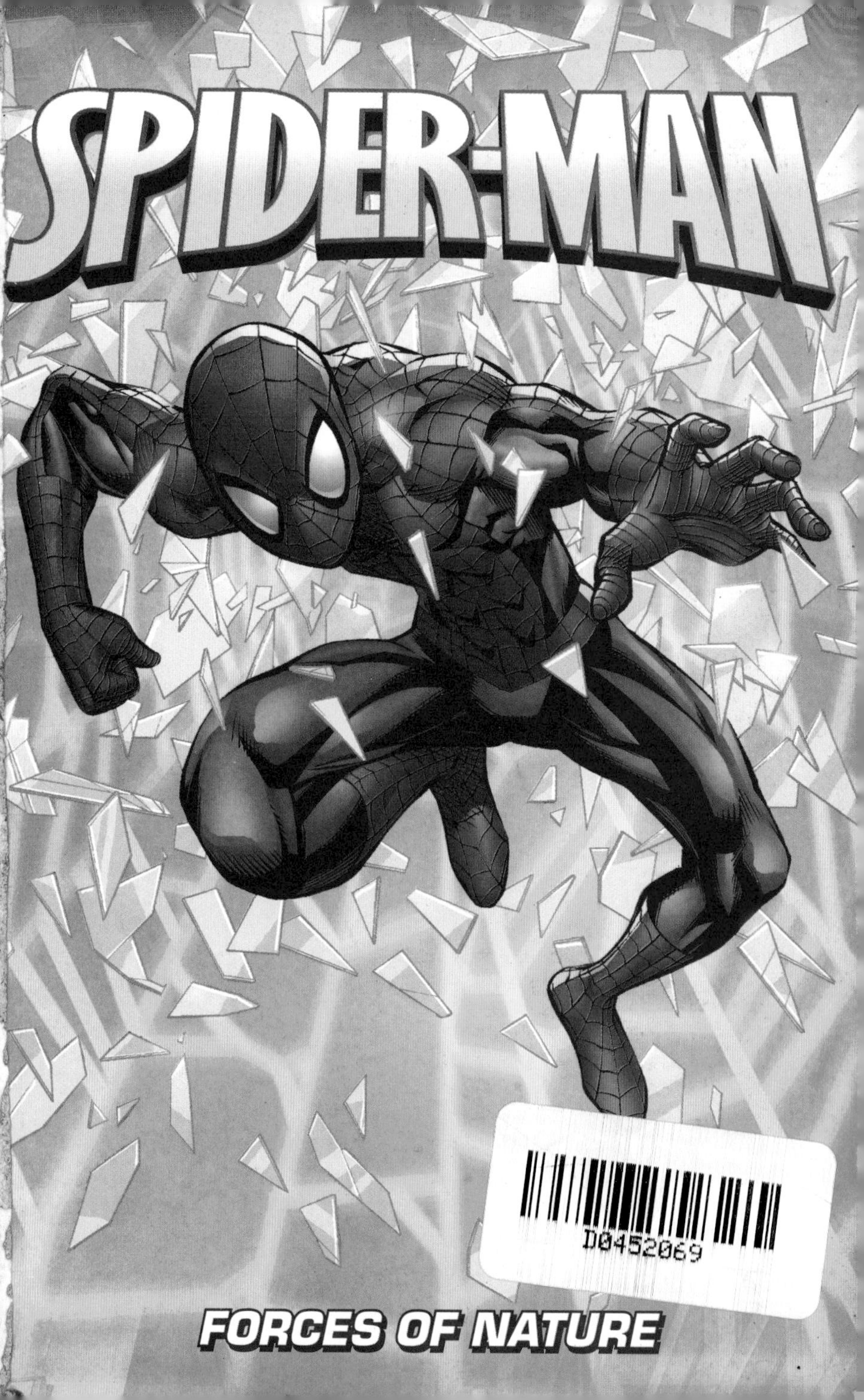
SPIDER-MAN
FORCES OF NATURE

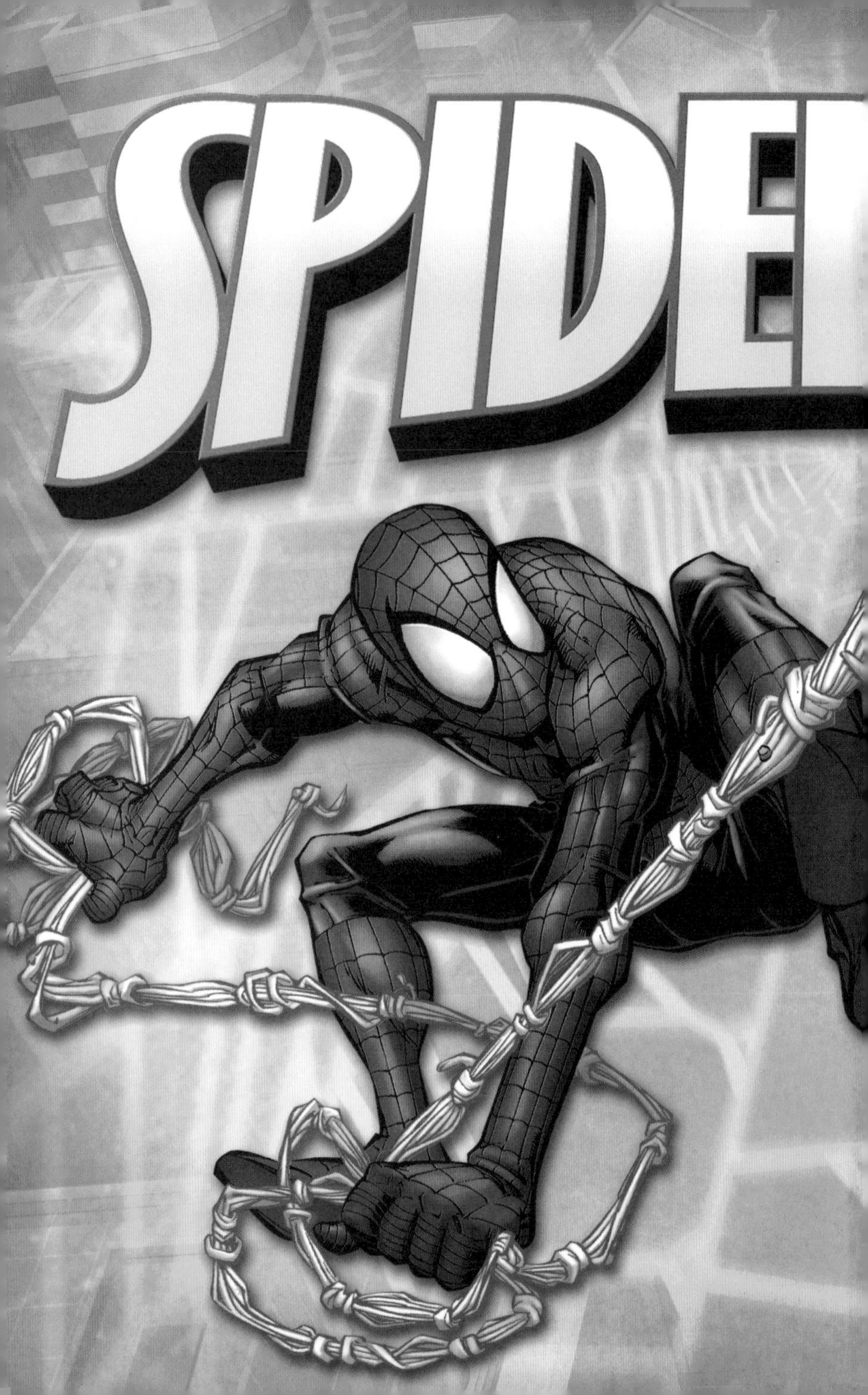
SPIDE

R-MAN

FORCES OF NATURE

Writer
Peter David
Pencils
Pop Mhan
Inks
Norman Lee
Colors
Guru eFX
Letters
Dave Sharpe
Cover Art: **Patrick Scherberger, Norman Lee
& Guru eFX**
Assistant Editor: **Nathan Cosby**
Editor: **Mark Paniccia**

Collection Editor: **Jennifer Grünwald**
Assistant Editors: **Cory Levine & John Denning**
Associate Editor: **Mark D. Beazley**
Senior Editor, Special Projects: **Jeff Youngquist**
Senior Vice President of Sales: **David Gabriel**
Vice President of Creative: **Tom Marvelli**

Editor in Chief: **Joe Quesada**
Publisher: **Dan Buckley**

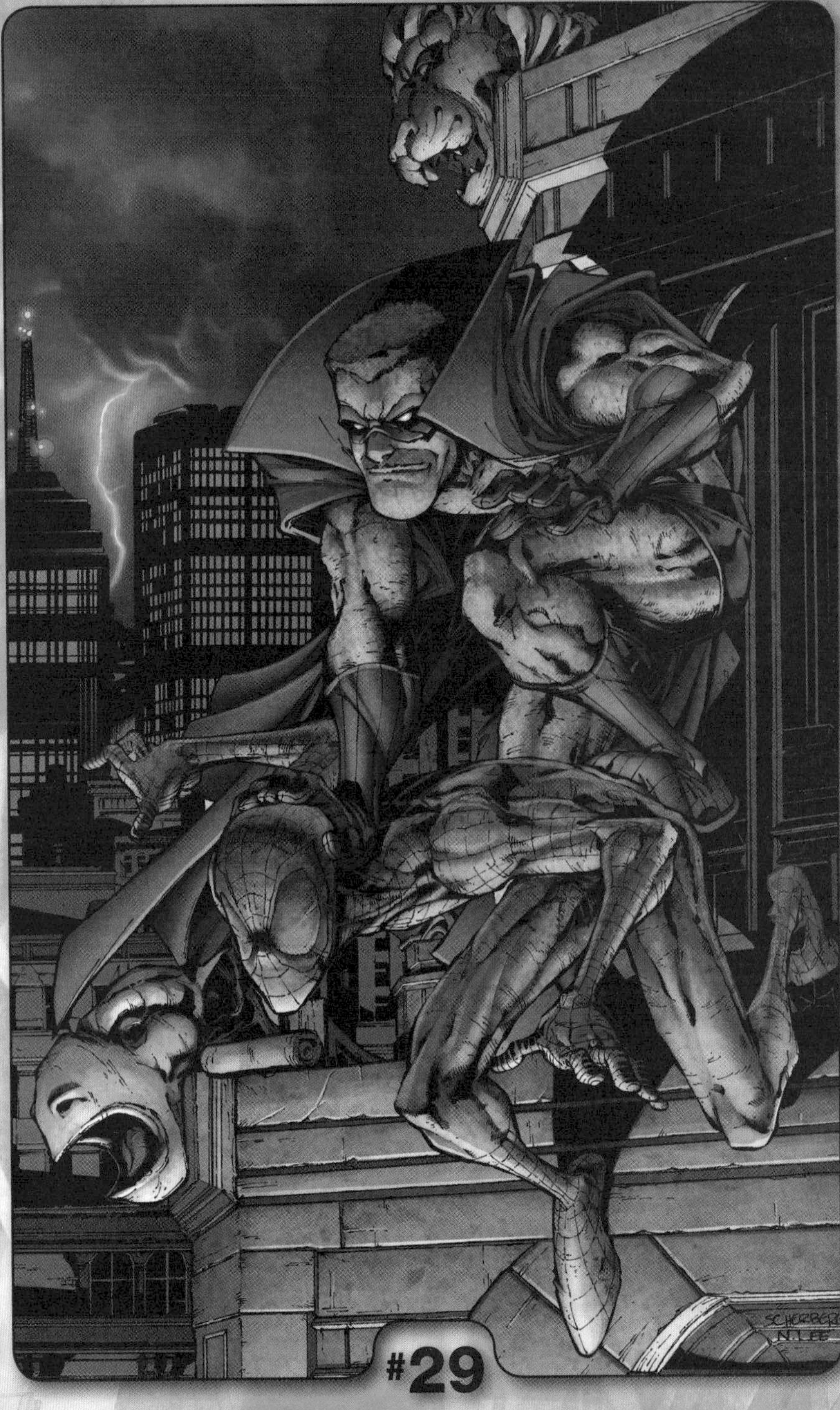
N. LEE
#29

BITTEN BY AN IRRADIATED SPIDER, WHICH GRANTED HIM INCREDIBLE ABILITIES, **PETER PARKER** LEARNED THE ALL-IMPORTANT LESSON, THAT WITH GREAT POWER THERE MUST ALSO COME GREAT RESPONSIBILITY. AND SO HE BECAME THE AMAZING **SPIDER-MAN**

Spider-Man may have thought that he's had some rocky encounters before...

...but nothing's prepared him for going head-to-head with a villain whose very touch could turn him into a stone statue for the rest of his life!

One wrong move and Spidey is going to become a permanent part of the Manhattan Museum of Art's collection!

You'd think that, just once, Peter Parker could go on a class trip and not have everything go wrong.

Unfortunately, this time was no different than any other...

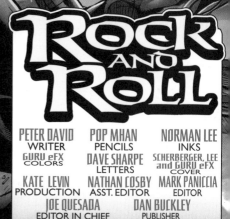

ROCK AND ROLL

PETER DAVID
WRITER

POP MHAN
PENCILS

NORMAN LEE
INKS

GURU eFX
COLORS

DAVE SHARPE
LETTERS

SCHERBERGER, LEE and GURU eFX
COVER

KATE LEVIN
PRODUCTION

NATHAN COSBY
ASST. EDITOR

MARK PANICCIA
EDITOR

JOE QUESADA
EDITOR IN CHIEF

DAN BUCKLEY
PUBLISHER

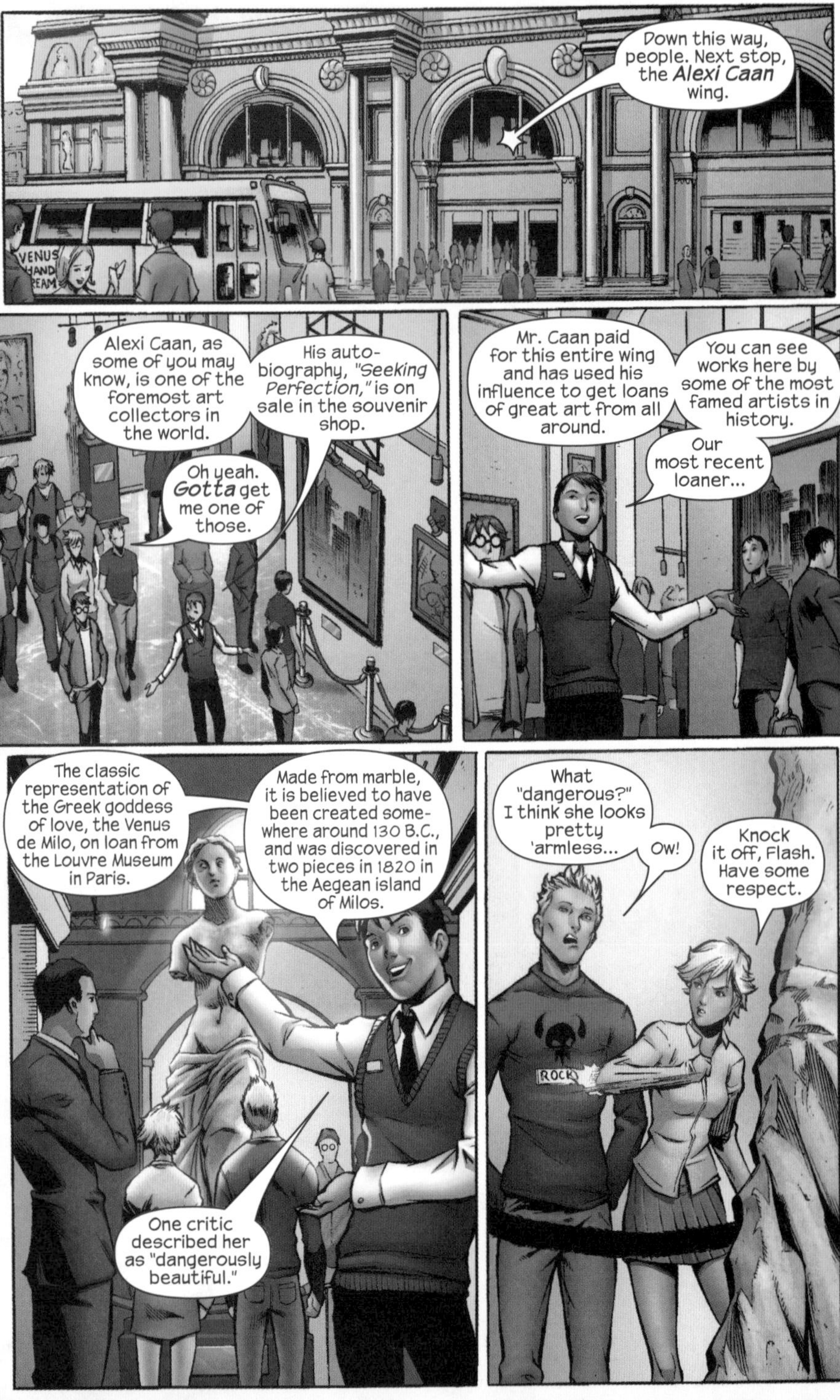

VENUS HAND CREAM
Down this way, people. Next stop, the *Alexi Caan* wing.
Alexi Caan, as some of you may know, is one of the foremost art collectors in the world.
His auto-biography, "*Seeking Perfection,*" is on sale in the souvenir shop.
Oh yeah. *Gotta* get me one of those.
Mr. Caan paid for this entire wing and has used his influence to get loans of great art from all around.
You can see works here by some of the most famed artists in history.
Our most recent loaner...
The classic representation of the Greek goddess of love, the Venus de Milo, on loan from the Louvre Museum in Paris.
Made from marble, it is believed to have been created some-where around 130 B.C., and was discovered in two pieces in 1820 in the Aegean island of Milos.
One critic described her as "dangerously beautiful."
What "dangerous?" I think she looks pretty 'armless...
Ow!
Knock it off, Flash. Have some respect.
ROCK

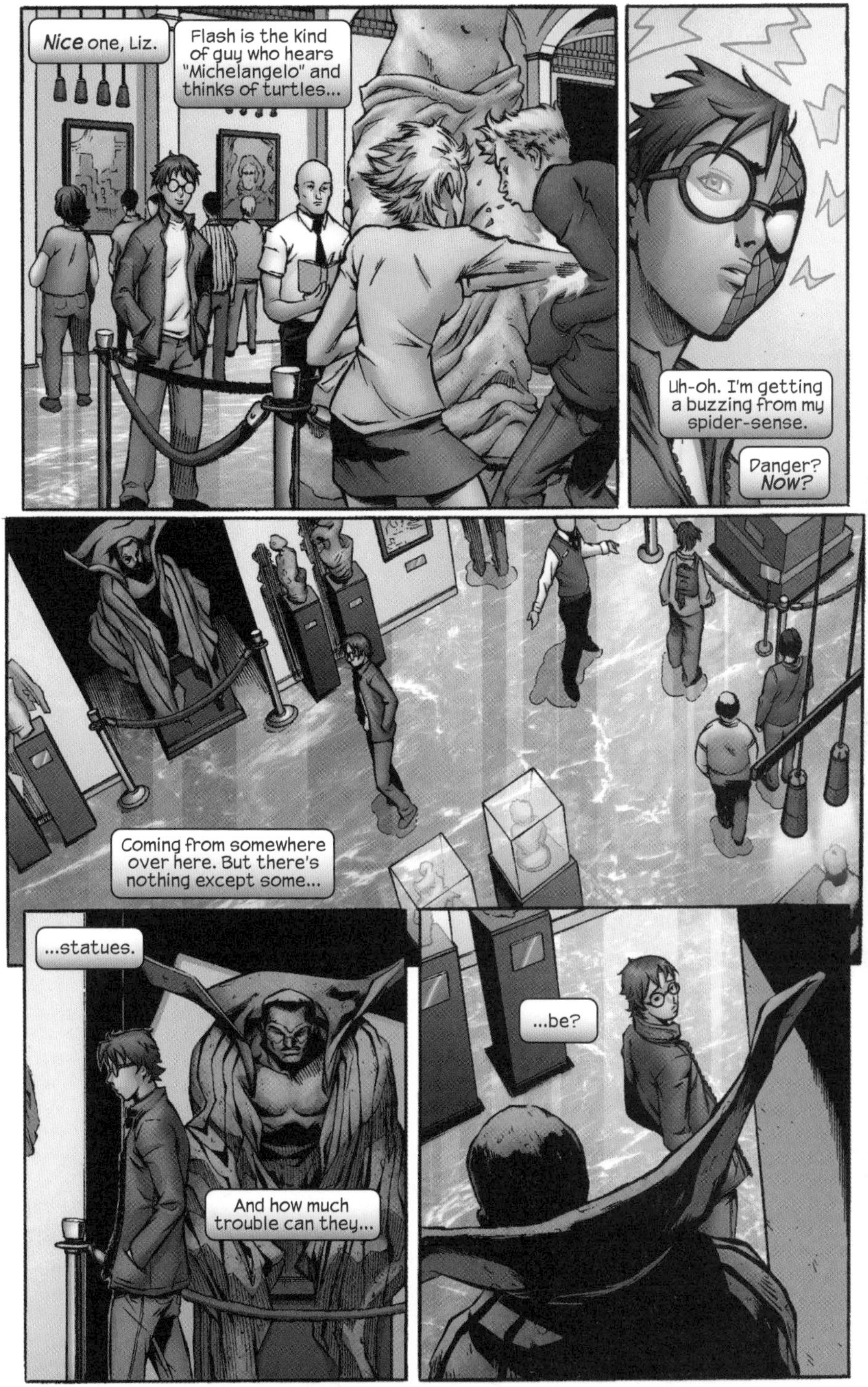
Nice one, Liz.
Flash is the kind of guy who hears "Michelangelo" and thinks of turtles...
Uh-oh. I'm getting a buzzing from my spider-sense.
Danger? NOW?
Coming from somewhere over here. But there's nothing except some...
...statues.
And how much trouble can they...
...be?

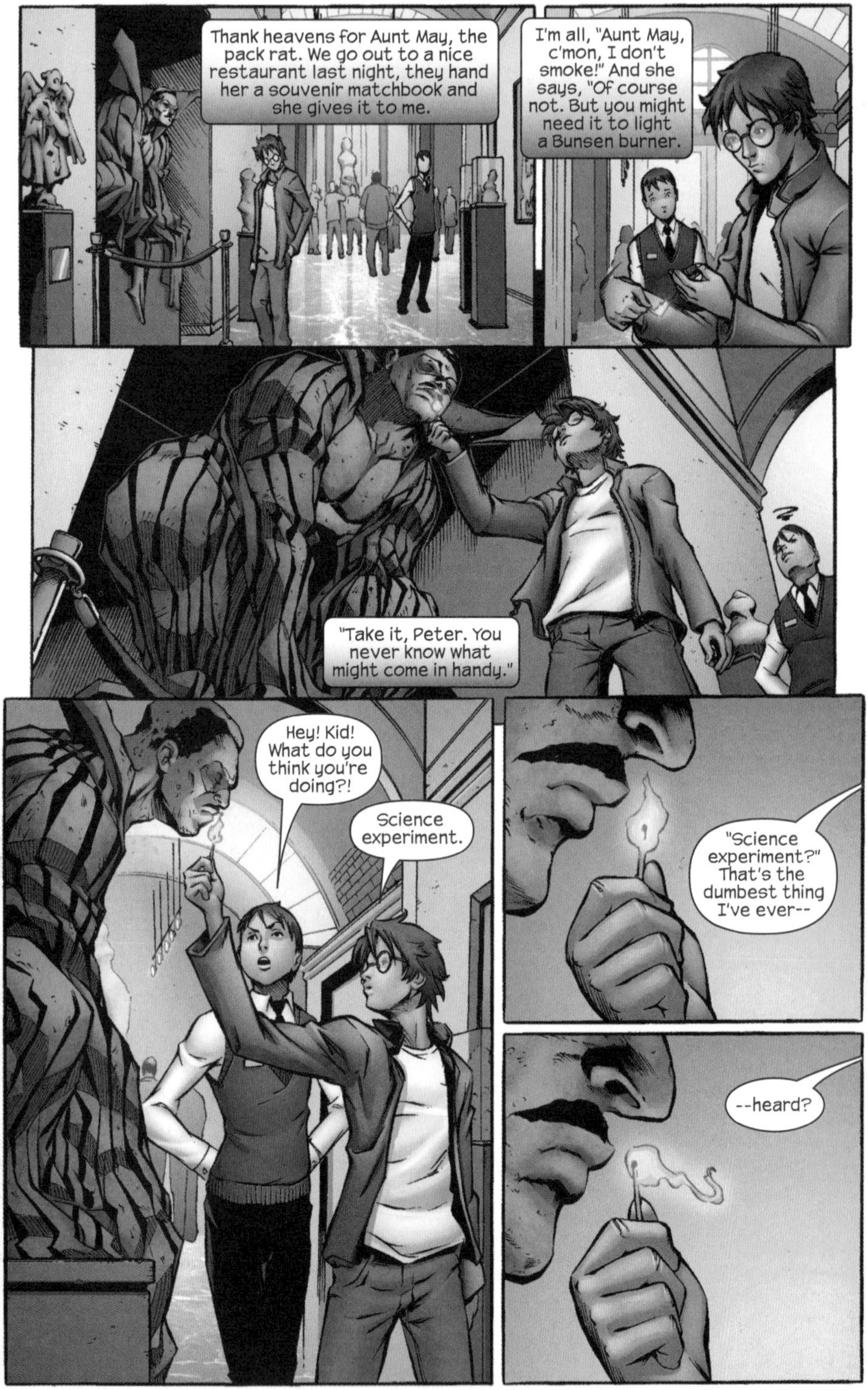
Thank heavens for Aunt May, the pack rat. We go out to a nice restaurant last night, they hand her a souvenir matchbook and she gives it to me.
I'm all, "Aunt May, c'mon, I don't smoke!" And she says, "Of course not. But you might need it to light a Bunsen burner.
"Take it, Peter. You never know what might come in handy."
Hey! Kid! What do you think you're doing?!
Science experiment.
"Science experiment?" That's the dumbest thing I've ever--
--heard?

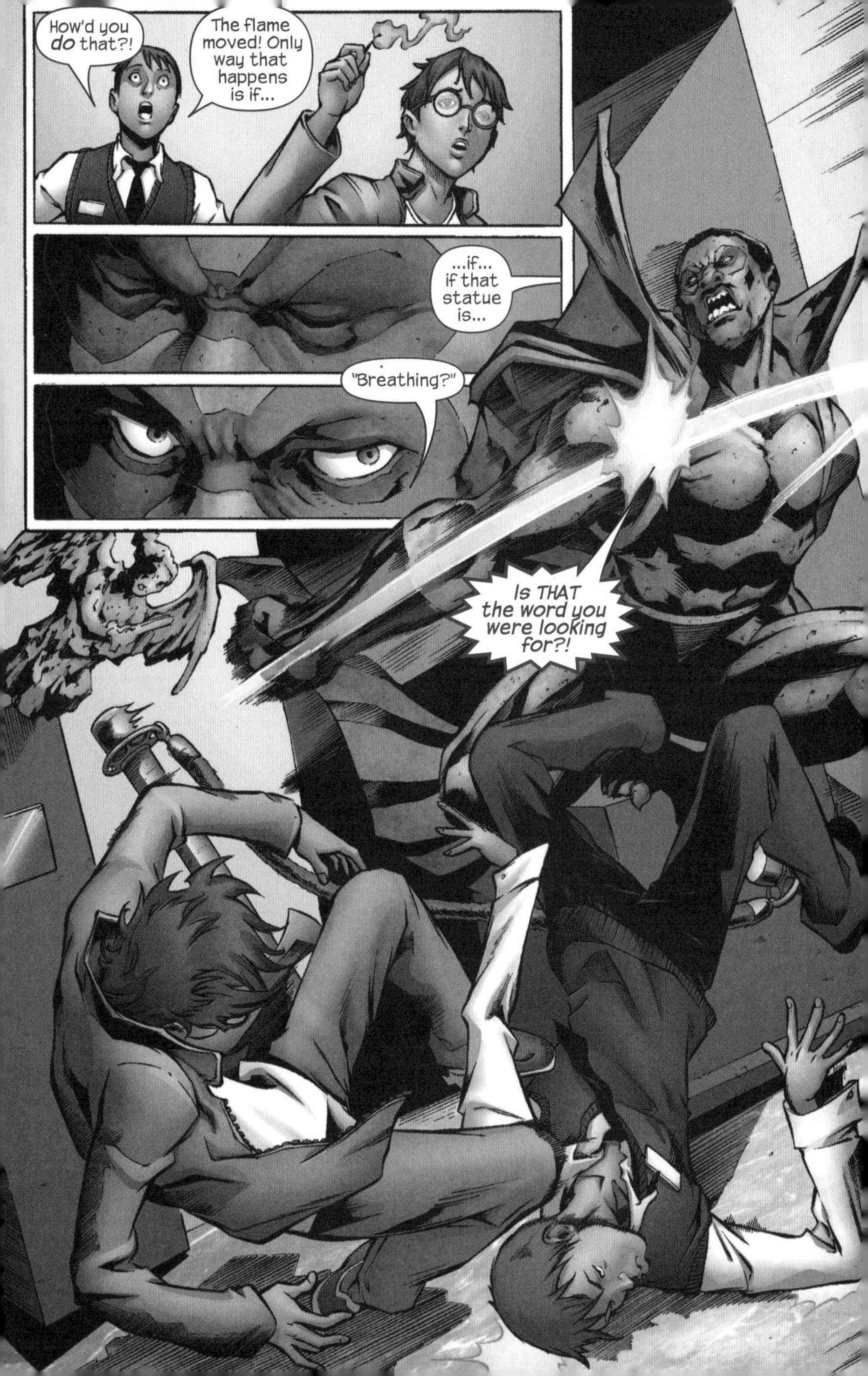
How'd you do that?!
The flame moved! Only way that happens is if...
...if... if that statue is...
"Breathing?"
Is THAT the word you were looking for?!

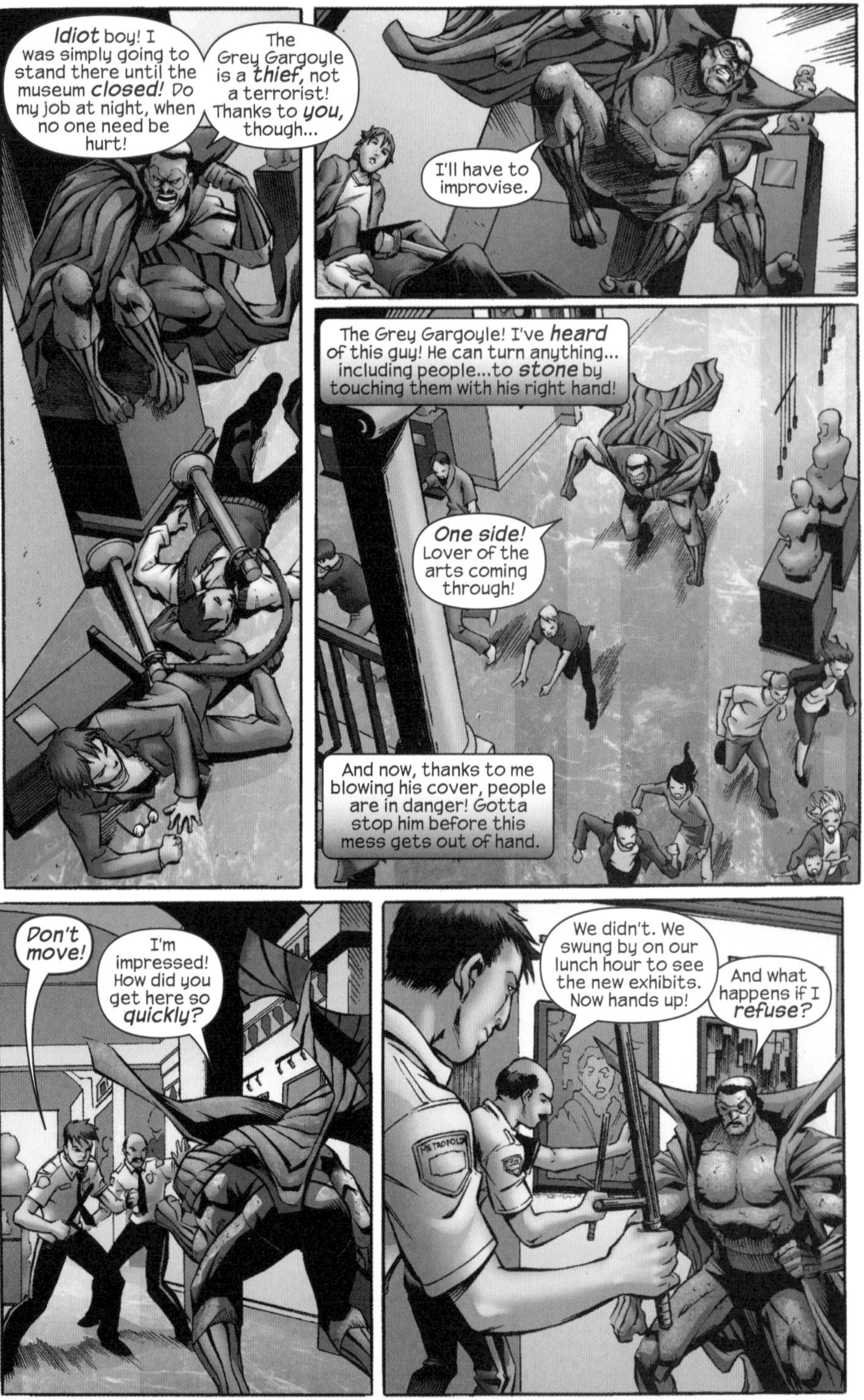
Idiot boy! I was simply going to stand there until the museum closed! Do my job at night, when no one need be hurt!
The Grey Gargoyle is a thief, not a terrorist! Thanks to you, though...
I'll have to improvise.
The Grey Gargoyle! I've heard of this guy! He can turn anything... including people...to stone by touching them with his right hand!
One side! Lover of the arts coming through!
And now, thanks to me blowing his cover, people are in danger! Gotta stop him before this mess gets out of hand.
Don't move!
I'm impressed! How did you get here so quickly?
We didn't. We swung by on our lunch hour to see the new exhibits. Now hands up!
And what happens if I refuse?
METROPOLI

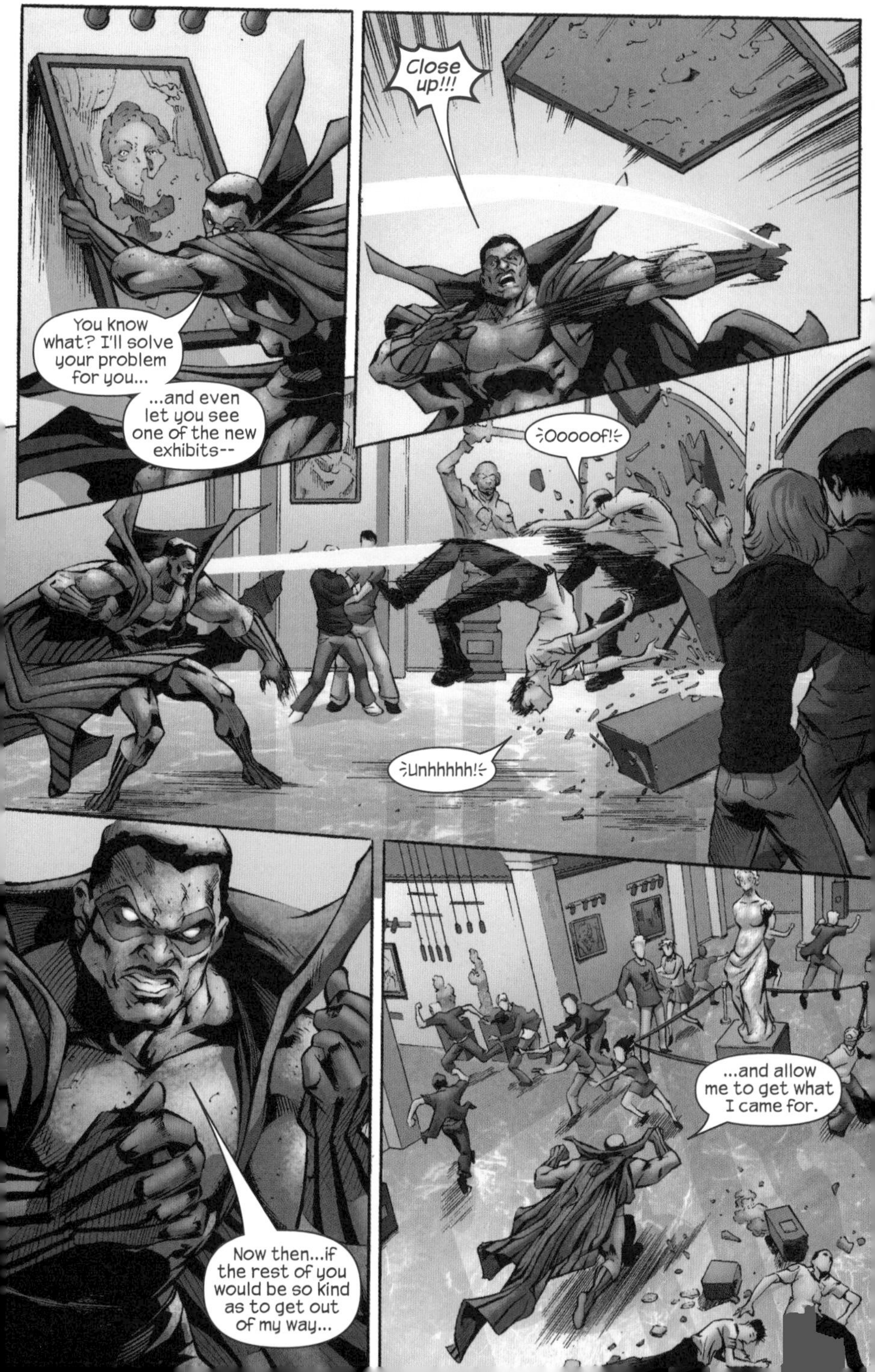
You know what? I'll solve your problem for you...
...and even let you see one of the new exhibits--
Close up!!!
Ooooof!
Unhhhhh!
Now then...if the rest of you would be so kind as to get out of my way...
...and allow me to get what I came for.

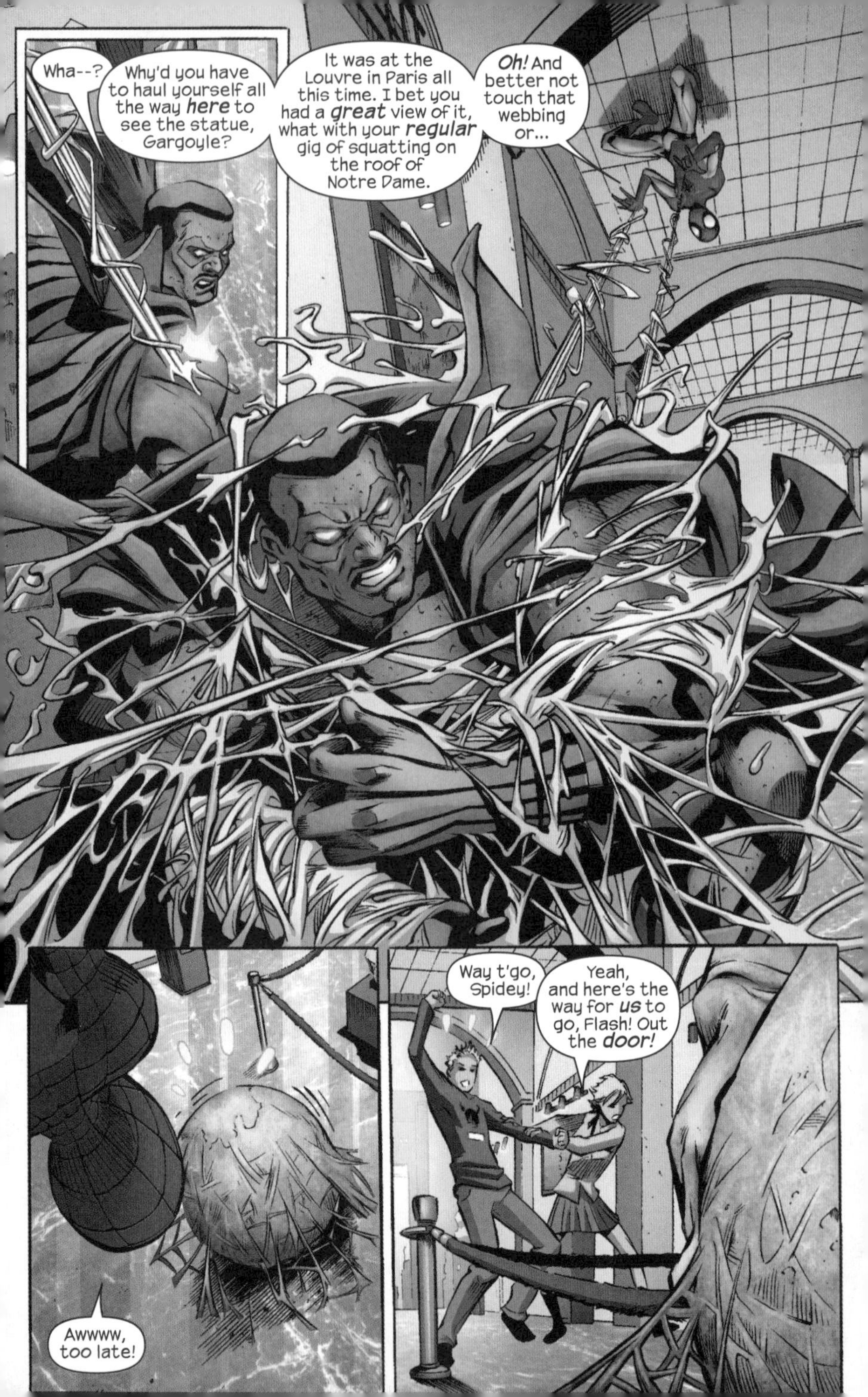
Wha--?
Why'd you have to haul yourself all the way here to see the statue, Gargoyle?
It was at the Louvre in Paris all this time. I bet you had a great view of it, what with your regular gig of squatting on the roof of Notre Dame.
Oh! And better not touch that webbing or...
Awwww, too late!
Way t'go, Spidey!
Yeah, and here's the way for us to go, Flash! Out the door!

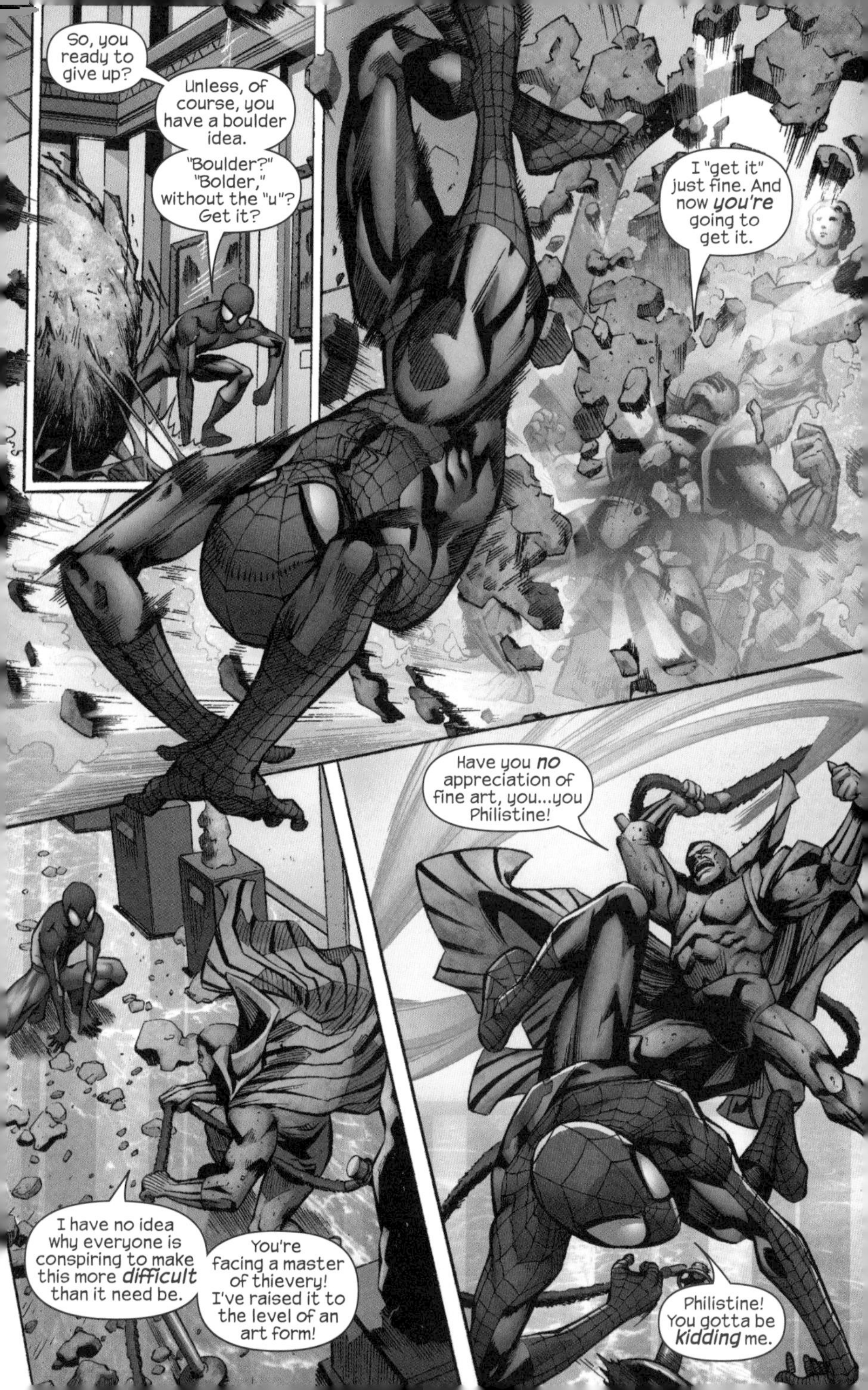

So, you ready to give up?
Unless, of course, you have a boulder idea.
"Boulder?" "Bolder," without the "u"? Get it?
I "get it" just fine. And now *you're* going to get it.
I have no idea why everyone is conspiring to make this more *difficult* than it need be.
You're facing a master of thievery! I've raised it to the level of an art form!
Have you *no* appreciation of fine art, you...you Philistine!
Philistine! You gotta be *kidding* me.

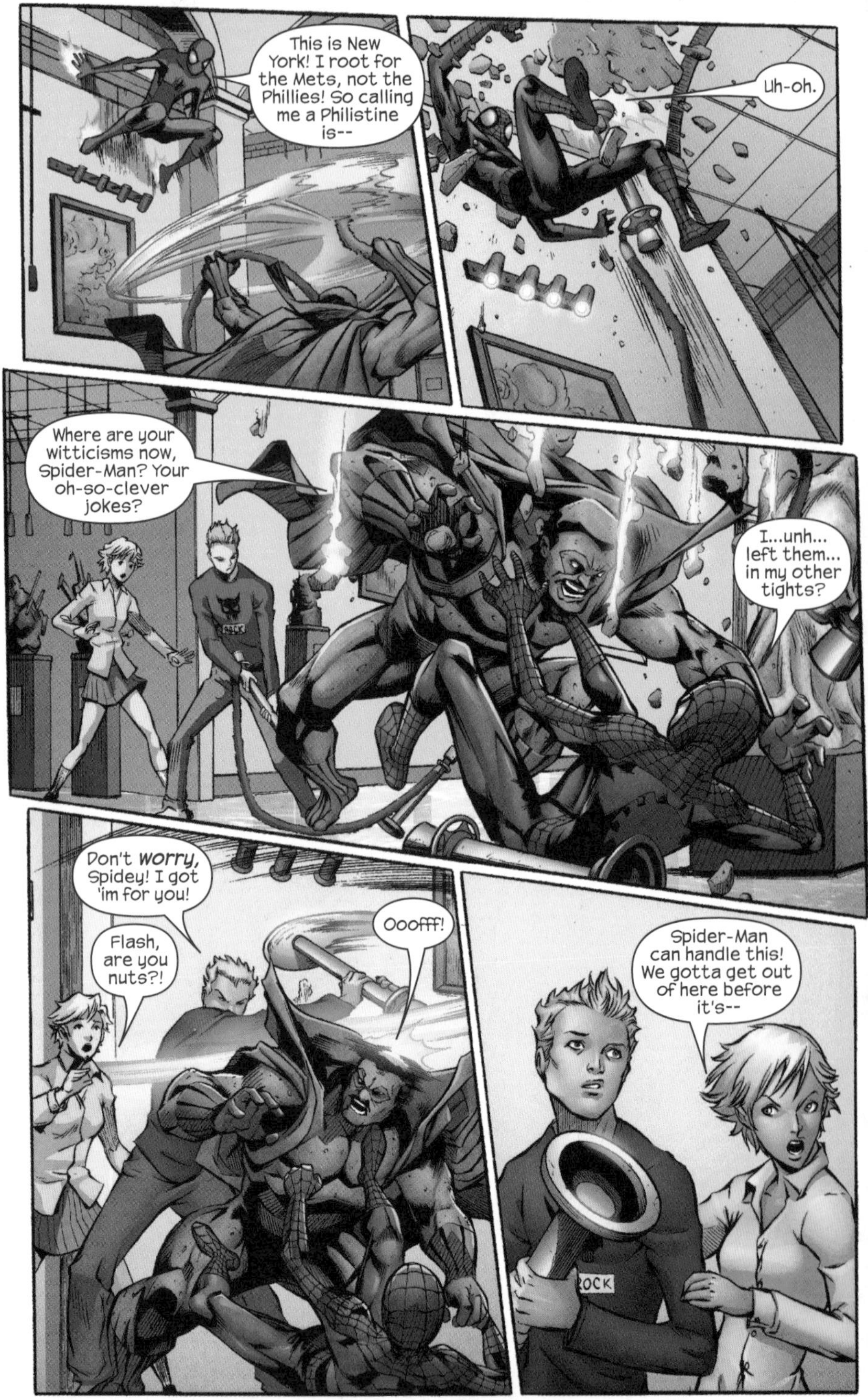
This is New York! I root for the Mets, not the Phillies! So calling me a Philistine is--
Uh-oh.
Where are your witticisms now, Spider-Man? Your oh-so-clever jokes?
I...unh... left them... in my other tights?
ROCK
Don't *worry,* Spidey! I got 'im for you!
Flash, are you nuts?!
Ooofff!
Spider-Man can handle this! We gotta get out of here before it's--
ROCK

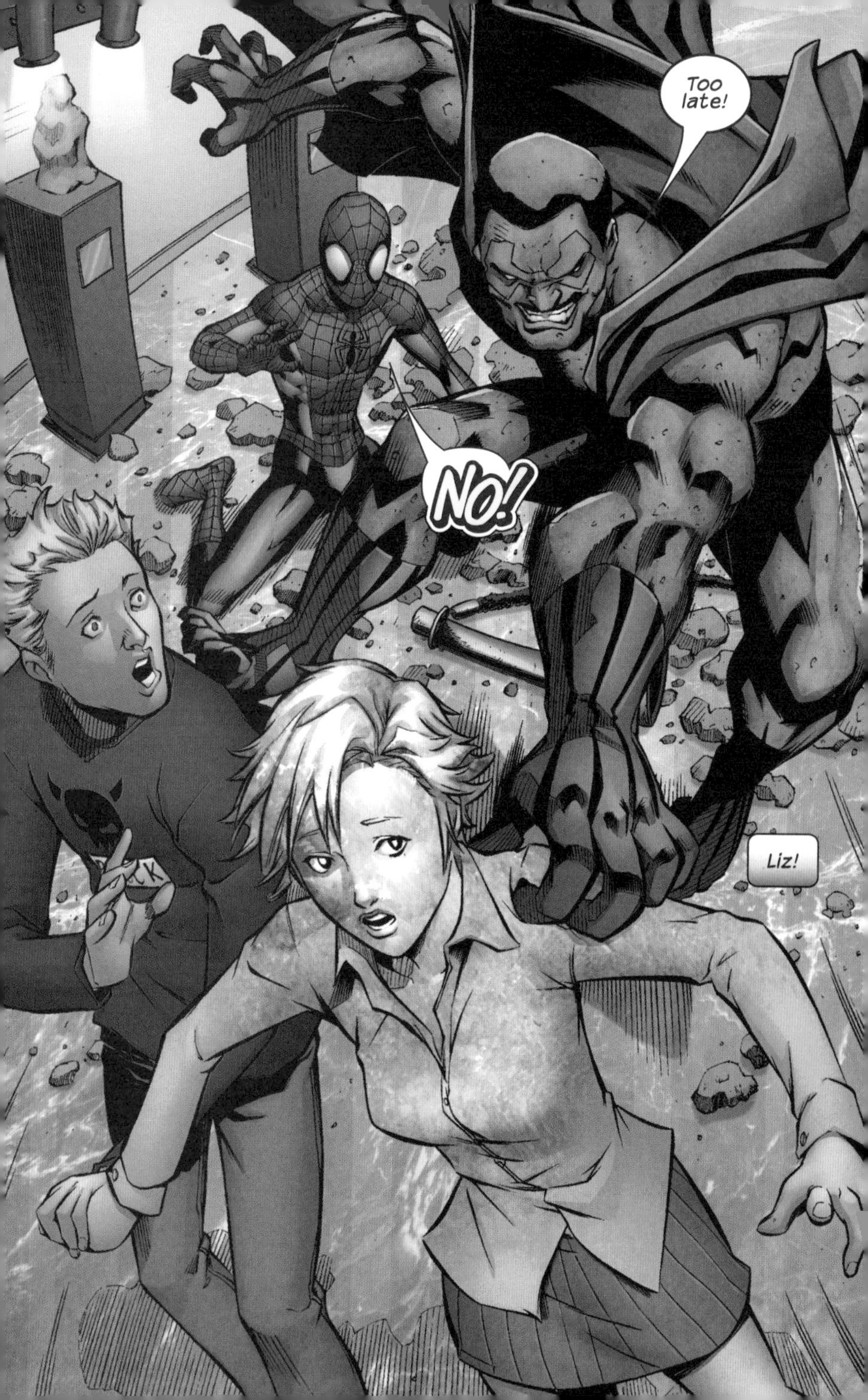
Too late!
NO!
Liz!

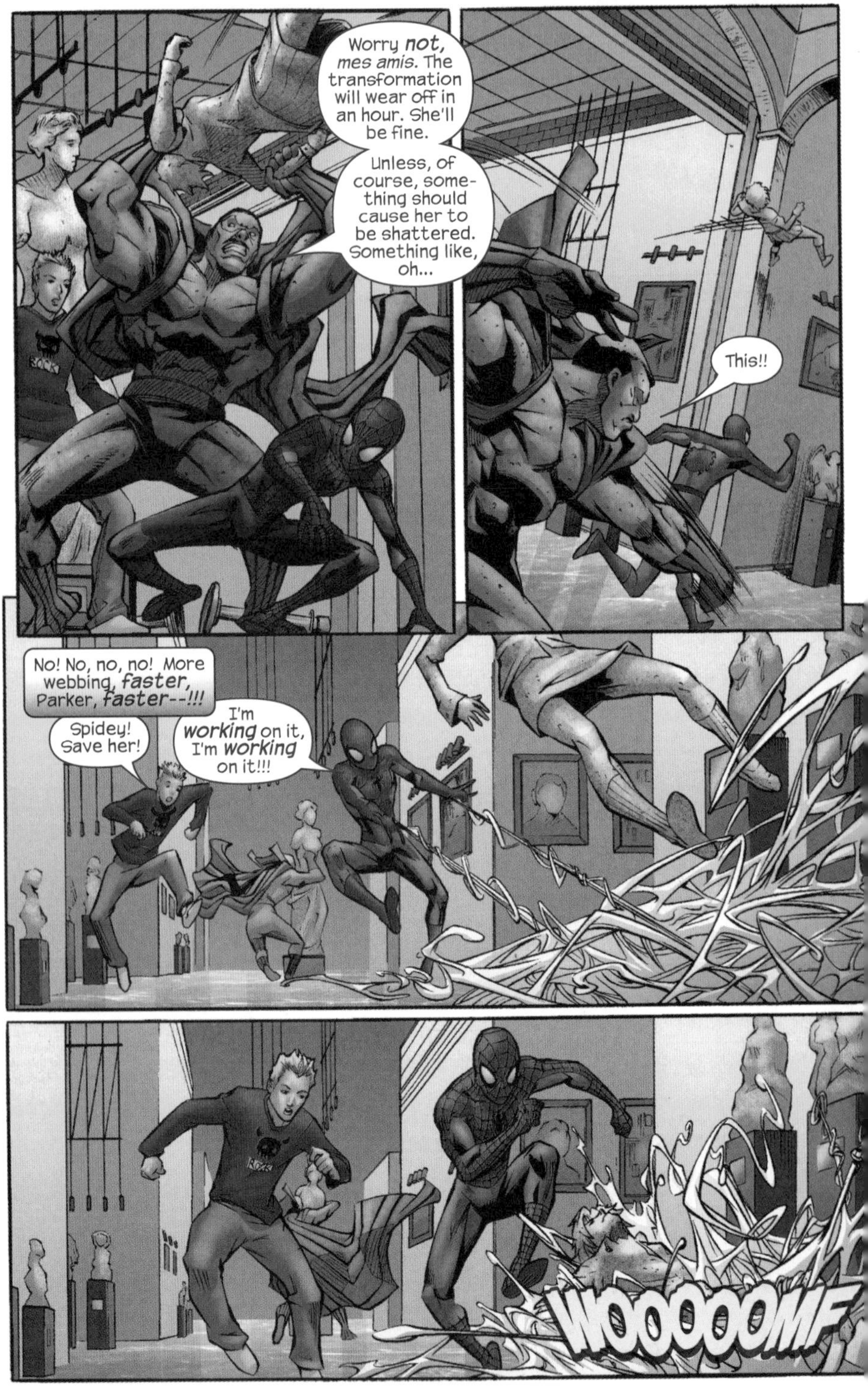
Worry *not*, *mes amis*. The transformation will wear off in an hour. She'll be fine.
Unless, of course, some-thing should cause her to be shattered. Something like, oh...
This!!
No! No, no, no! More webbing, *faster*, Parker, *faster*--!!!
Spidey! Save her!
I'm *working* on it, I'm *working* on it!!!
WOOOOOOMF

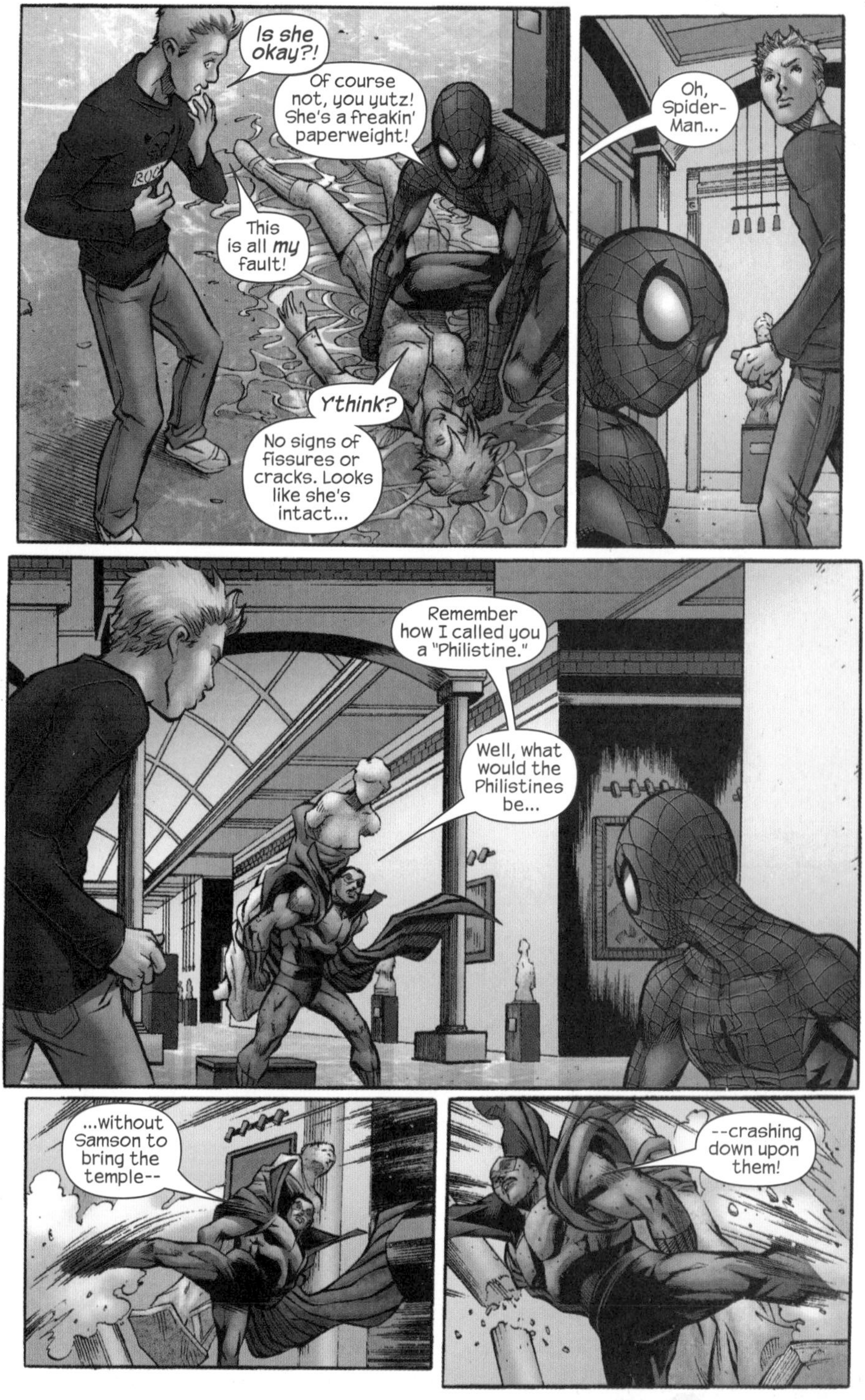
Is she okay?!
Of course not, you yutz! She's a freakin' paperweight!
This is all my fault!
Y'think?
No signs of fissures or cracks. Looks like she's intact...
Oh, Spider-Man...
Remember how I called you a "Philistine."
Well, what would the Philistines be...
...without Samson to bring the temple--
--crashing down upon them!

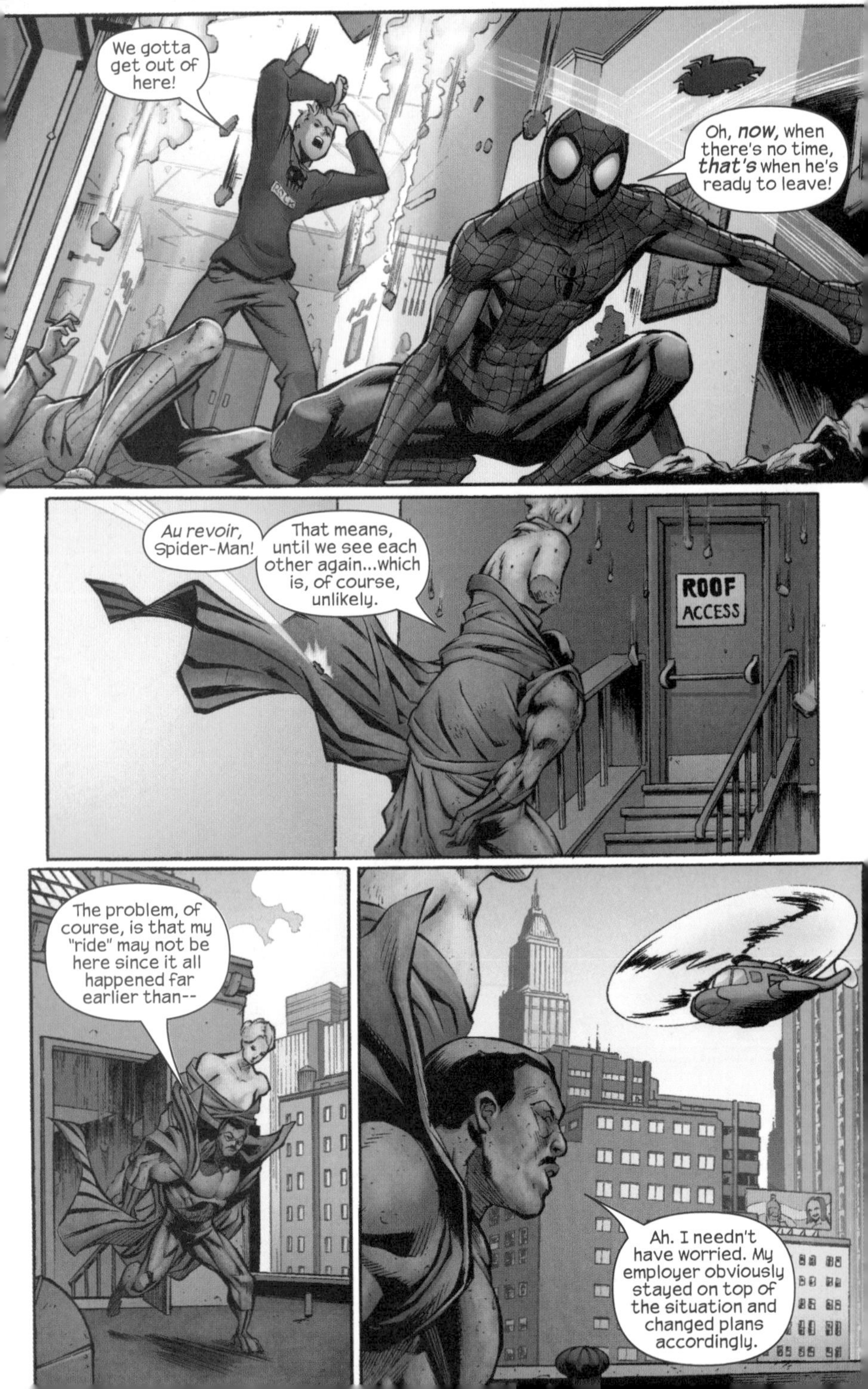

We gotta get out of here!
Oh, *now*, when there's no time, *that's* when he's ready to leave!
Au revoir, Spider-Man!
That means, until we see each other again...which is, of course, unlikely.
ROOF ACCESS
The problem, of course, is that my "ride" may not be here since it all happened far earlier than--
Ah. I needn't have worried. My employer obviously stayed on top of the situation and changed plans accordingly.

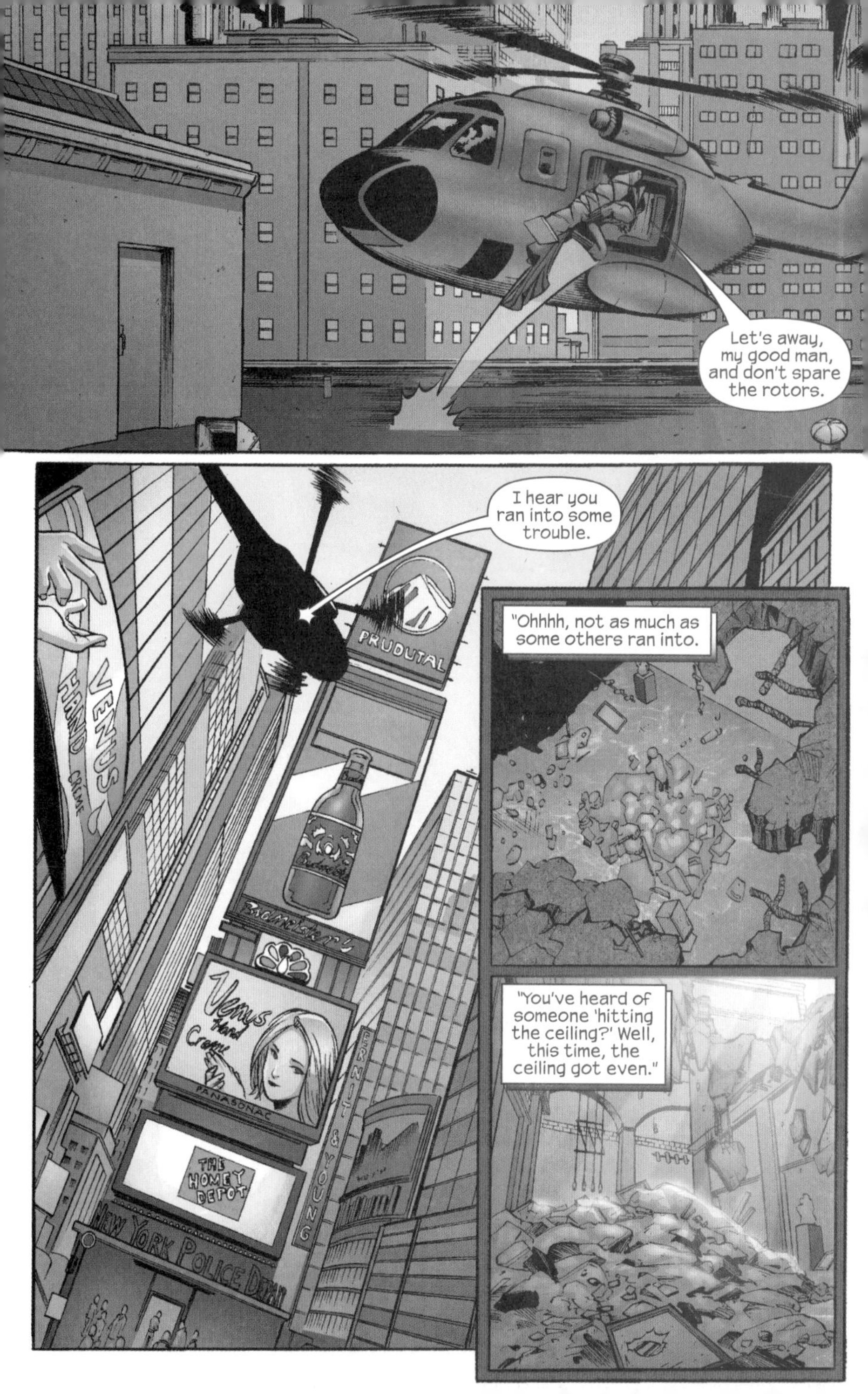
Let's away, my good man, and don't spare the rotors.
I hear you ran into some trouble.
"Ohhhh, not as much as some others ran into.
"You've heard of someone 'hitting the ceiling?' Well, this time, the ceiling got even."
VENUS HAND CRÈME
PRUDUTAL
PANASONAC
THE HOMEY DEPOT
NEW YORK POLICE DEPART

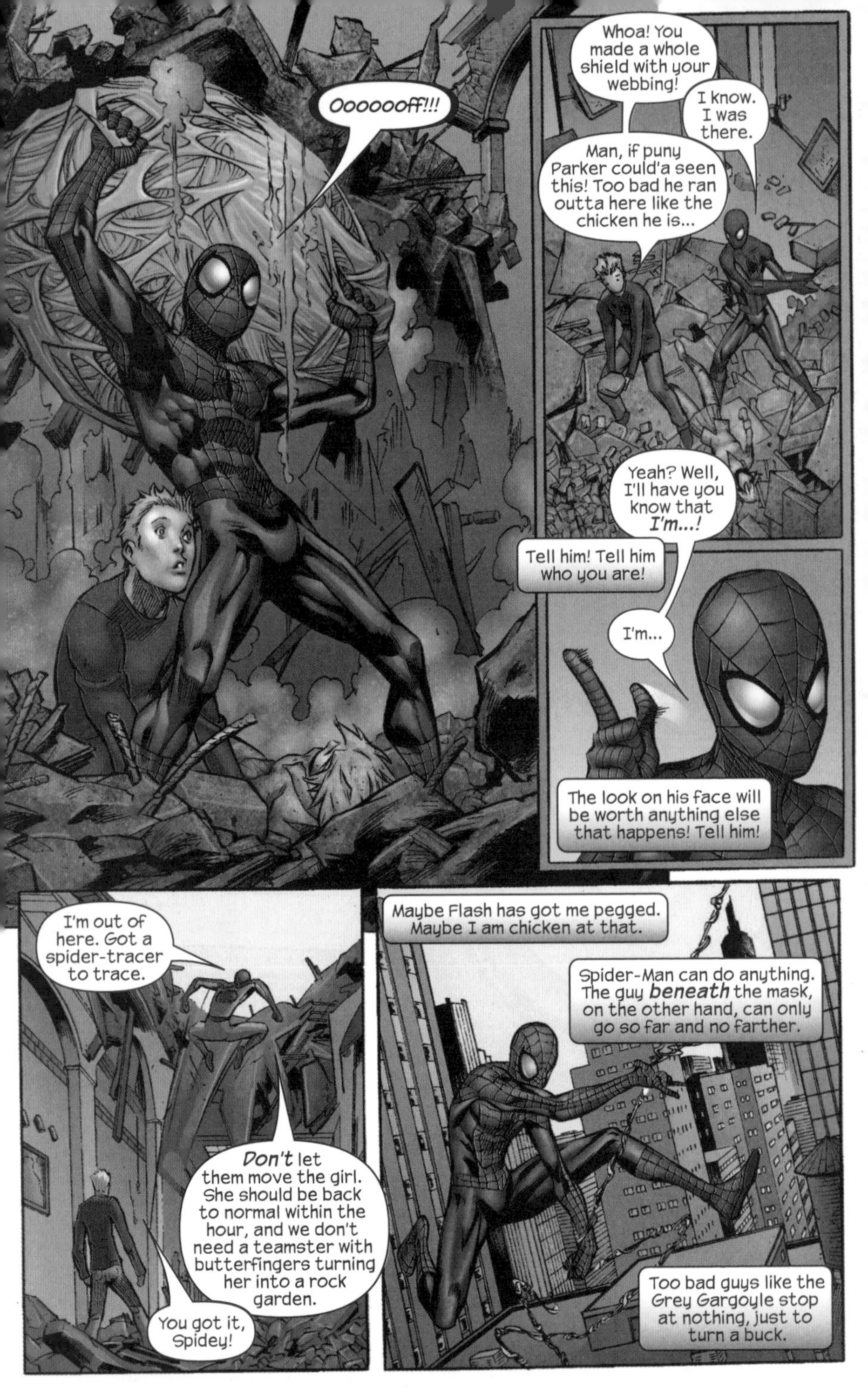
Ooooooff!!!
Whoa! You made a whole shield with your webbing!
I know. I was there.
Man, if puny Parker could'a seen this! Too bad he ran outta here like the chicken he is...
Yeah? Well, I'll have you know that I'm...!
Tell him! Tell him who you are!
I'm...
The look on his face will be worth anything else that happens! Tell him!
I'm out of here. Got a spider-tracer to trace.
Don't let them move the girl. She should be back to normal within the hour, and we don't need a teamster with butterfingers turning her into a rock garden.
You got it, Spidey!
Maybe Flash has got me pegged. Maybe I am chicken at that.
Spider-Man can do anything. The guy beneath the mask, on the other hand, can only go so far and no farther.
Too bad guys like the Grey Gargoyle stop at nothing, just to turn a buck.

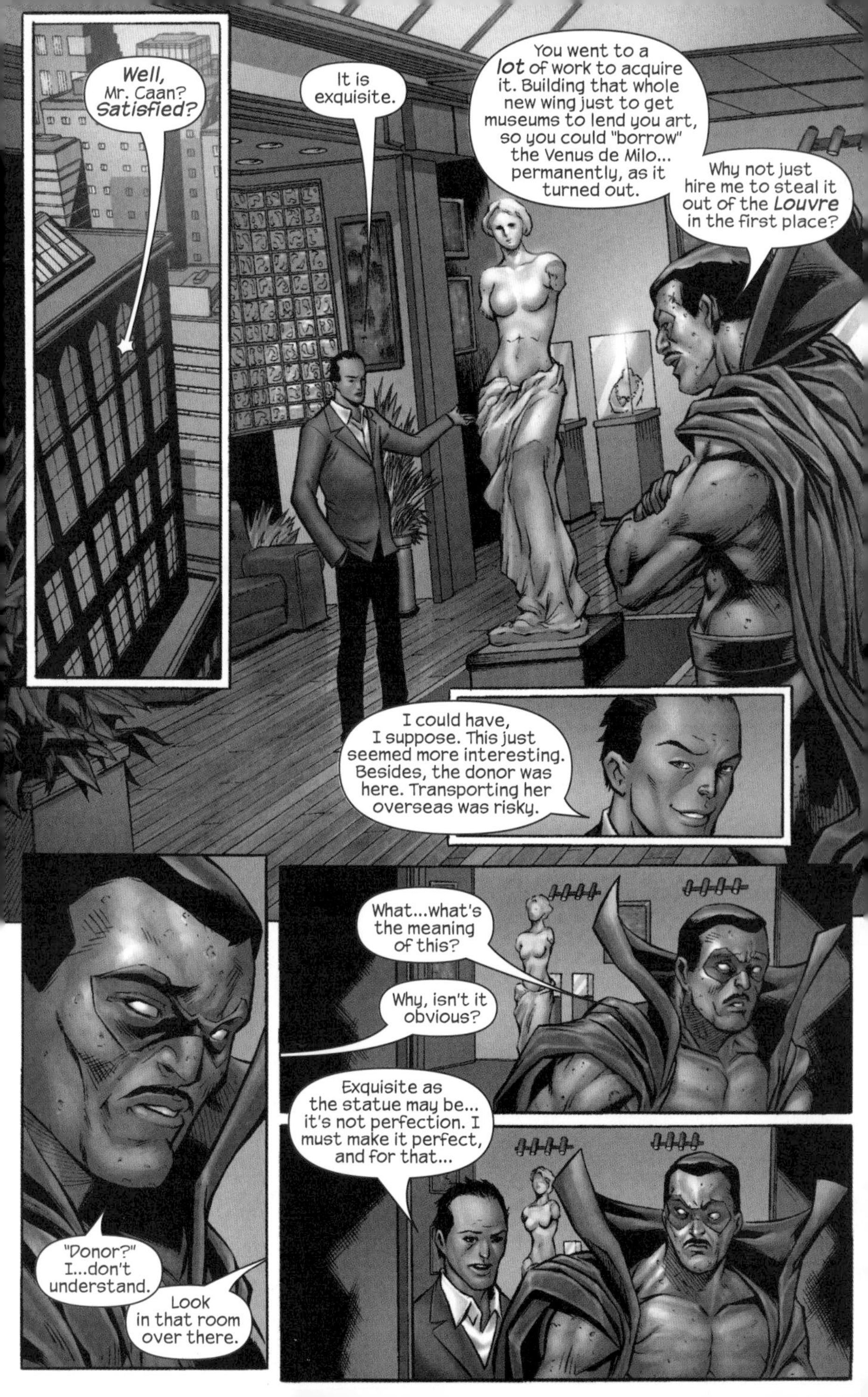
Well, Mr. Caan? Satisfied?
It is exquisite.
You went to a lot of work to acquire it. Building that whole new wing just to get museums to lend you art, so you could "borrow" the Venus de Milo... permanently, as it turned out.
Why not just hire me to steal it out of the Louvre in the first place?
I could have, I suppose. This just seemed more interesting. Besides, the donor was here. Transporting her overseas was risky.
"Donor?" I...don't understand.
Look in that room over there.
What...what's the meaning of this?
Why, isn't it obvious?
Exquisite as the statue may be... it's not perfection. I must make it perfect, and for that...

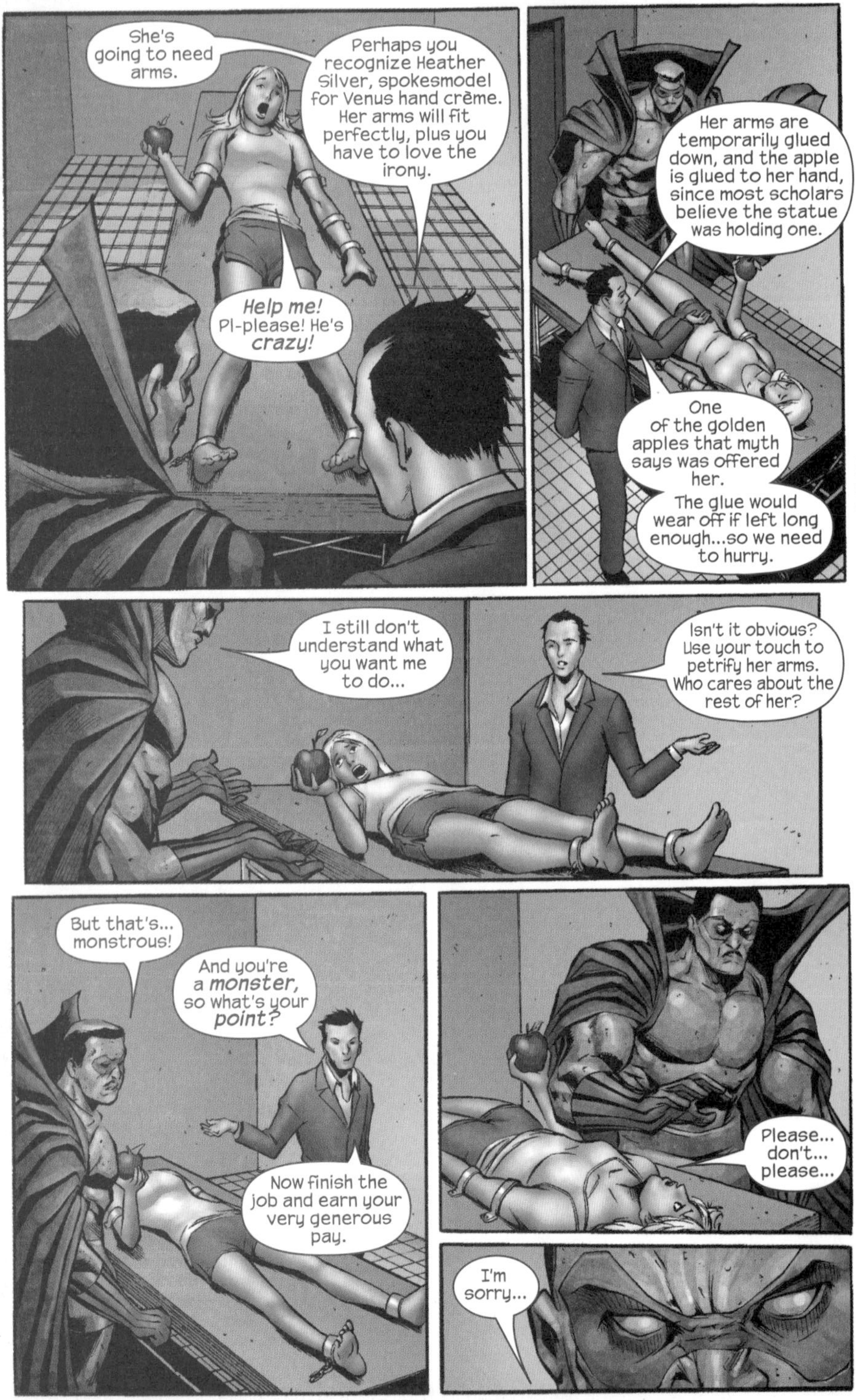
She's going to need arms.
Perhaps you recognize Heather Silver, spokesmodel for Venus hand crème. Her arms will fit perfectly, plus you have to love the irony.
Help me! Pl-please! He's crazy!
Her arms are temporarily glued down, and the apple is glued to her hand, since most scholars believe the statue was holding one.
One of the golden apples that myth says was offered her.
The glue would wear off if left long enough...so we need to hurry.
I still don't understand what you want me to do...
Isn't it obvious? Use your touch to petrify her arms. Who cares about the rest of her?
But that's... monstrous!
And you're a monster, so what's your point?
Now finish the job and earn your very generous pay.
Please... don't... please...
I'm sorry...

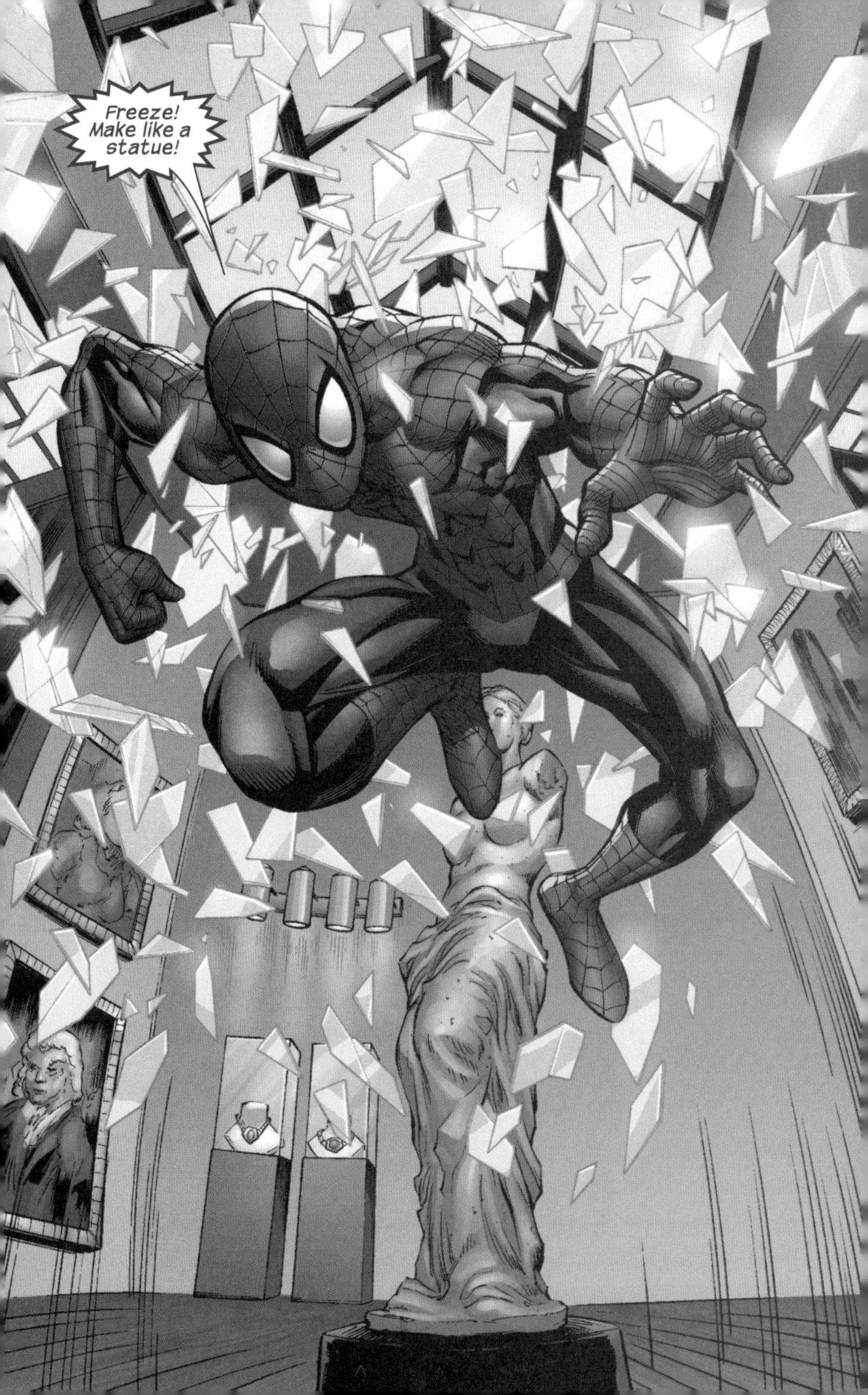
Freeze! Make like a statue!

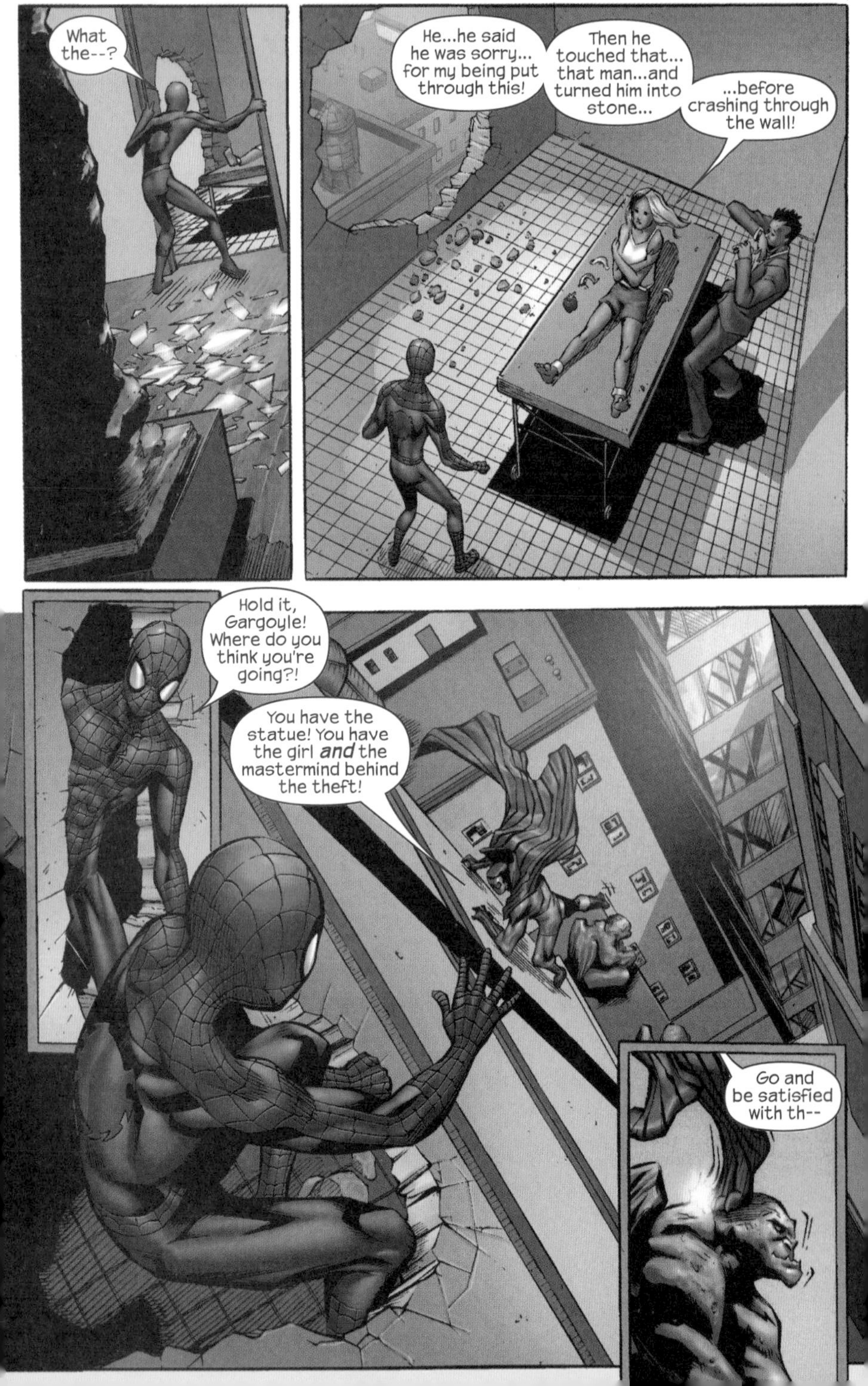
What the--?
He...he said he was sorry... for my being put through this!
Then he touched that... that man...and turned him into stone...
...before crashing through the wall!
Hold it, Gargoyle! Where do you think you're going?!
You have the statue! You have the girl *and* the mastermind behind the theft!
Go and be satisfied with th--

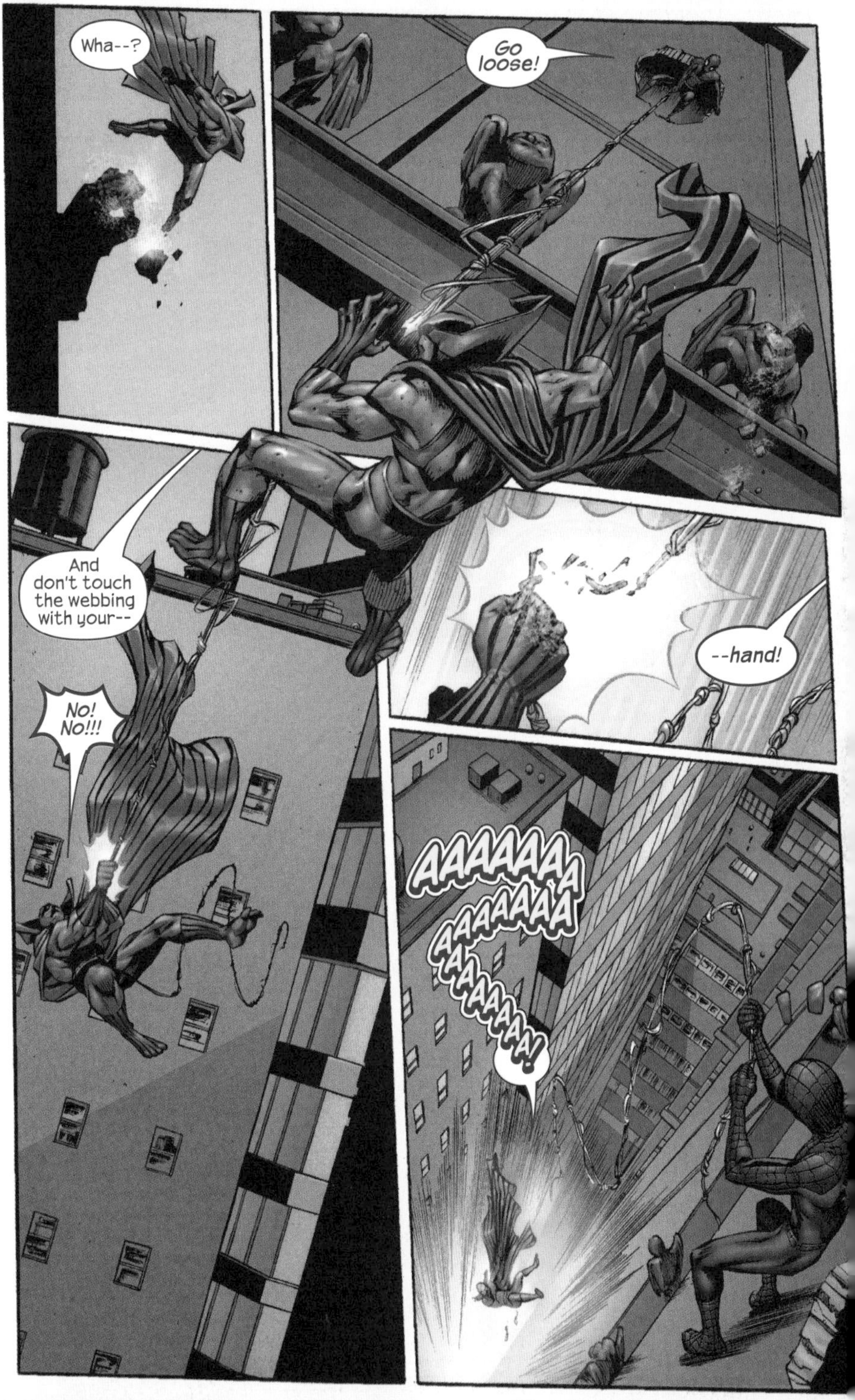
Wha--?
Go loose!
And don't touch the webbing with your--
No! No!!!
--hand!
AAAAAAAAAAAAAAAAAAAAAAAAAAA!

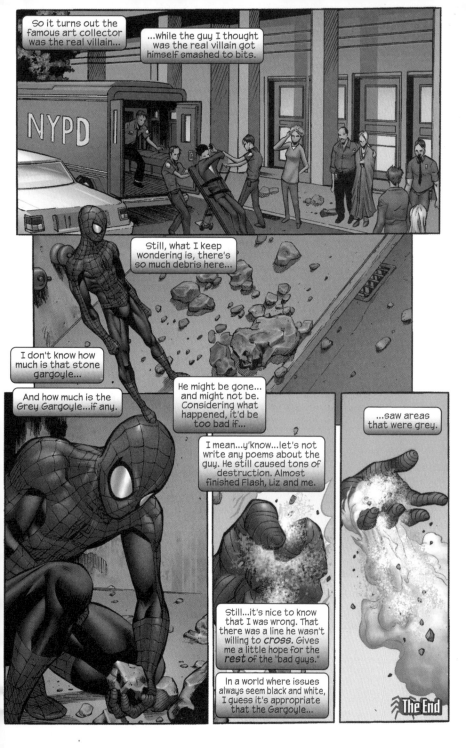

So it turns out the famous art collector was the real villain...

...while the guy I thought was the real villain got himself smashed to bits.

Still, what I keep wondering is, there's so much debris here...

I don't know how much is that stone gargoyle...

And how much is the Grey Gargoyle...if any.

He might be gone... and might not be. Considering what happened, it'd be too bad if...

I mean...y'know...let's not write any poems about the guy. He still caused tons of destruction. Almost finished Flash, Liz and me.

...saw areas that were grey.

Still...it's nice to know that I was wrong. That there was a line he wasn't willing to *cross*. Gives me a little hope for the *rest* of the "bad guys."

In a world where issues always seem black and white, I guess it's appropriate that the Gargoyle...

The End

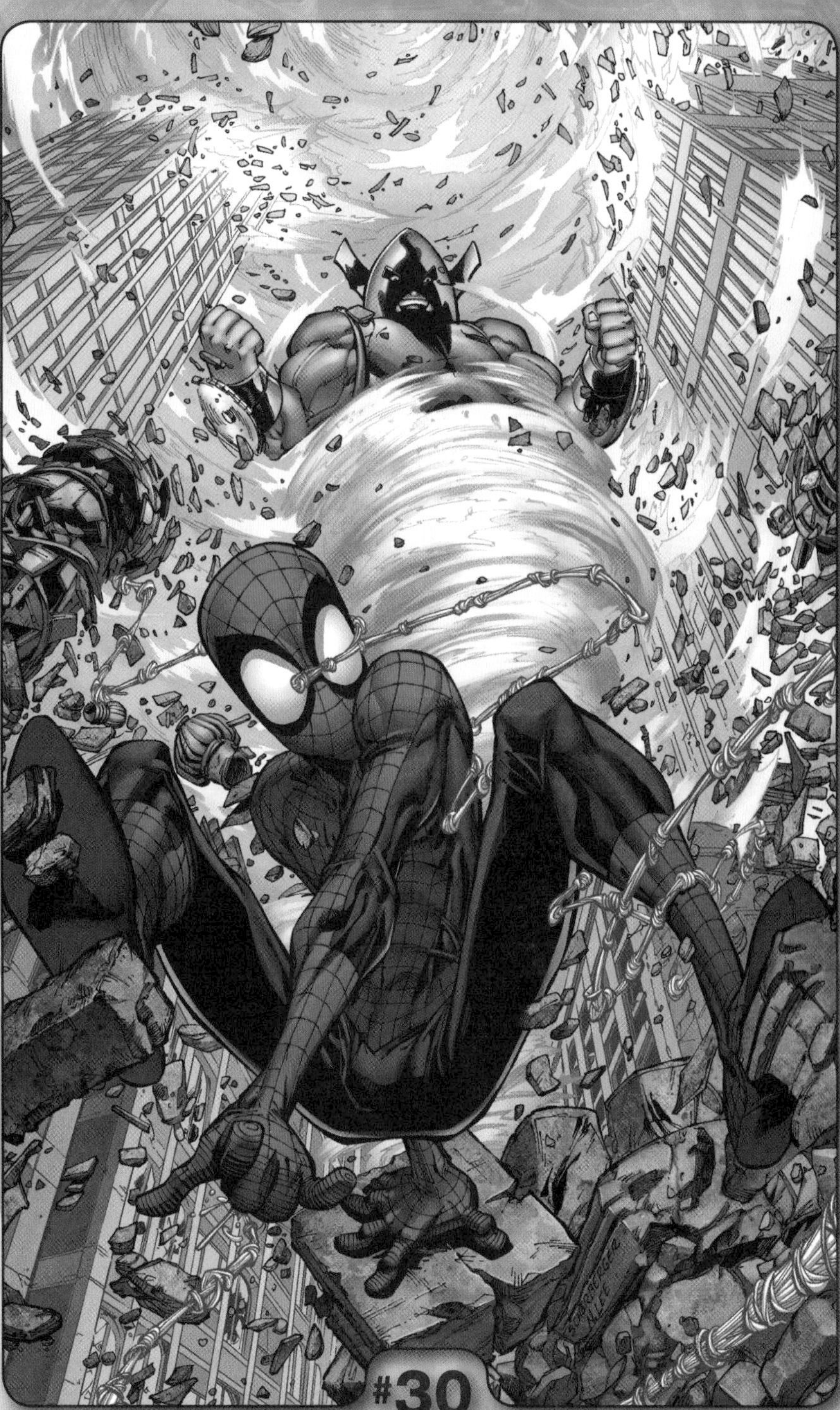

#30

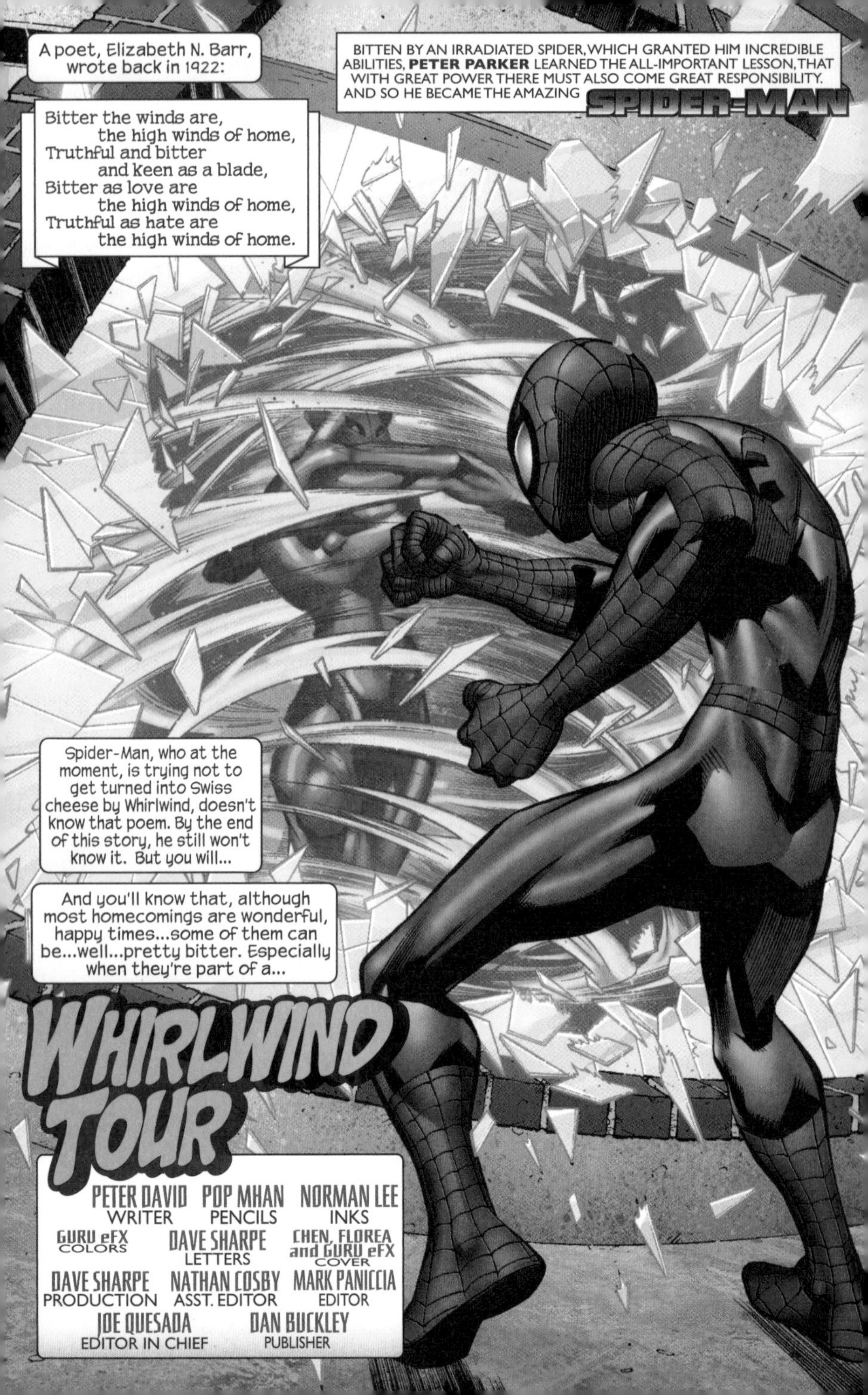
A poet, Elizabeth N. Barr, wrote back in 1922:
BITTEN BY AN IRRADIATED SPIDER, WHICH GRANTED HIM INCREDIBLE ABILITIES, PETER PARKER LEARNED THE ALL-IMPORTANT LESSON, THAT WITH GREAT POWER THERE MUST ALSO COME GREAT RESPONSIBILITY. AND SO HE BECAME THE AMAZING SPIDER-MAN
Bitter the winds are, the high winds of home, Truthful and bitter and keen as a blade, Bitter as love are the high winds of home, Truthful as hate are the high winds of home.
Spider-Man, who at the moment, is trying not to get turned into Swiss cheese by Whirlwind, doesn't know that poem. By the end of this story, he still won't know it. But you will...
And you'll know that, although most homecomings are wonderful, happy times...some of them can be...well...pretty bitter. Especially when they're part of a...
WHIRLWIND TOUR
PETER DAVID WRITER
POP MHAN PENCILS
NORMAN LEE INKS
GURU eFX COLORS
DAVE SHARPE LETTERS
CHEN, FLOREA and GURU eFX COVER
DAVE SHARPE PRODUCTION
NATHAN COSBY ASST. EDITOR
MARK PANICCIA EDITOR
JOE QUESADA EDITOR IN CHIEF
DAN BUCKLEY PUBLISHER

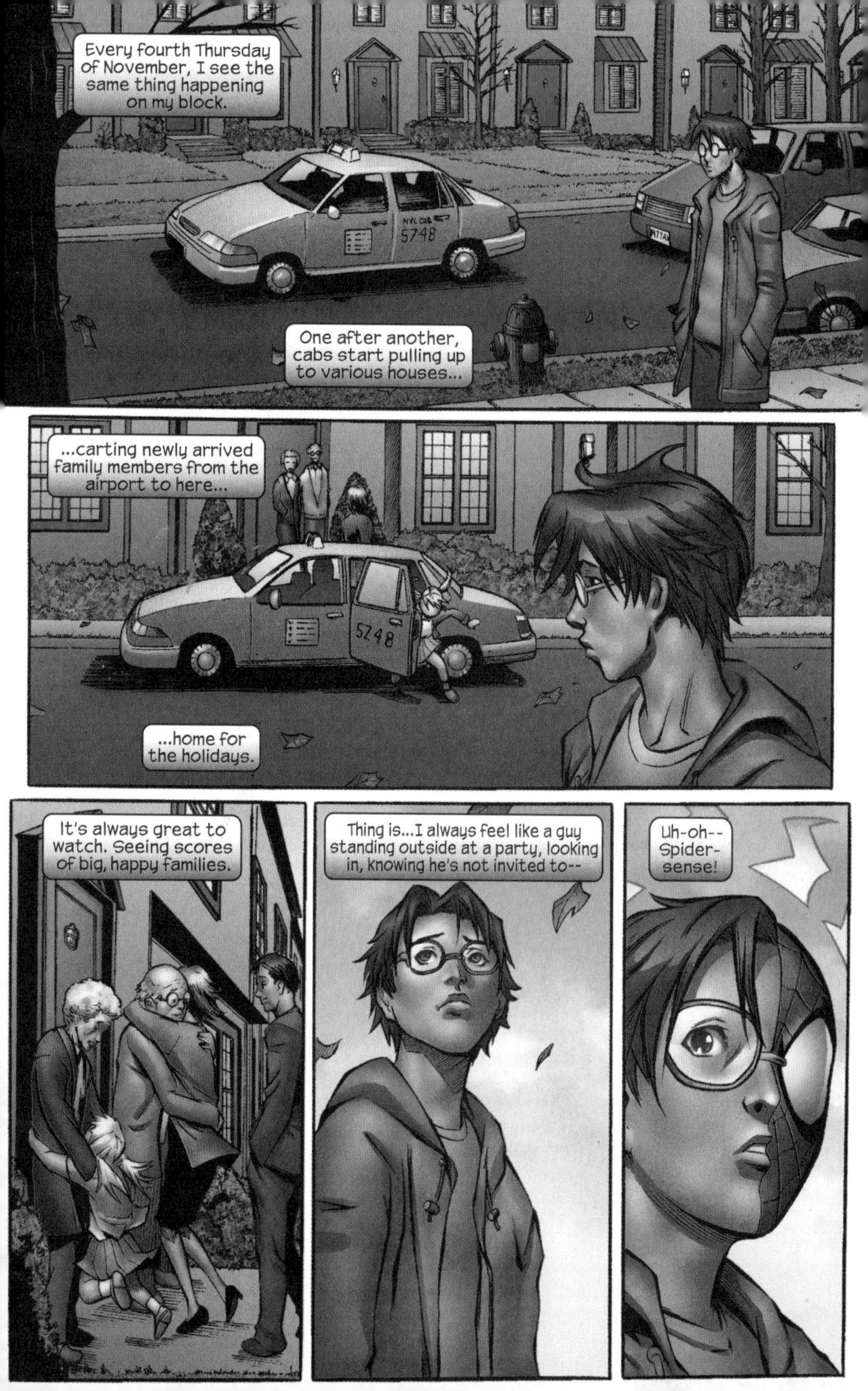
Every fourth Thursday of November, I see the same thing happening on my block.
One after another, cabs start pulling up to various houses...
NYC CAB 5748
...carting newly arrived family members from the airport to here...
5748
...home for the holidays.
It's always great to watch. Seeing scores of big, happy families.
Thing is...I always feel like a guy standing outside at a party, looking in, knowing he's not invited to--
Uh-oh-- Spider-sense!

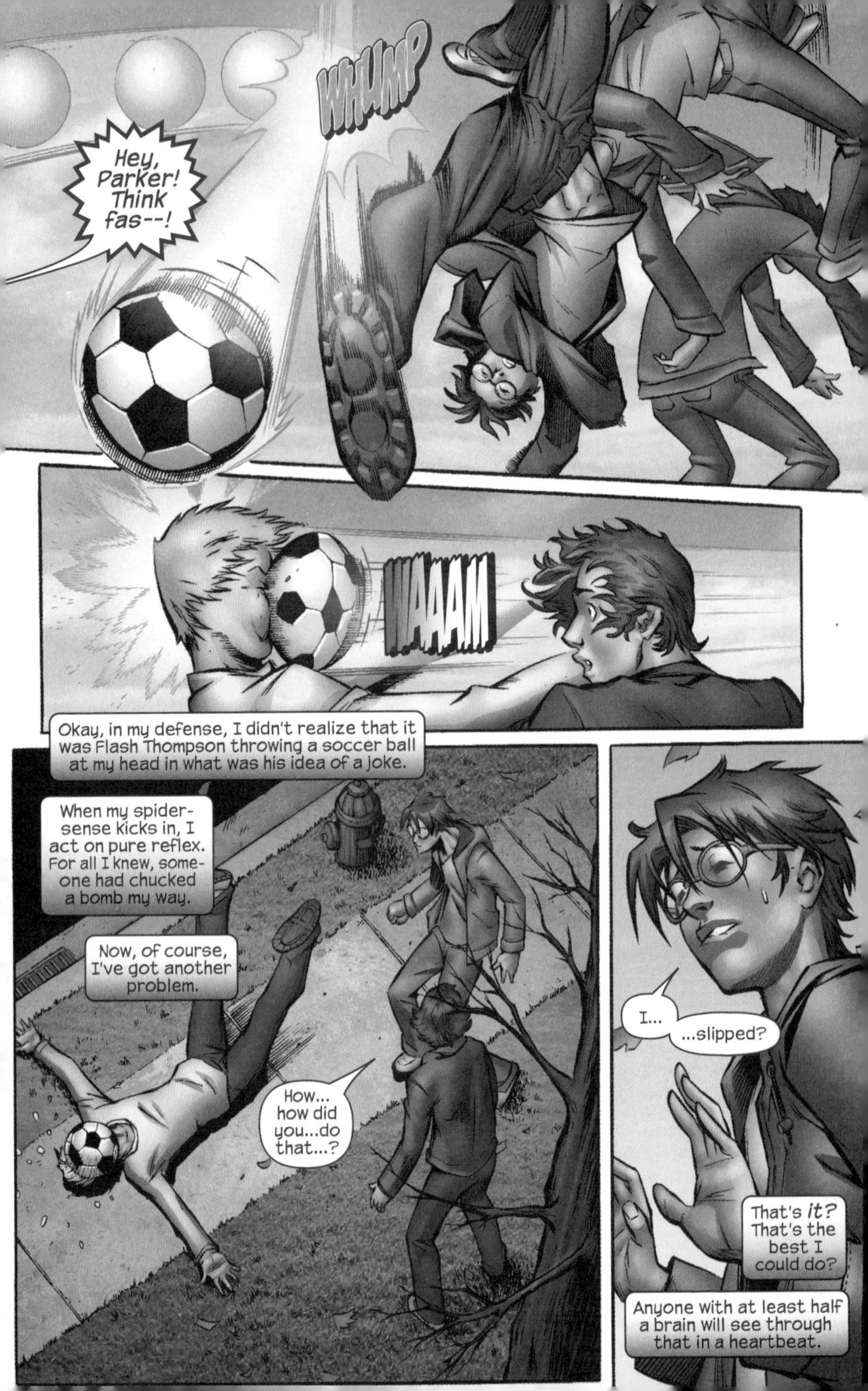
Hey, Parker! Think fas--!
WHUMP
WAAAM
Okay, in my defense, I didn't realize that it was Flash Thompson throwing a soccer ball at my head in what was his idea of a joke.
When my spider-sense kicks in, I act on pure reflex. For all I knew, some-one had chucked a bomb my way.
Now, of course, I've got another problem.
How... how did you...do that...?
I...
...slipped?
That's *it*? That's the best I could do?
Anyone with at least half a brain will see through that in a heartbeat.

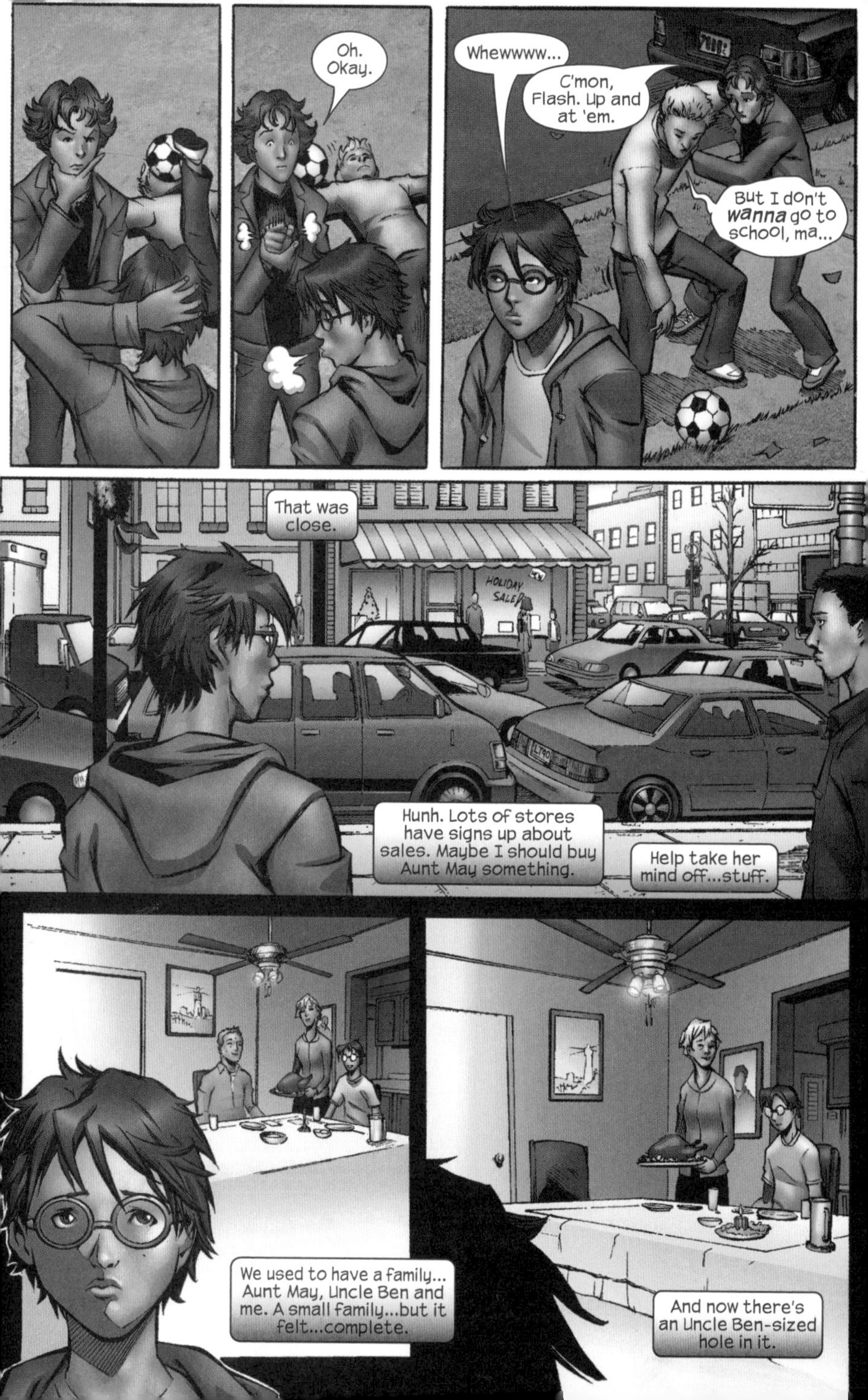
Oh. Okay.
Whewwww...
C'mon, Flash. Up and at 'em.
But I don't wanna go to school, ma...
That was close.
HOLIDAY SALE
Hunh. Lots of stores have signs up about sales. Maybe I should buy Aunt May something.
Help take her mind off...stuff.
We used to have a family... Aunt May, Uncle Ben and me. A small family...but it felt...complete.
And now there's an Uncle Ben-sized hole in it.

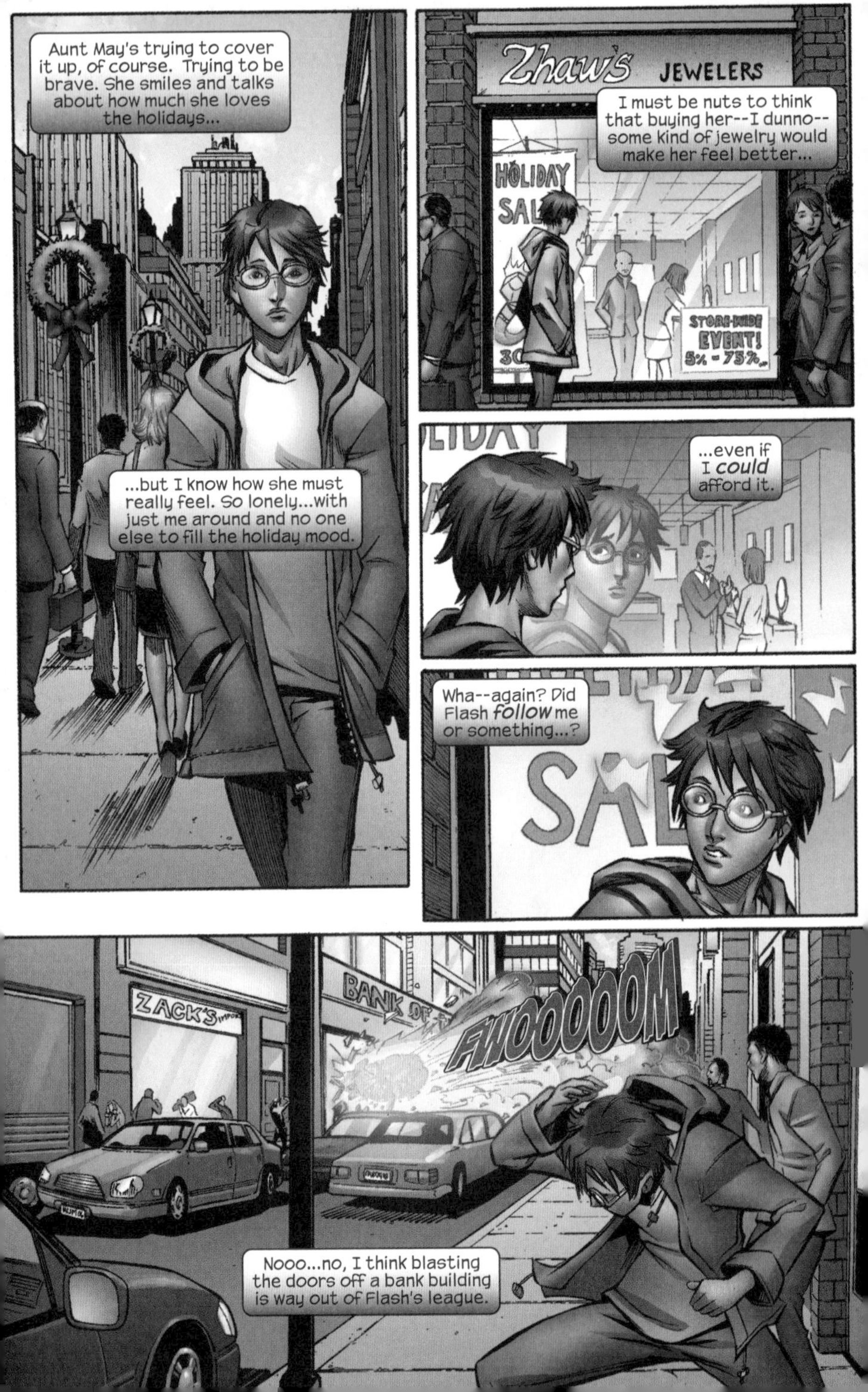
Aunt May's trying to cover it up, of course. Trying to be brave. She smiles and talks about how much she loves the holidays...
...but I know how she must really feel. So lonely...with just me around and no one else to fill the holiday mood.
Zhaw's JEWELERS
I must be nuts to think that buying her--I dunno--some kind of jewelry would make her feel better...
HOLIDAY SAL
STORE-WIDE EVENT! 5% - 75%
...even if I *could* afford it.
Wha--again? Did Flash *follow* me or something...?
SAL
ZACK'S
BANK OF
FWOOOOOOM
Nooo...no, I think blasting the doors off a bank building is way out of Flash's league.

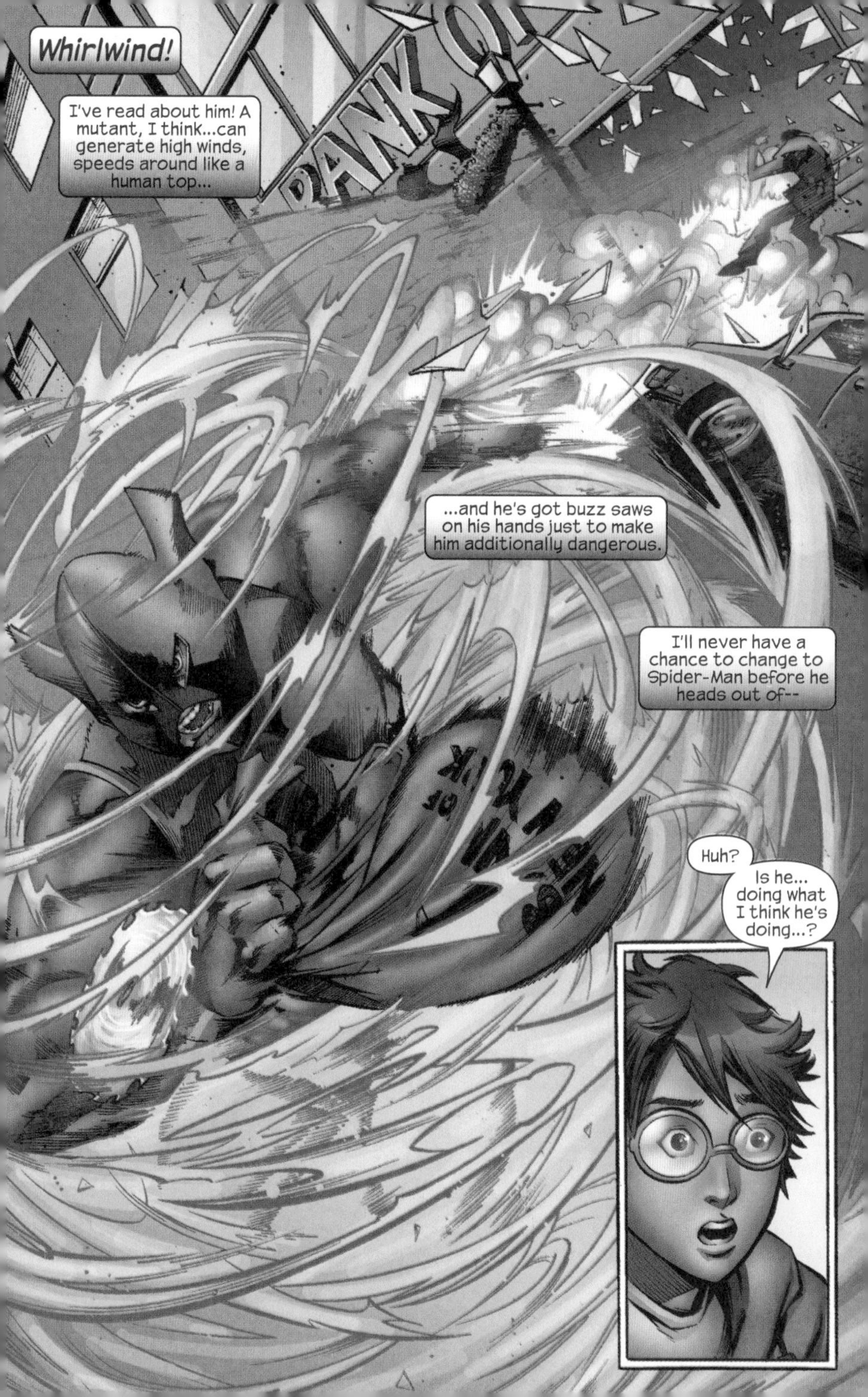
Whirlwind!
I've read about him! A mutant, I think...can generate high winds, speeds around like a human top...
BANK OF
...and he's got buzz saws on his hands just to make him additionally dangerous.
I'll never have a chance to change to Spider-Man before he heads out of--
Huh?
Is he... doing what I think he's doing...?

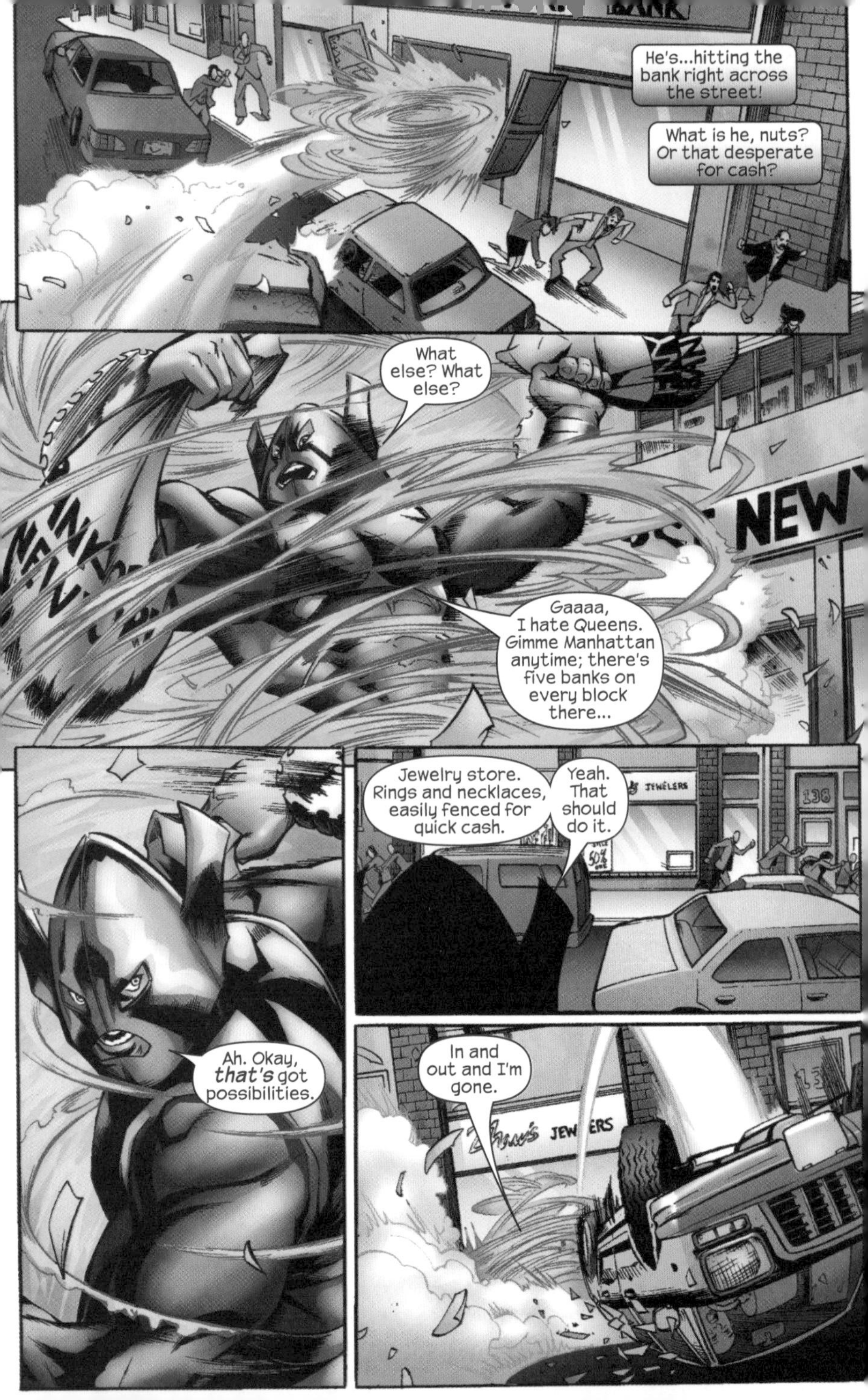

He's...hitting the bank right across the street!
What is he, nuts? Or that desperate for cash?
What else? What else?
NEW
Gaaaa, I hate Queens. Gimme Manhattan anytime; there's five banks on every block there...
Ah. Okay, ***that's*** got possibilities.
Jewelry store. Rings and necklaces, easily fenced for quick cash.
Yeah. That should do it.
JEWELERS
138
In and out and I'm gone.
JEW ERS

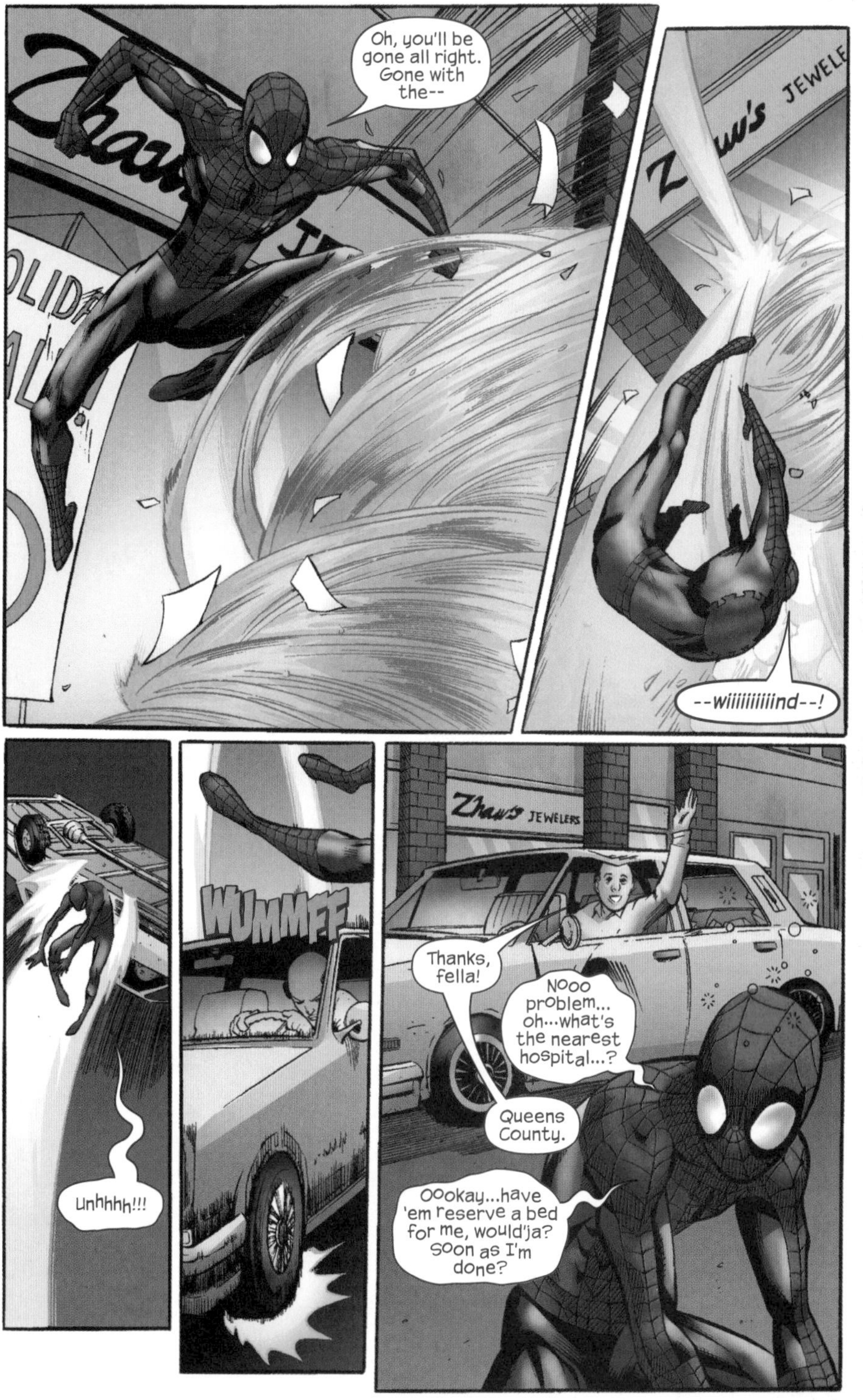
Oh, you'll be gone all right. Gone with the--
--wiiiiiiiiiind--!
Unhhhh!!!
WUMMFF
Thanks, fella!
Nooo problem... oh...what's the nearest hospital...?
Queens County.
Oookay...have 'em reserve a bed for me, would'ja? Soon as I'm done?

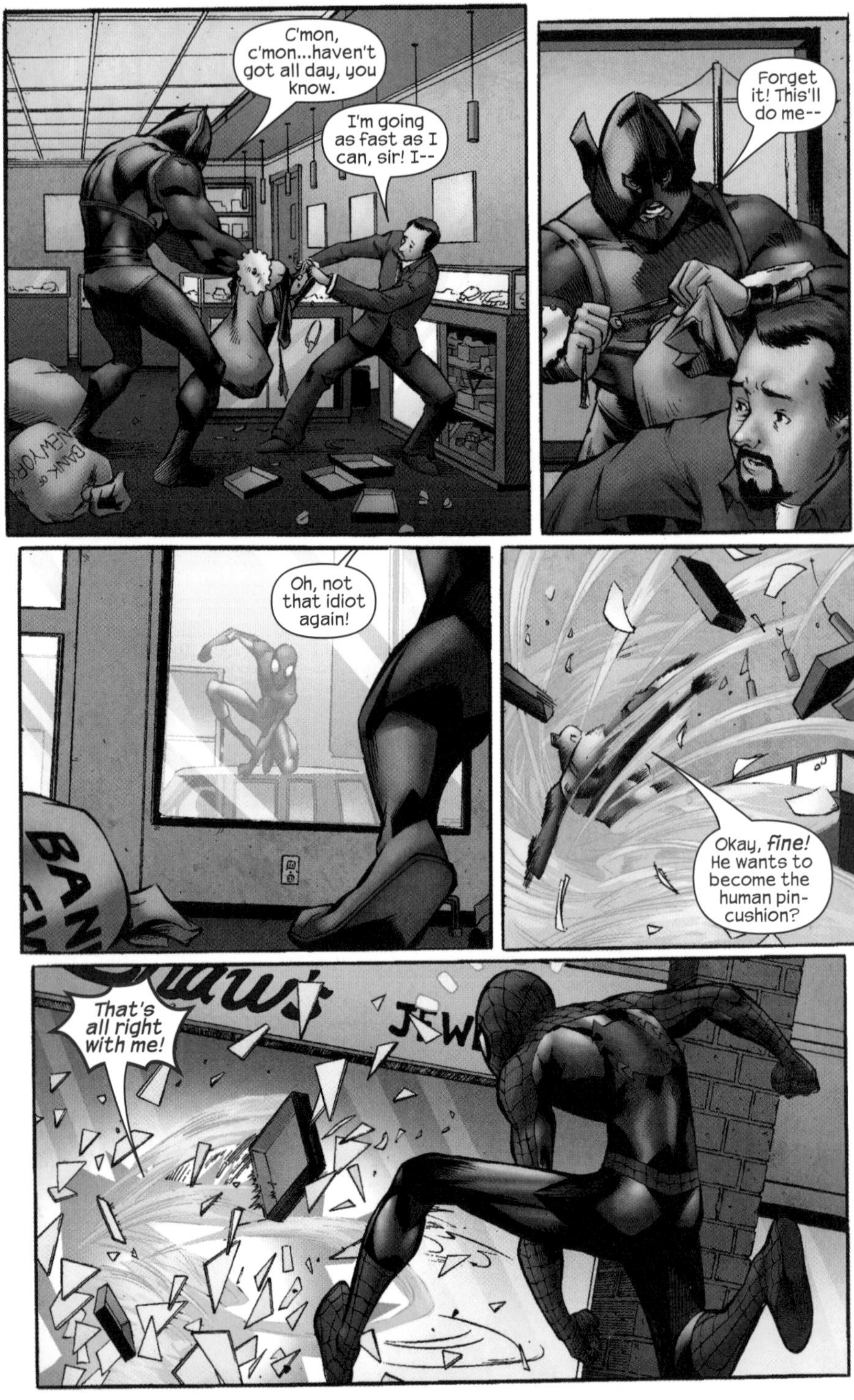
C'mon, c'mon...haven't got all day, you know.
I'm going as fast as I can, sir! I--
BANK of NEW YORK
Forget it! This'll do me--
Oh, not that idiot again!
Okay, *fine!* He wants to become the human pin-cushion?
That's all right with me!

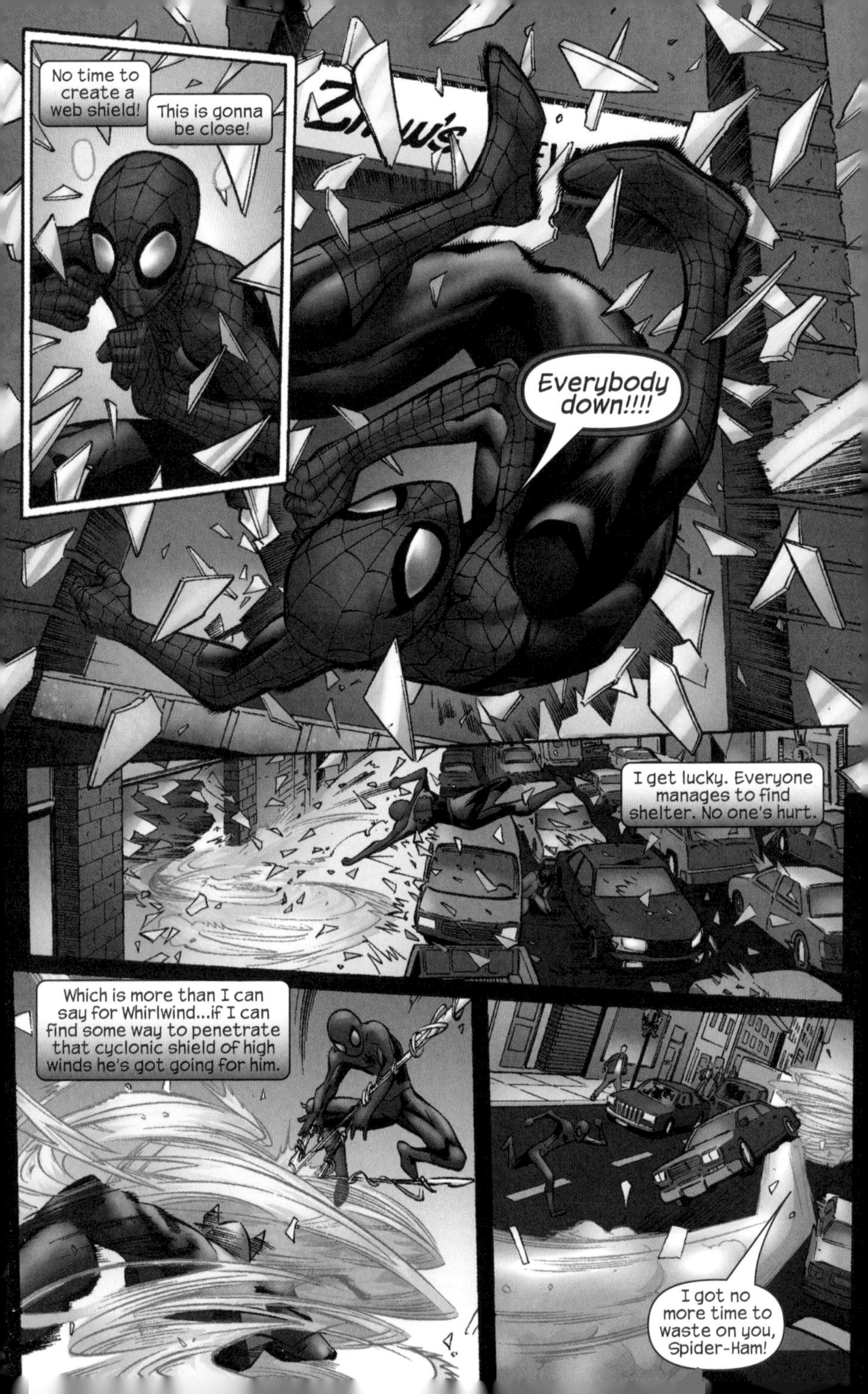
No time to create a web shield!
This is gonna be close!
Everybody down!!!!
I get lucky. Everyone manages to find shelter. No one's hurt.
Which is more than I can say for Whirlwind...if I can find some way to penetrate that cyclonic shield of high winds he's got going for him.
I got no more time to waste on you, Spider-Ham!

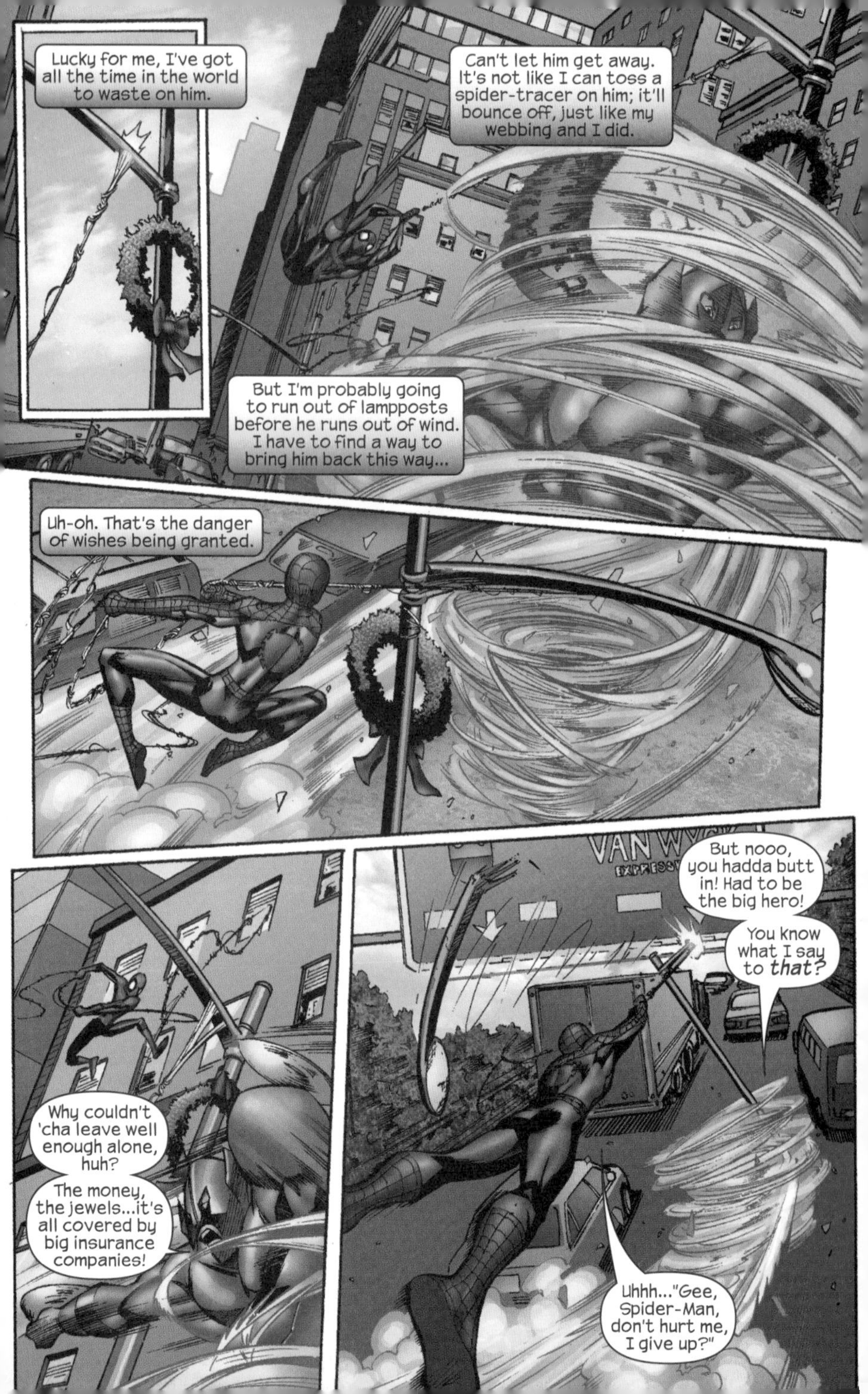

Lucky for me, I've got all the time in the world to waste on him.
Can't let him get away. It's not like I can toss a spider-tracer on him; it'll bounce off, just like my webbing and I did.
But I'm probably going to run out of lampposts before he runs out of wind. I have to find a way to bring him back this way...
Uh-oh. That's the danger of wishes being granted.
Why couldn't 'cha leave well enough alone, huh?
The money, the jewels...it's all covered by big insurance companies!
VAN WY
EXPRESS
But nooo, you hadda butt in! Had to be the big hero!
You know what I say to *that?*
Uhhh..."Gee, Spider-Man, don't hurt me, I give up?"

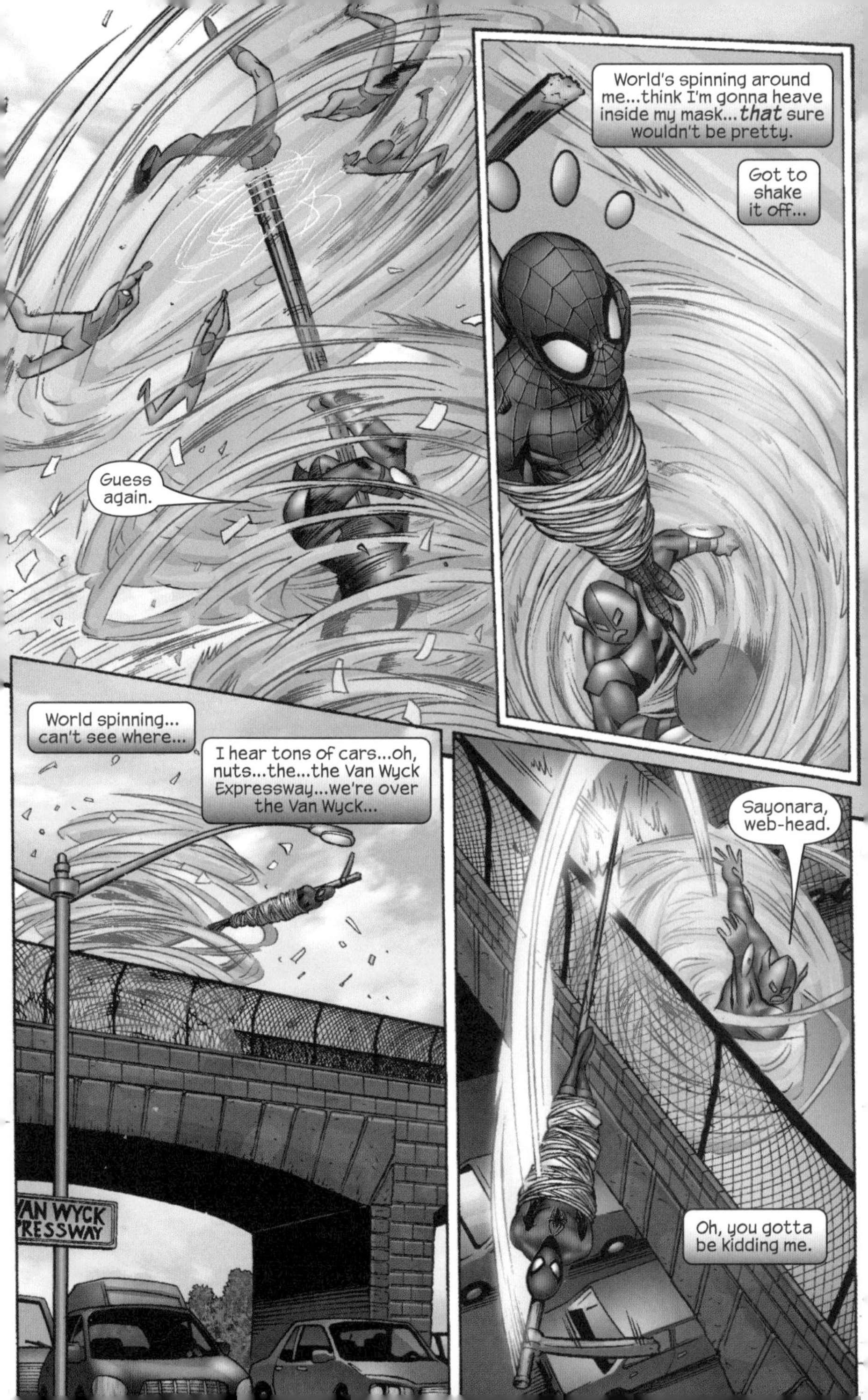
Guess again.
World's spinning around me...think I'm gonna heave inside my mask...*that* sure wouldn't be pretty.
Got to shake it off...
World spinning... can't see where...
I hear tons of cars...oh, nuts...the...the Van Wyck Expressway...we're over the Van Wyck...
VAN WYCK
PRESSWAY
Sayonara, web-head.
Oh, you gotta be kidding me.

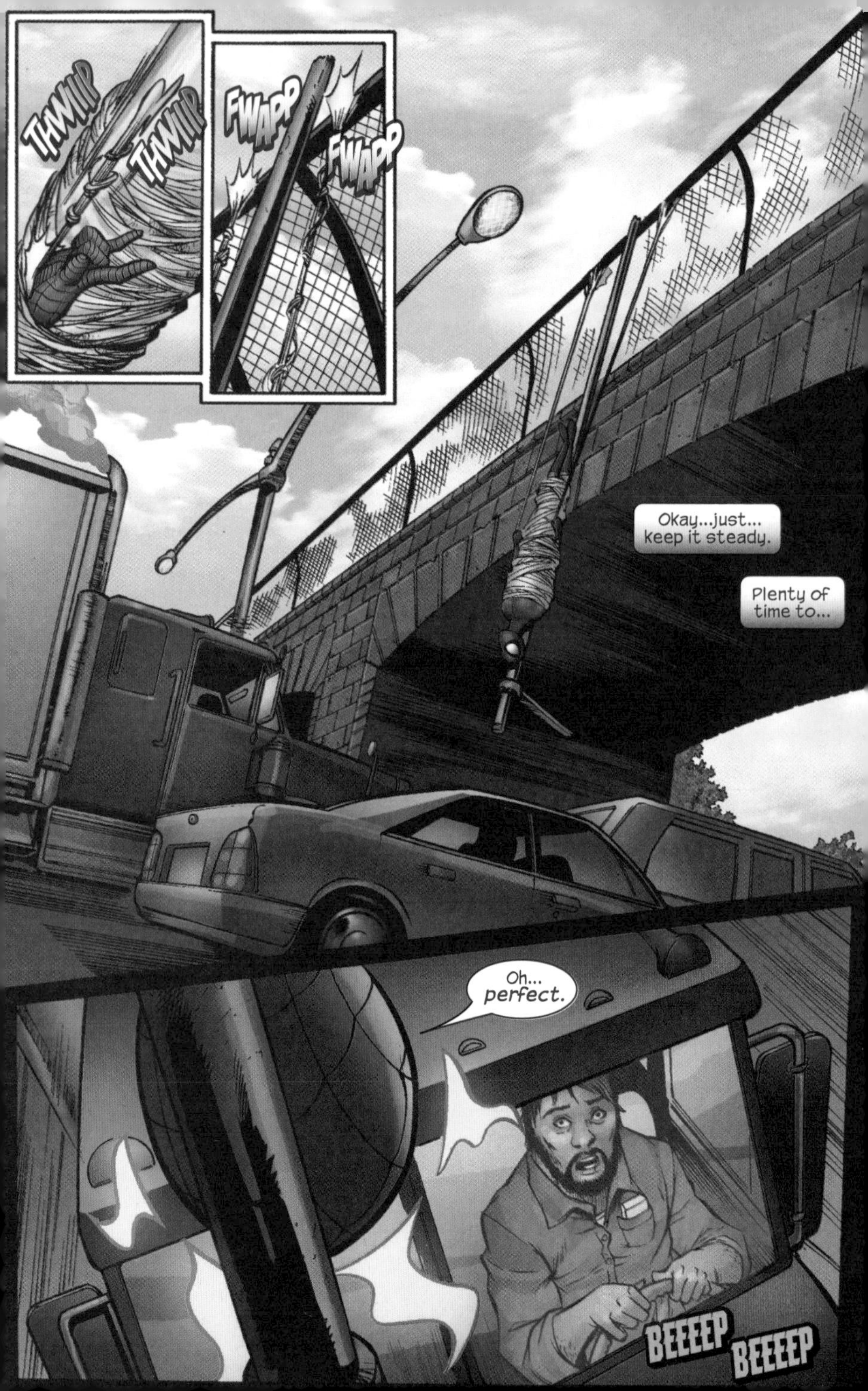
THWIP
THWIP
FWAPP
FWAPP
Okay...just... keep it steady.
Plenty of time to...
Oh... perfect.
BEEEEP
BEEEEP

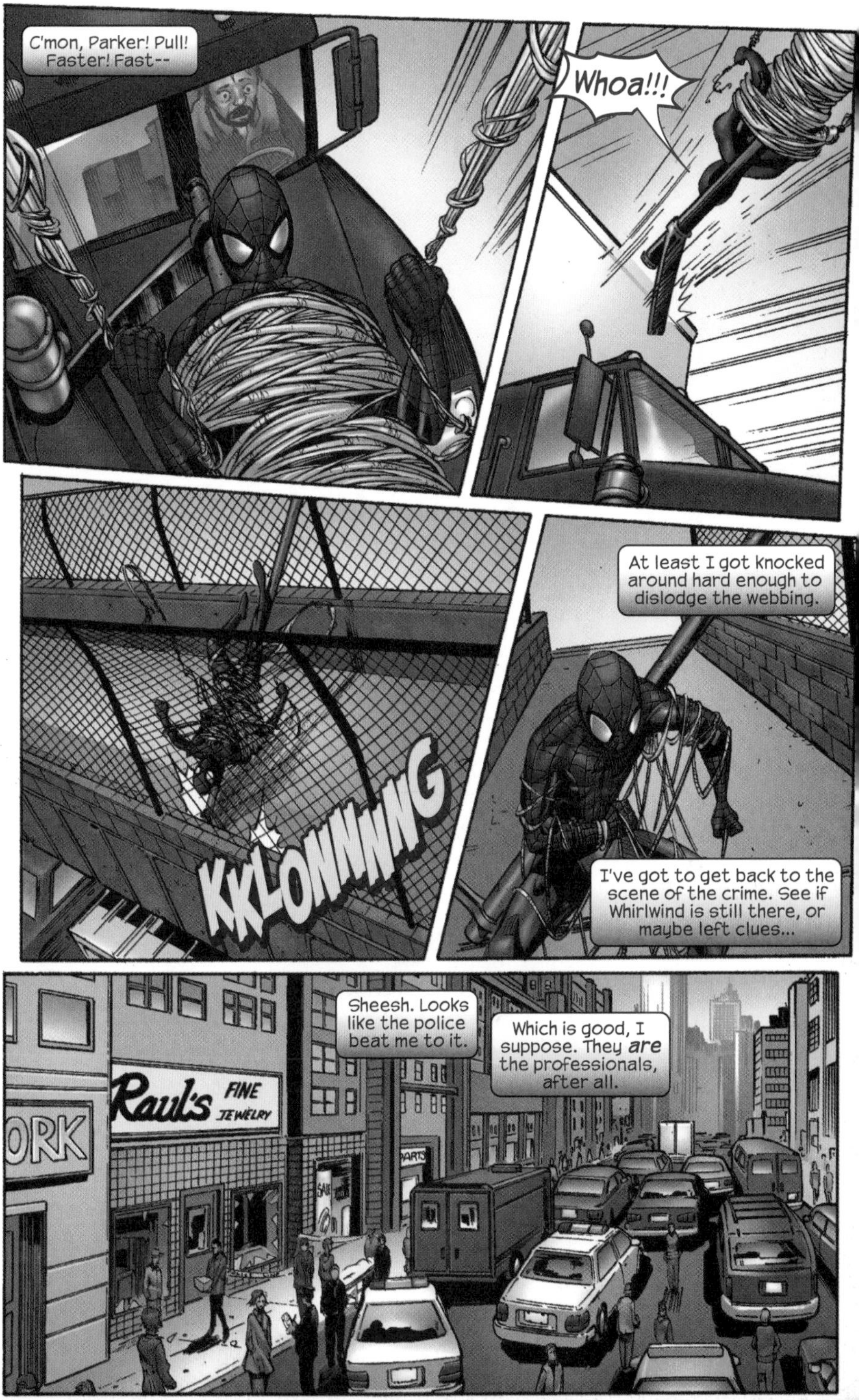
C'mon, Parker! Pull! Faster! Fast--
Whoa!!!
KKLONNNNG
At least I got knocked around hard enough to dislodge the webbing.
I've got to get back to the scene of the crime. See if Whirlwind is still there, or maybe left clues...
Raul's FINE JEWELRY
Sheesh. Looks like the police beat me to it.
Which is good, I suppose. They *are* the professionals, after all.

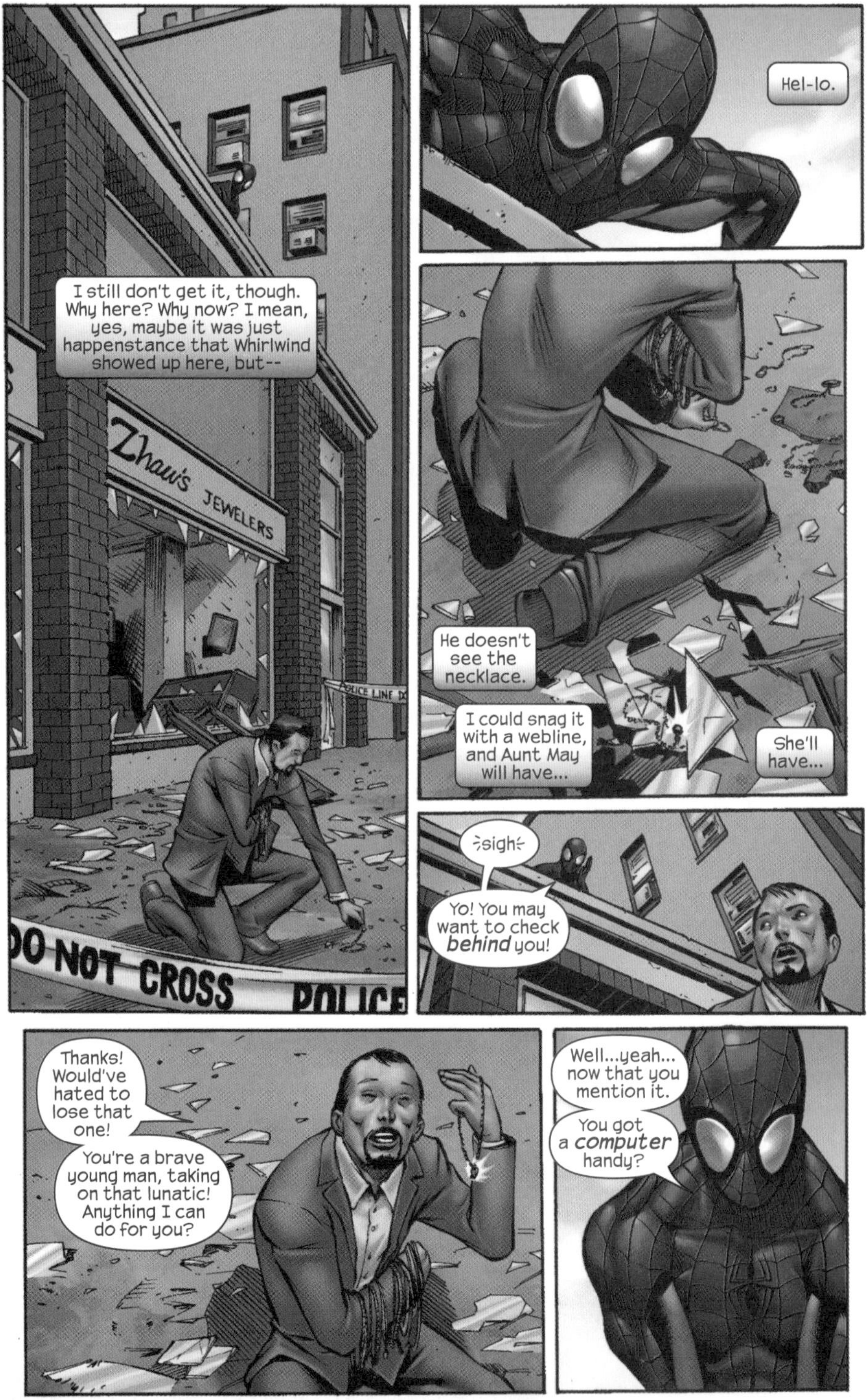

I still don't get it, though. Why here? Why now? I mean, yes, maybe it was just happenstance that Whirlwind showed up here, but--
Zhaw's JEWELERS
POLICE LINE DO
DO NOT CROSS
POLICE
Hel-lo.
He doesn't see the necklace.
I could snag it with a webline, and Aunt May will have...
She'll have...
sigh
Yo! You may want to check *behind* you!
Thanks! Would've hated to lose that one!
You're a brave young man, taking on that lunatic! Anything I can do for you?
Well...yeah... now that you mention it.
You got a *computer* handy?

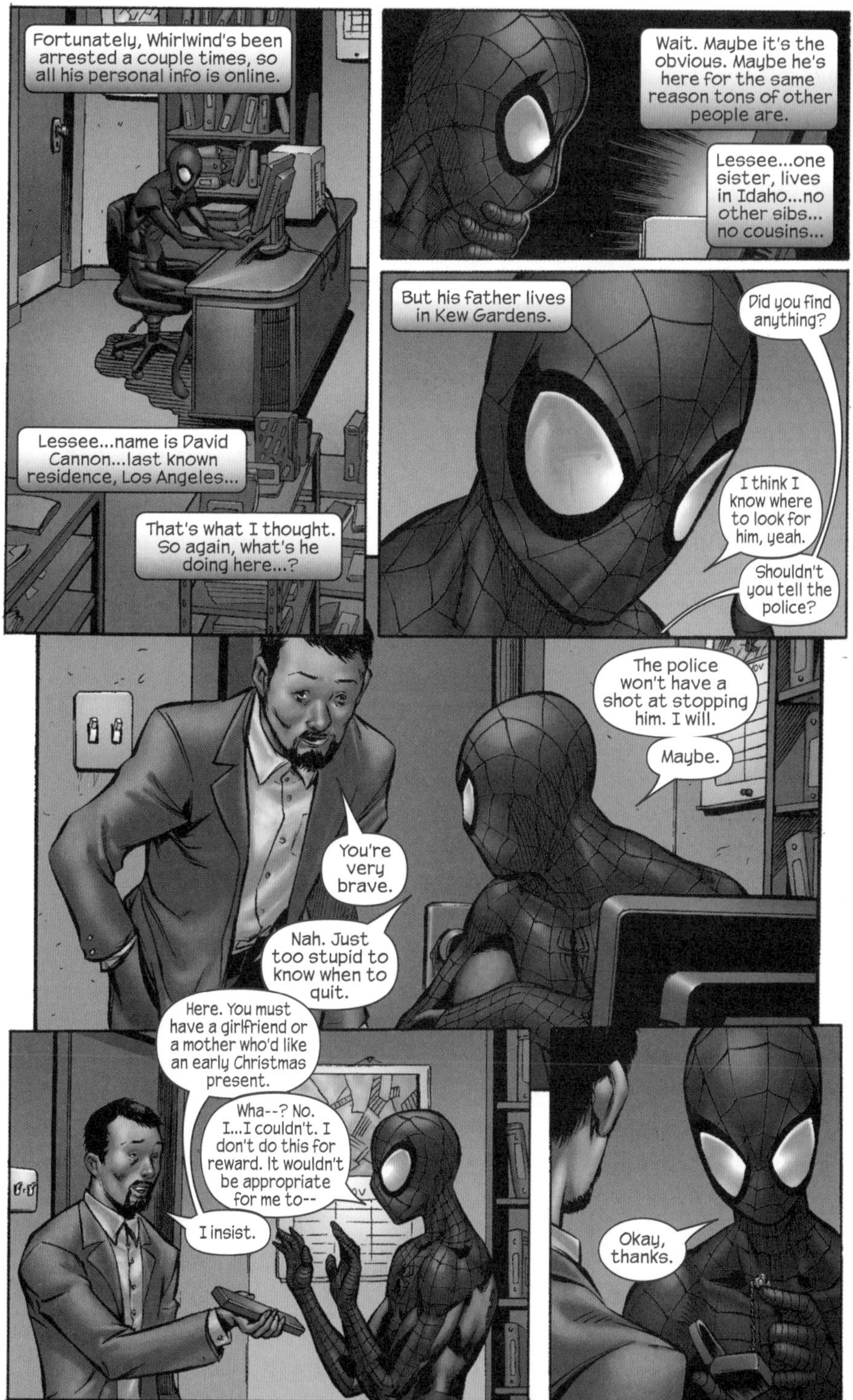
Fortunately, Whirlwind's been arrested a couple times, so all his personal info is online.
Lessee...name is David Cannon...last known residence, Los Angeles...
That's what I thought. So again, what's he doing here...?
Wait. Maybe it's the obvious. Maybe he's here for the same reason tons of other people are.
Lessee...one sister, lives in Idaho...no other sibs... no cousins...
But his father lives in Kew Gardens.
Did you find anything?
I think I know where to look for him, yeah.
Shouldn't you tell the police?
The police won't have a shot at stopping him. I will.
Maybe.
You're very brave.
Nah. Just too stupid to know when to quit.
Here. You must have a girlfriend or a mother who'd like an early Christmas present.
Wha--? No. I...I couldn't. I don't do this for reward. It wouldn't be appropriate for me to--
I insist.
Okay, thanks.

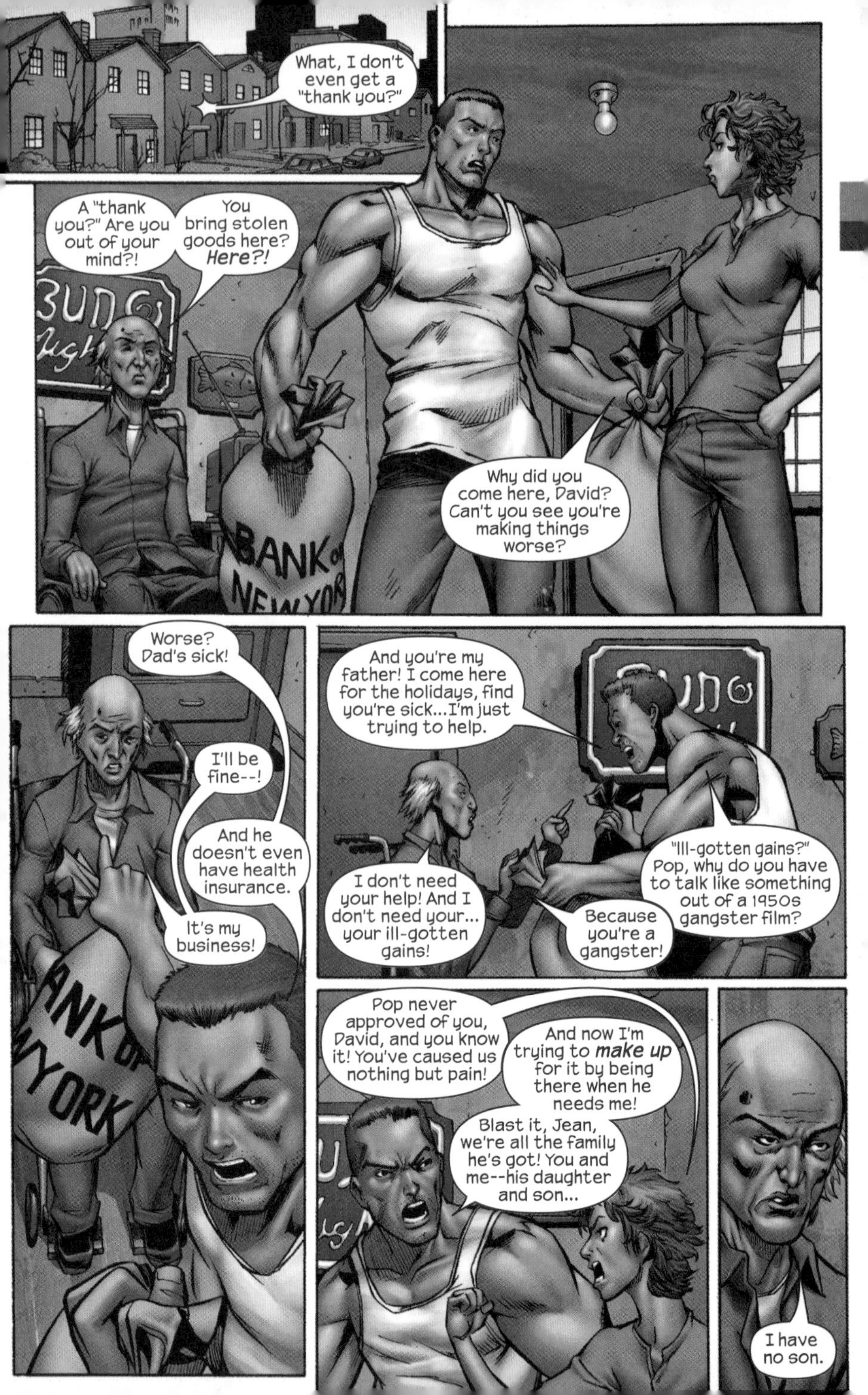
What, I don't even get a "thank you?"
A "thank you?" Are you out of your mind?!
You bring stolen goods here? Here?!
Why did you come here, David? Can't you see you're making things worse?
Worse? Dad's sick!
I'll be fine--!
And he doesn't even have health insurance.
It's my business!
And you're my father! I come here for the holidays, find you're sick...I'm just trying to help.
I don't need your help! And I don't need your... your ill-gotten gains!
"Ill-gotten gains?" Pop, why do you have to talk like something out of a 1950s gangster film?
Because you're a gangster!
Pop never approved of you, David, and you know it! You've caused us nothing but pain!
And now I'm trying to make up for it by being there when he needs me!
Blast it, Jean, we're all the family he's got! You and me--his daughter and son...
I have no son.

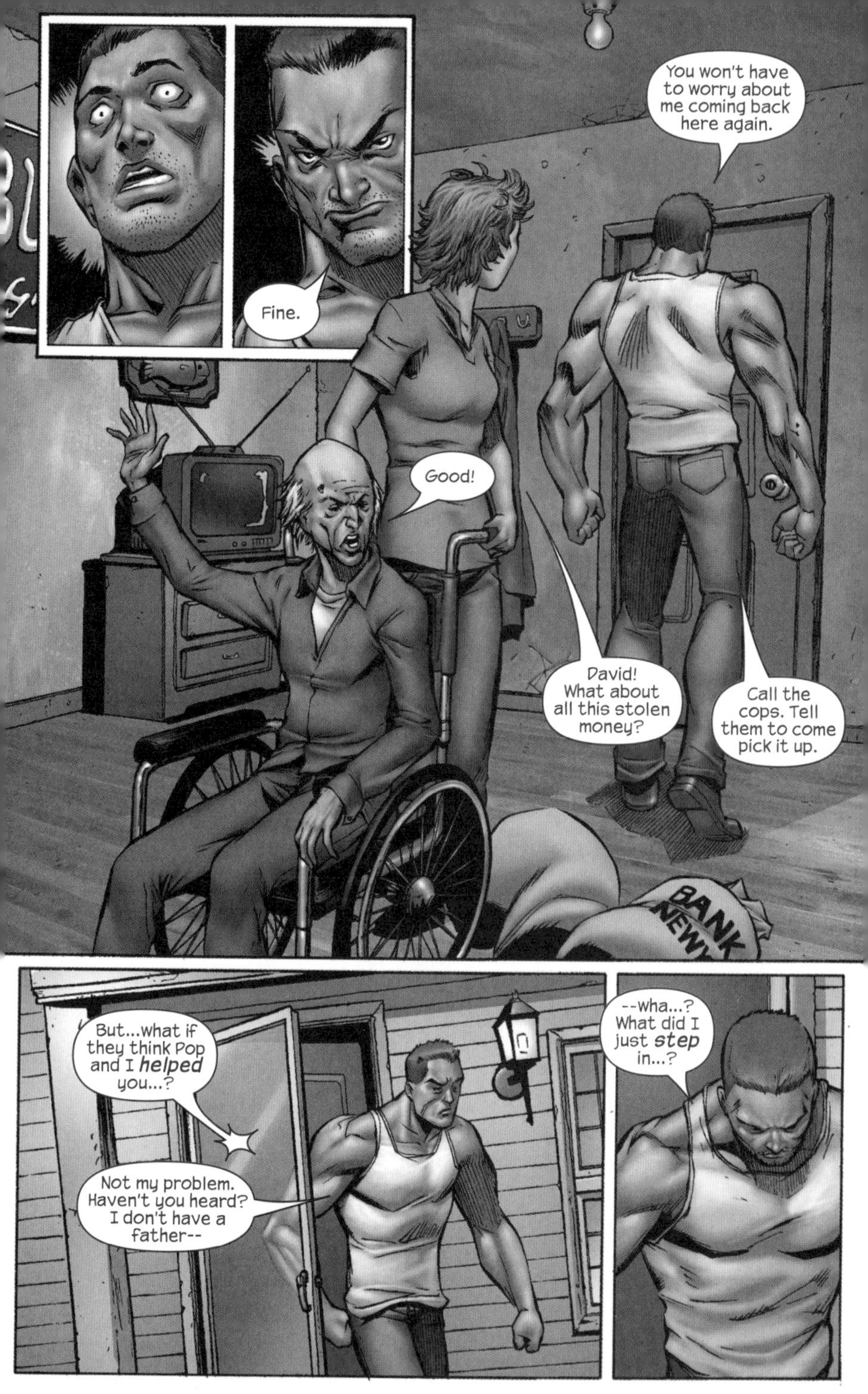
Fine.
You won't have to worry about me coming back here again.
Good!
David! What about all this stolen money?
Call the cops. Tell them to come pick it up.
BANK
NEWY
But...what if they think Pop and I *helped* you...?
Not my problem. Haven't you heard? I don't have a father--
--wha...? What did I just *step* in...?

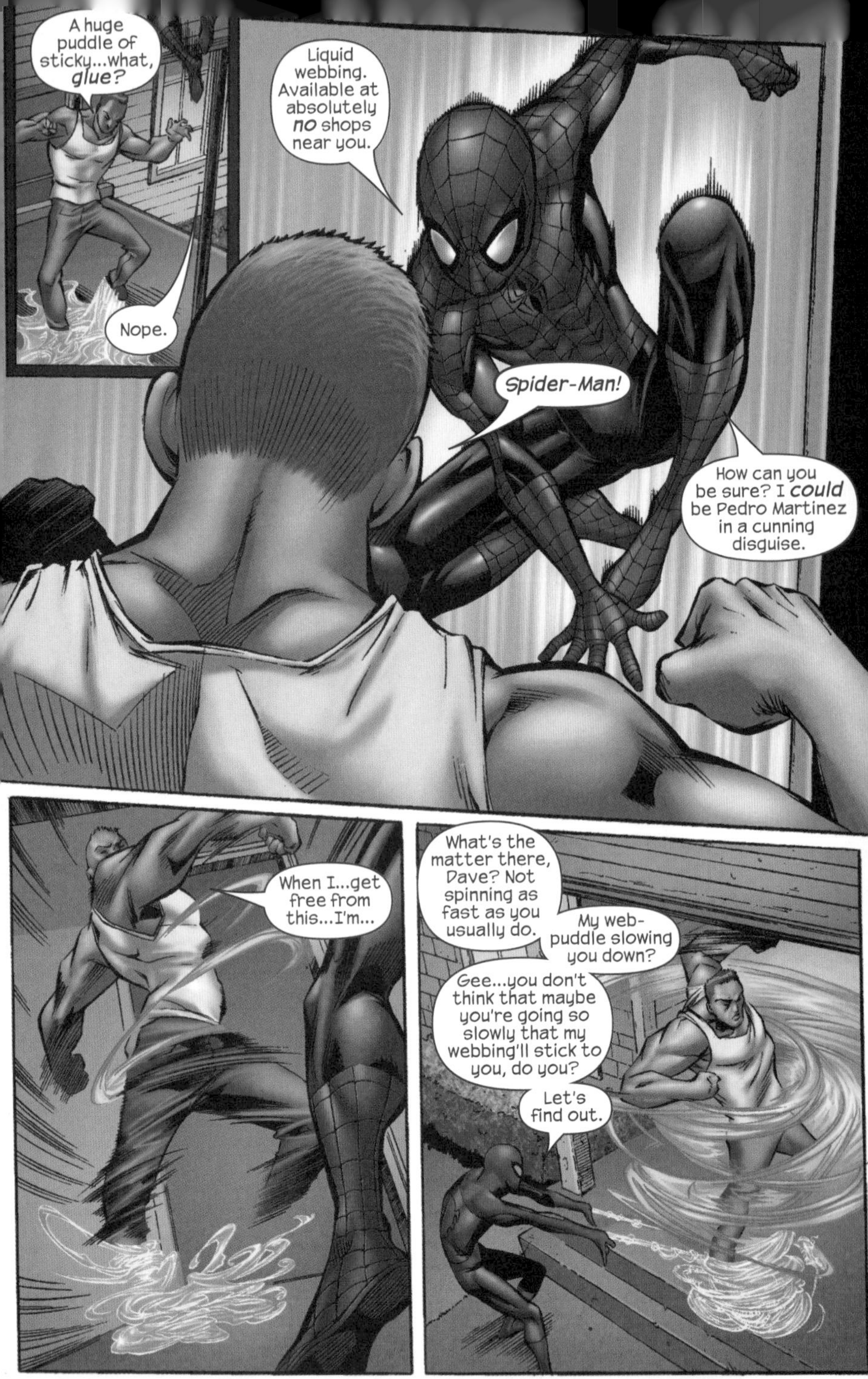

A huge puddle of sticky...what, *glue?*
Liquid webbing. Available at absolutely *no* shops near you.
Nope.
Spider-Man!
How can you be sure? I *could* be Pedro Martinez in a cunning disguise.
When I...get free from this...I'm...
What's the matter there, Dave? Not spinning as fast as you usually do.
My web-puddle slowing you down?
Gee...you don't think that maybe you're going so slowly that my webbing'll stick to you, do you?
Let's find out.

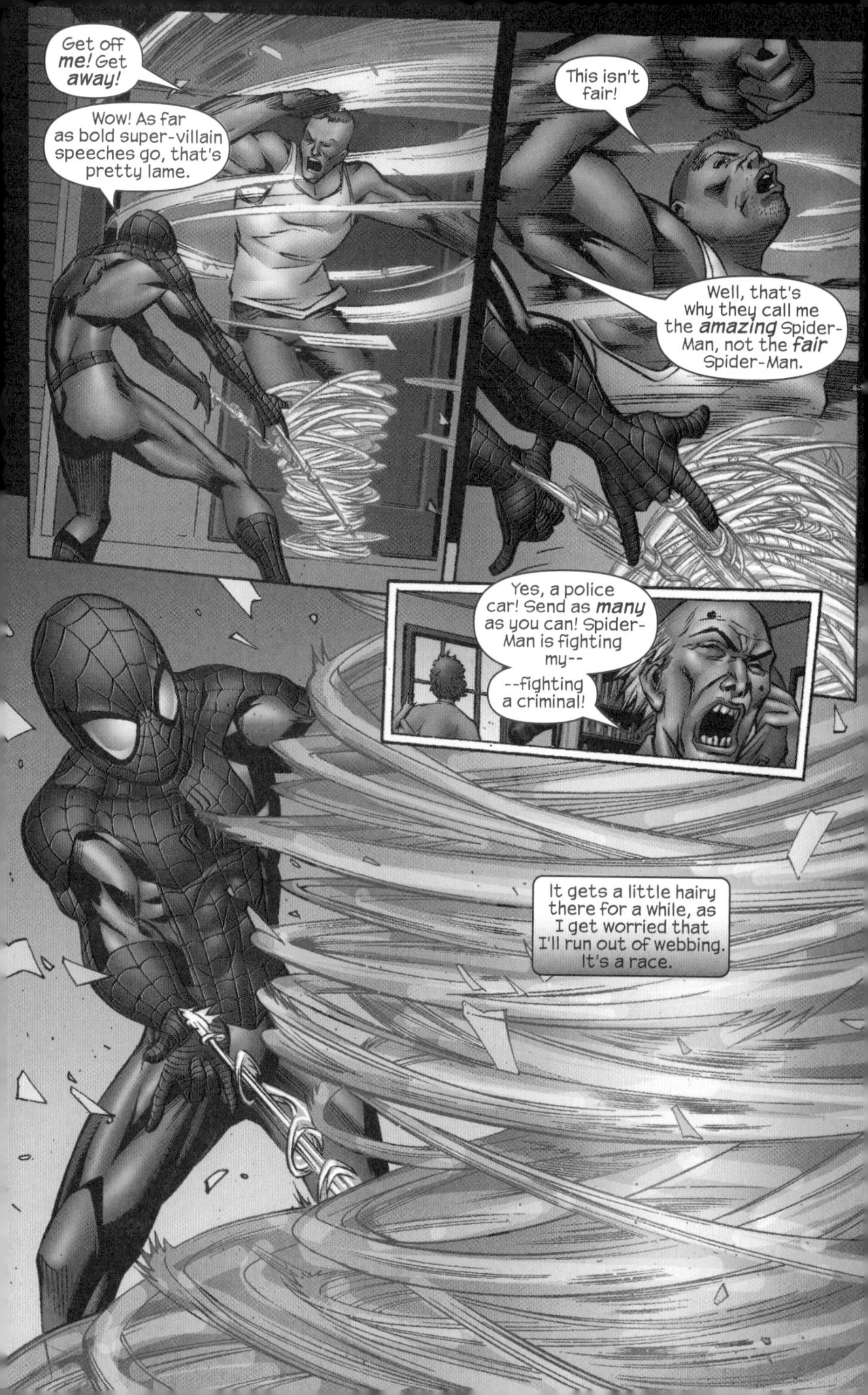
Get off me! Get away!
Wow! As far as bold super-villain speeches go, that's pretty lame.
This isn't fair!
Well, that's why they call me the amazing Spider-Man, not the fair Spider-Man.
Yes, a police car! Send as many as you can! Spider-Man is fighting my--
--fighting a criminal!
It gets a little hairy there for a while, as I get worried that I'll run out of webbing. It's a race.

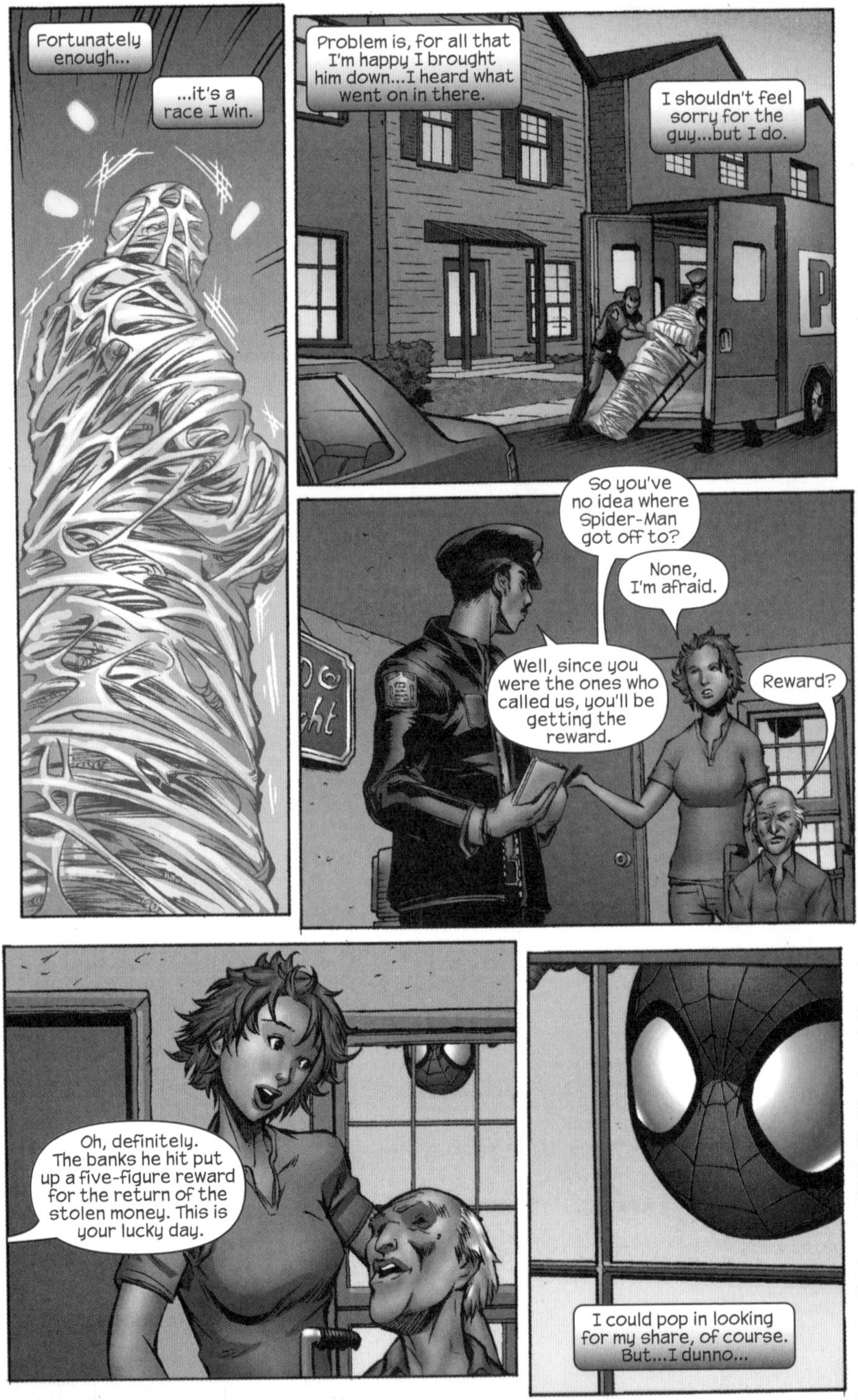
Fortunately enough...
...it's a race I win.
Problem is, for all that I'm happy I brought him down...I heard what went on in there.
I shouldn't feel sorry for the guy...but I do.
So you've no idea where Spider-Man got off to?
None, I'm afraid.
Well, since you were the ones who called us, you'll be getting the reward.
Reward?
Oh, definitely. The banks he hit put up a five-figure reward for the return of the stolen money. This is your lucky day.
I could pop in looking for my share, of course. But...I dunno...

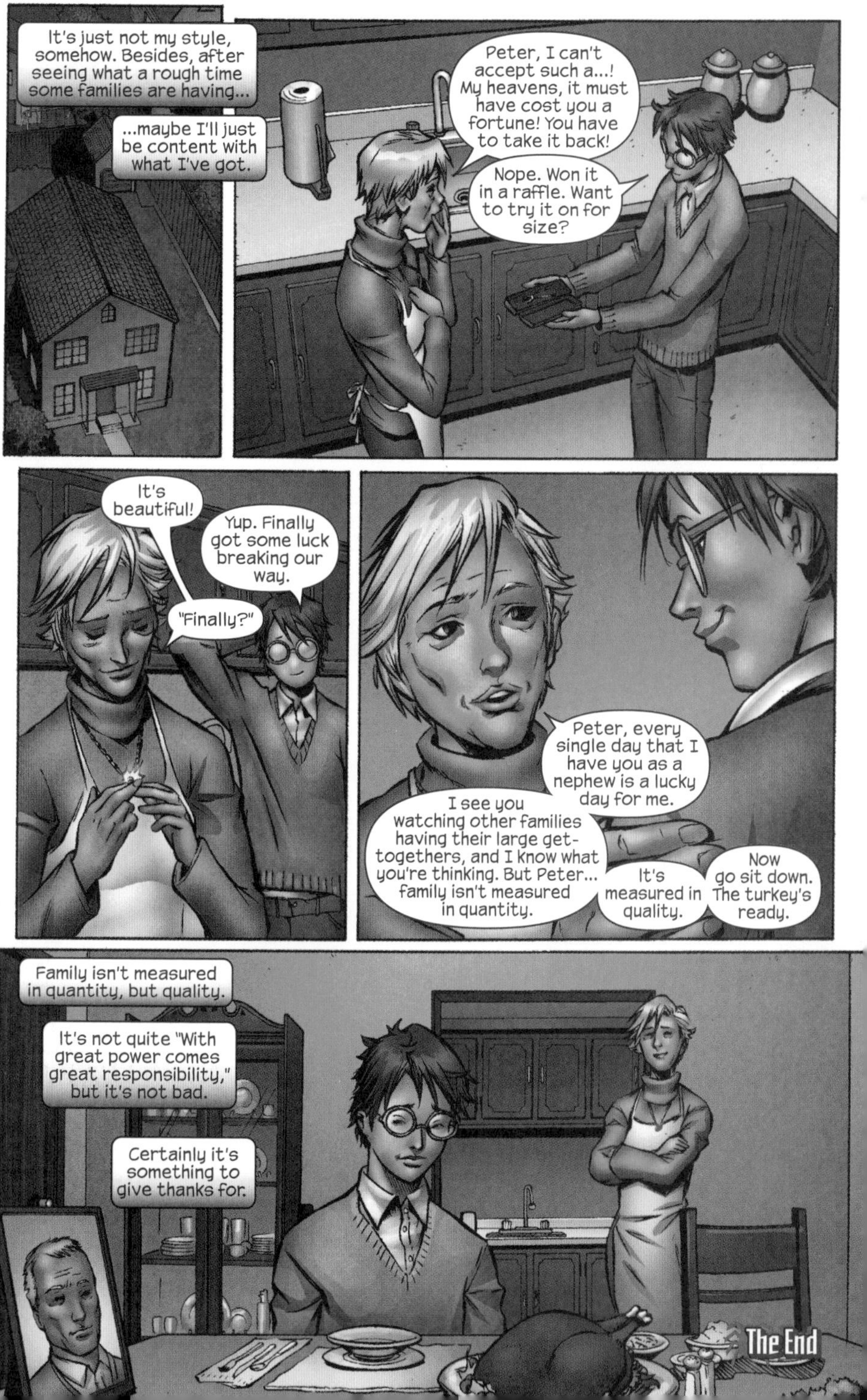
It's just not my style, somehow. Besides, after seeing what a rough time some families are having...
...maybe I'll just be content with what I've got.
Peter, I can't accept such a...! My heavens, it must have cost you a fortune! You have to take it back!
Nope. Won it in a raffle. Want to try it on for size?
It's beautiful!
Yup. Finally got some luck breaking our way.
"Finally?"
Peter, every single day that I have you as a nephew is a lucky day for me.
I see you watching other families having their large get-togethers, and I know what you're thinking. But Peter... family isn't measured in quantity.
It's measured in quality.
Now go sit down. The turkey's ready.
Family isn't measured in quantity, but quality.
It's not quite "With great power comes great responsibility," but it's not bad.
Certainly it's something to give thanks for.
The End

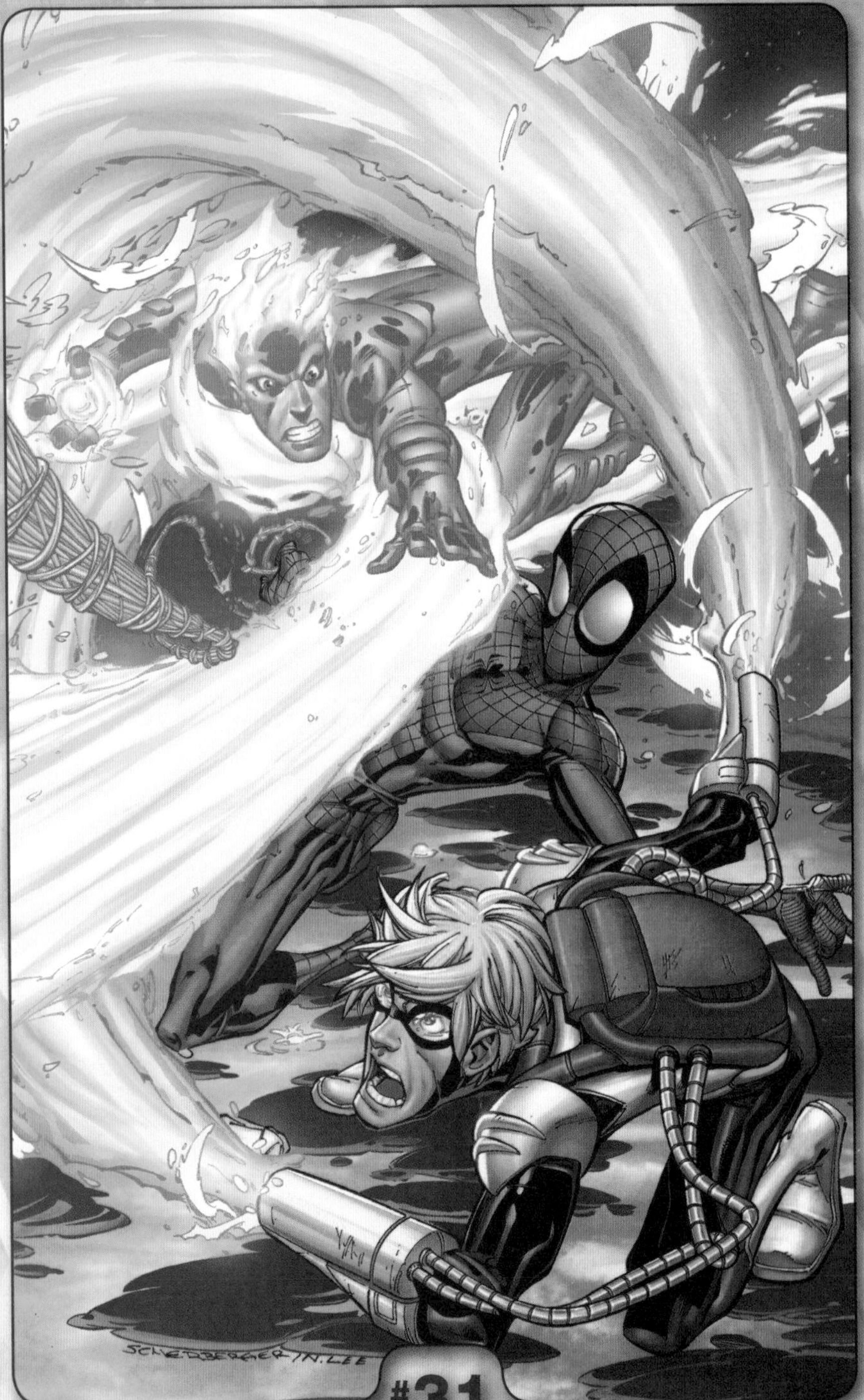

#31

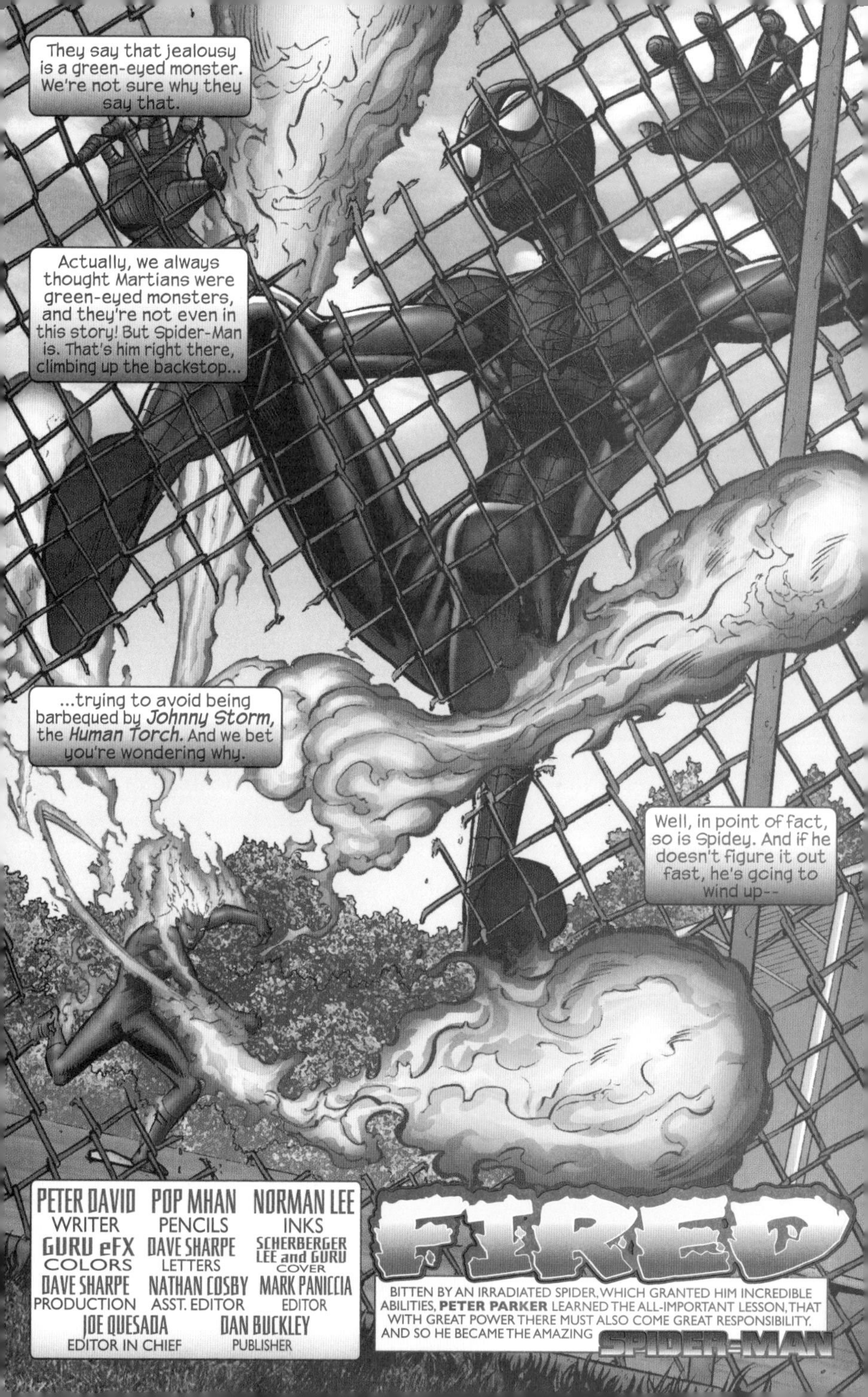
They say that jealousy is a green-eyed monster. We're not sure why they say that.
Actually, we always thought Martians were green-eyed monsters, and they're not even in this story! But Spider-Man is. That's him right there, climbing up the backstop...
...trying to avoid being barbequed by *Johnny Storm*, the *Human Torch*. And we bet you're wondering why.
Well, in point of fact, so is Spidey. And if he doesn't figure it out fast, he's going to wind up--
FIRED
PETER DAVID WRITER
POP MHAN PENCILS
NORMAN LEE INKS
GURU eFX COLORS
DAVE SHARPE LETTERS
SCHERBERGER LEE and GURU COVER
DAVE SHARPE PRODUCTION
NATHAN COSBY ASST. EDITOR
MARK PANICCIA EDITOR
JOE QUESADA EDITOR IN CHIEF
DAN BUCKLEY PUBLISHER
BITTEN BY AN IRRADIATED SPIDER, WHICH GRANTED HIM INCREDIBLE ABILITIES, **PETER PARKER** LEARNED THE ALL-IMPORTANT LESSON, THAT WITH GREAT POWER THERE MUST ALSO COME GREAT RESPONSIBILITY. AND SO HE BECAME THE AMAZING SPIDER-MAN

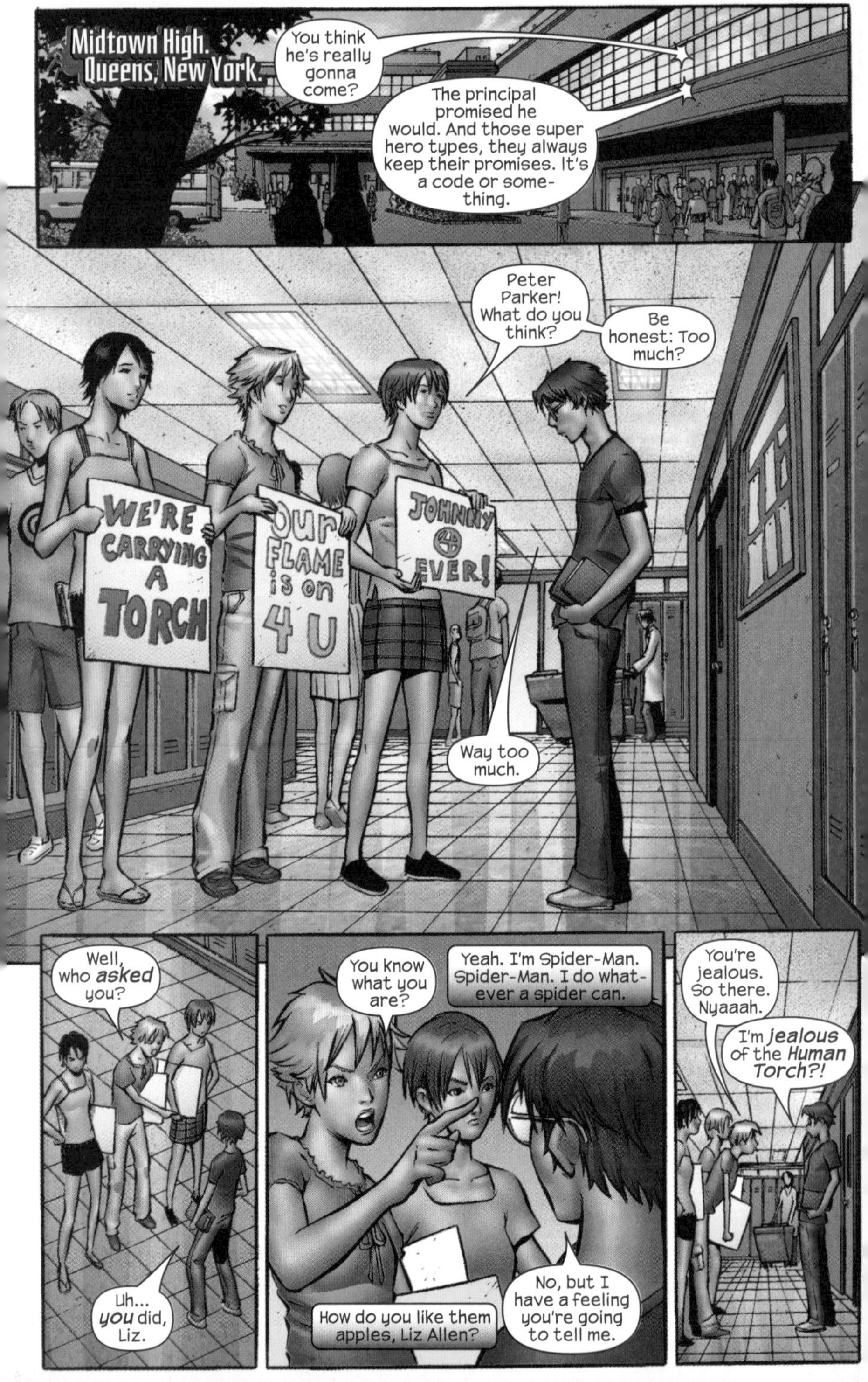

Midtown High. Queens, New York.
You think he's really gonna come?
The principal promised he would. And those super hero types, they always keep their promises. It's a code or some-thing.
WE'RE CARRYING A TORCH
OUR FLAME is on 4 U
JOHNNY 4 EVER!
Peter Parker! What do you think?
Be honest: Too much?
Way too much.
Well, who *asked* you?
Uh... *you* did, Liz.
You know what you are?
Yeah. I'm Spider-Man. Spider-Man. I do what-ever a spider can.
No, but I have a feeling you're going to tell me.
How do you like them apples, Liz Allen?
You're jealous. So there. Nyaaah.
I'm *jealous* of the *Human Torch?!*

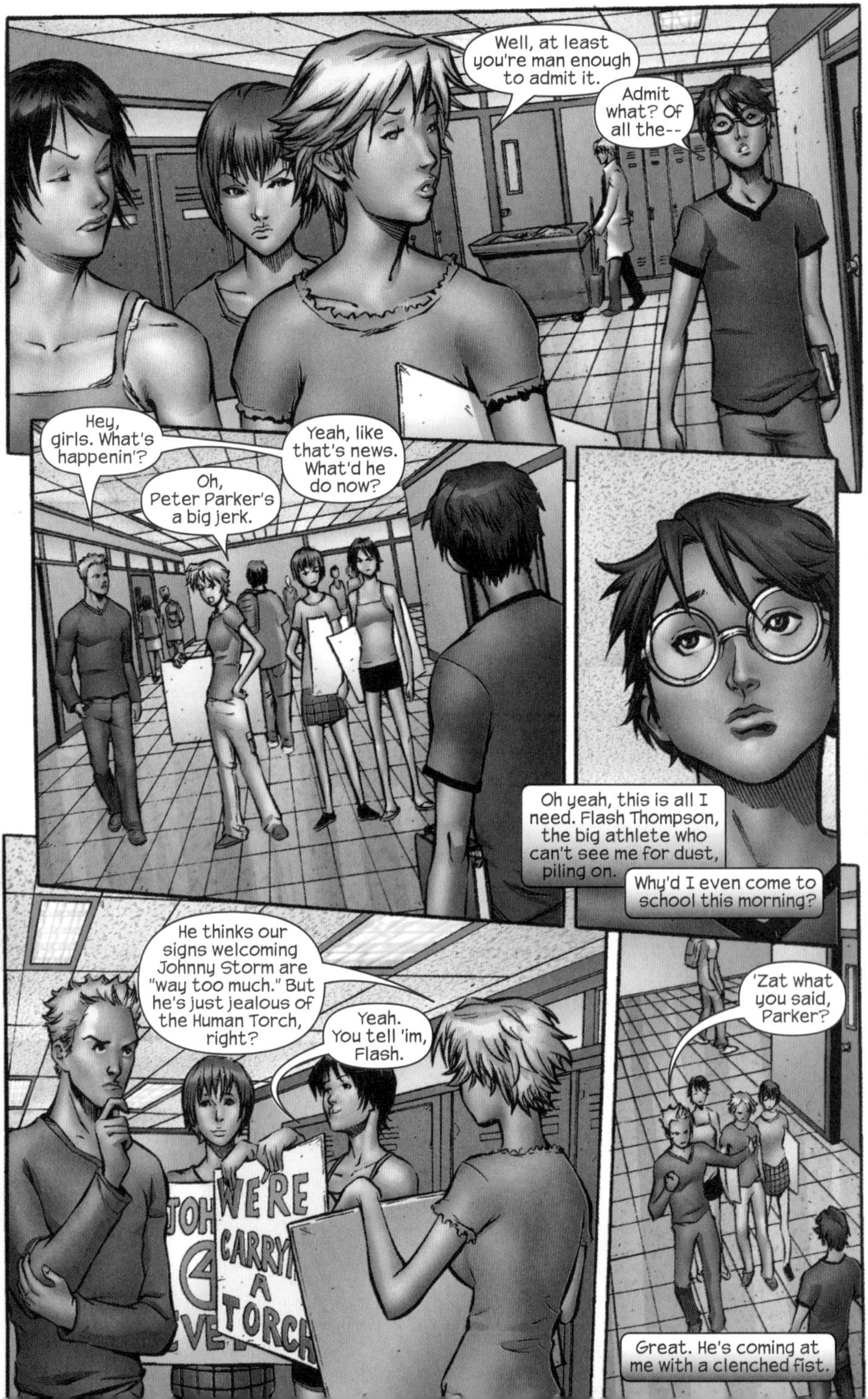
Well, at least you're man enough to admit it.
Admit what? Of all the--
Hey, girls. What's happenin'?
Yeah, like that's news. What'd he do now?
Oh, Peter Parker's a big jerk.
Oh yeah, this is all I need. Flash Thompson, the big athlete who can't see me for dust, piling on.
Why'd I even come to school this morning?
He thinks our signs welcoming Johnny Storm are "way too much." But he's just jealous of the Human Torch, right?
Yeah. You tell 'im, Flash.
WE'RE CARRYI A TORCH
'Zat what you said, Parker?
Great. He's coming at me with a clenched fist.

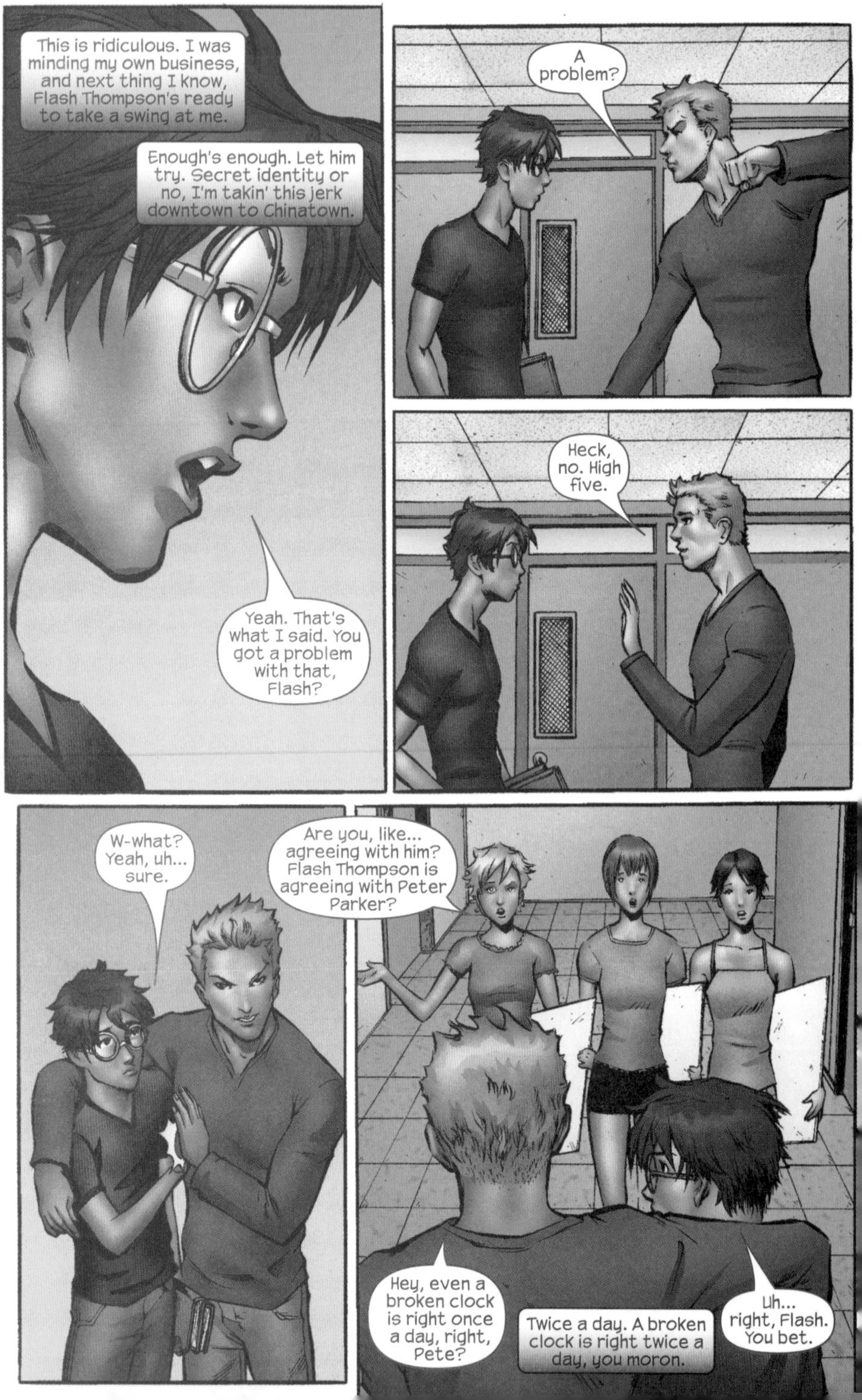
This is ridiculous. I was minding my own business, and next thing I know, Flash Thompson's ready to take a swing at me.
Enough's enough. Let him try. Secret identity or no, I'm takin' this jerk downtown to Chinatown.
Yeah. That's what I said. You got a problem with that, Flash?
A problem?
Heck, no. High five.
W-what? Yeah, uh... sure.
Are you, like... agreeing with him? Flash Thompson is agreeing with Peter Parker?
Hey, even a broken clock is right once a day, right, Pete?
Twice a day. A broken clock is right twice a day, you moron.
Uh... right, Flash. You bet.

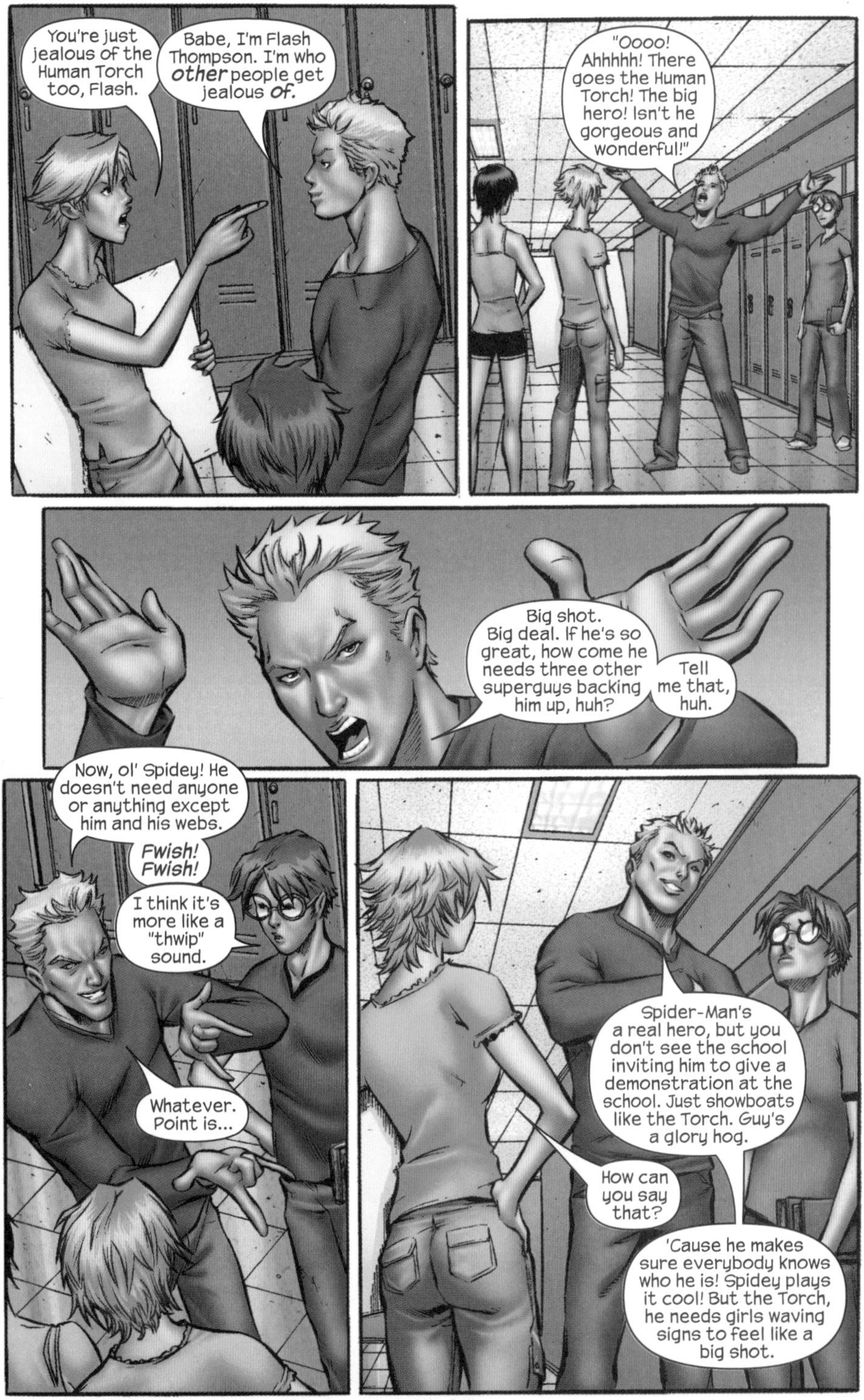
You're just jealous of the Human Torch too, Flash.
Babe, I'm Flash Thompson. I'm who *other* people get jealous *of.*
"Oooo! Ahhhhh! There goes the Human Torch! The big hero! Isn't he gorgeous and wonderful!"
Big shot. Big deal. If he's so great, how come he needs three other superguys backing him up, huh?
Tell me that, huh.
Now, ol' Spidey! He doesn't need anyone or anything except him and his webs.
Fwish! Fwish!
I think it's more like a "thwip" sound.
Whatever. Point is...
Spider-Man's a real hero, but you don't see the school inviting him to give a demonstration at the school. Just showboats like the Torch. Guy's a glory hog.
How can you say that?
'Cause he makes sure everybody knows who he is! Spidey plays it cool! But the Torch, he needs girls waving signs to feel like a big shot.

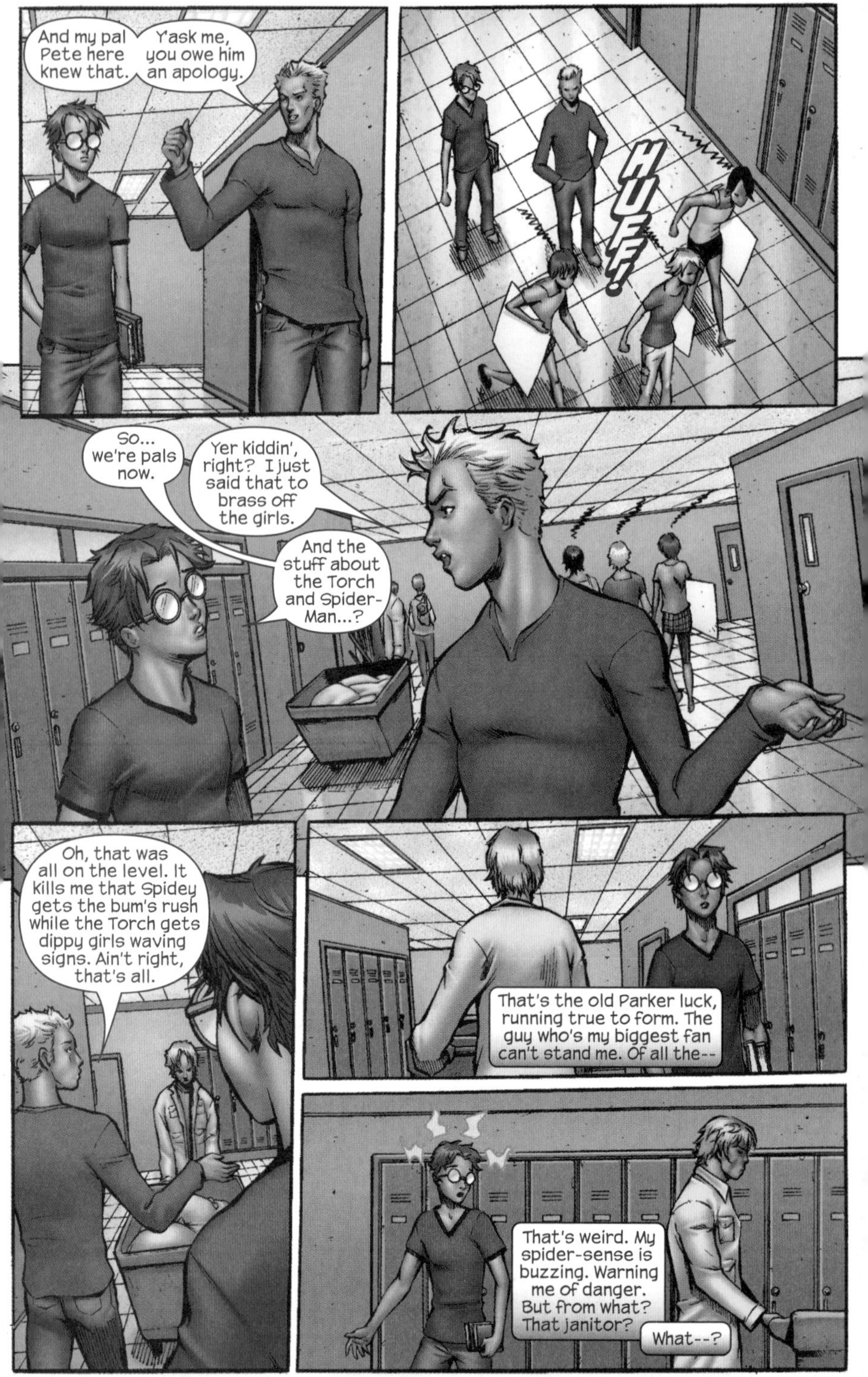
And my pal Pete here knew that.
Y'ask me, you owe him an apology.
HUFF!
So... we're pals now.
Yer kiddin', right? I just said that to brass off the girls.
And the stuff about the Torch and Spider-Man...?
Oh, that was all on the level. It kills me that Spidey gets the bum's rush while the Torch gets dippy girls waving signs. Ain't right, that's all.
That's the old Parker luck, running true to form. The guy who's my biggest fan can't stand me. Of all the--
That's weird. My spider-sense is buzzing. Warning me of danger. But from what? That janitor?
What--?

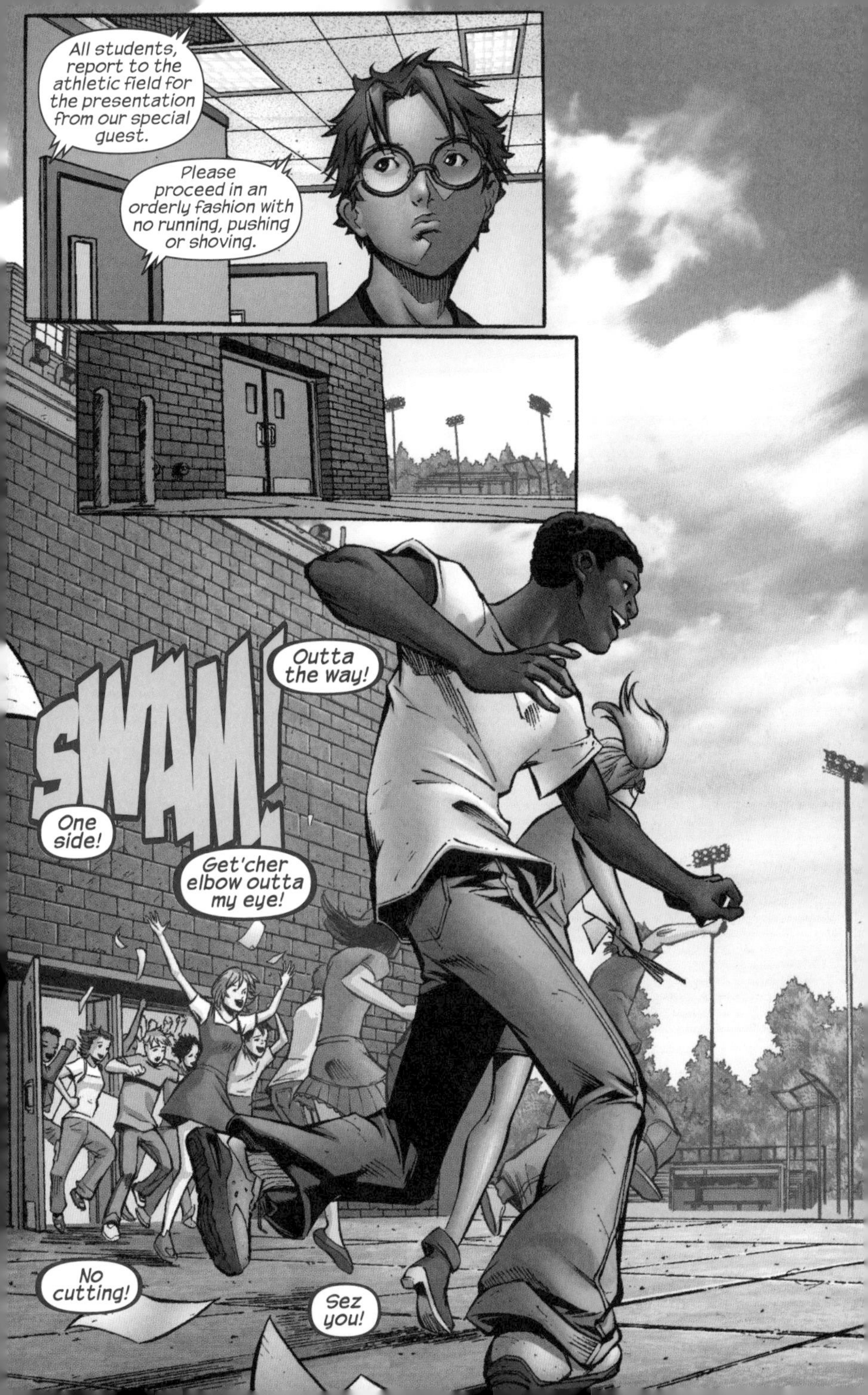
All students, report to the athletic field for the presentation from our special guest.
Please proceed in an orderly fashion with no running, pushing or shoving.
SWAM!
Outta the way!
One side!
Get'cher elbow outta my eye!
No cutting!
Sez you!

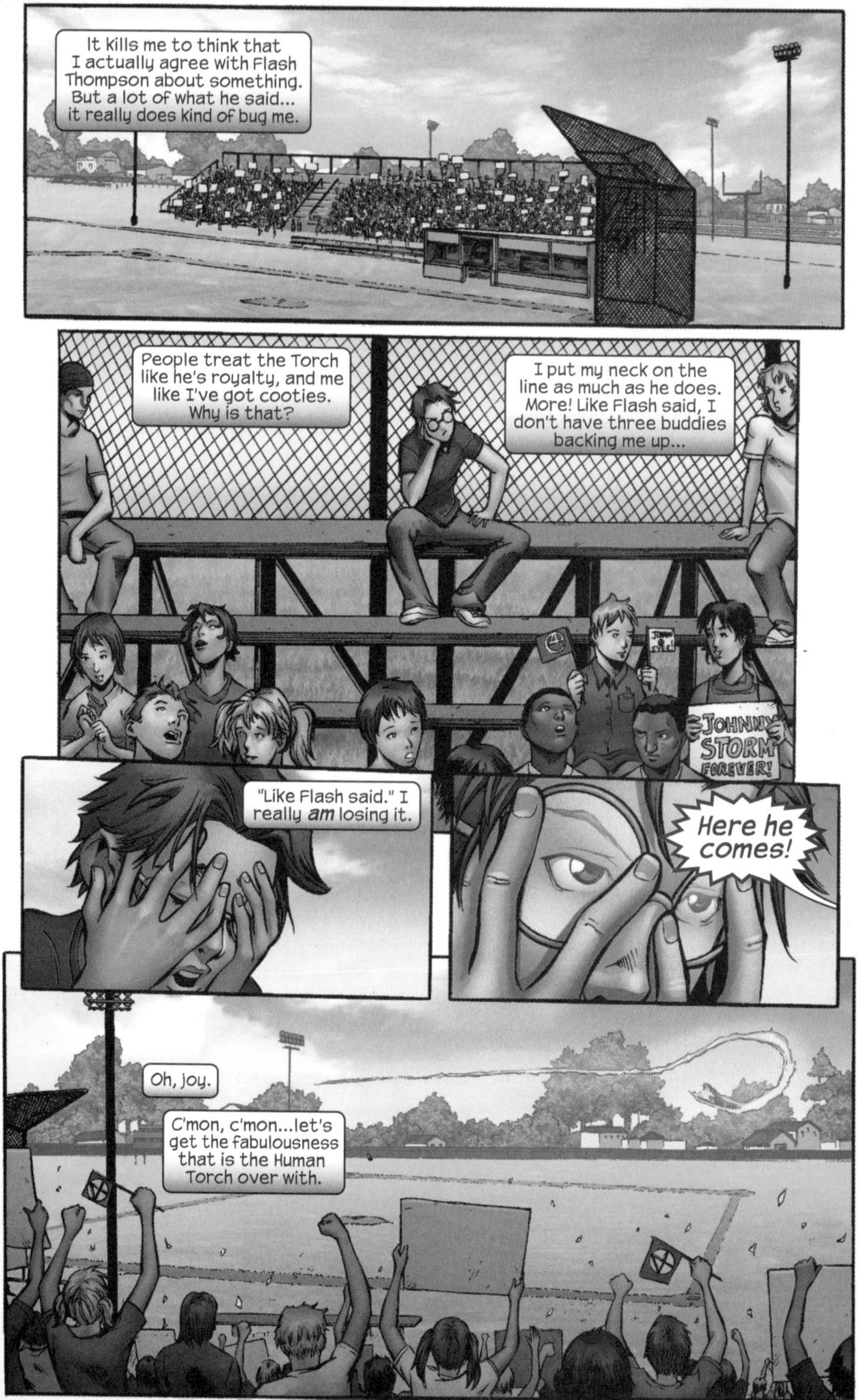
It kills me to think that I actually agree with Flash Thompson about something. But a lot of what he said... it really does kind of bug me.
People treat the Torch like he's royalty, and me like I've got cooties. Why is that?
I put my neck on the line as much as he does. More! Like Flash said, I don't have three buddies backing me up...
JOHNNY STORM FOREVER!
"Like Flash said." I really *am* losing it.
Here he comes!
Oh, joy.
C'mon, c'mon...let's get the fabulousness that is the Human Torch over with.

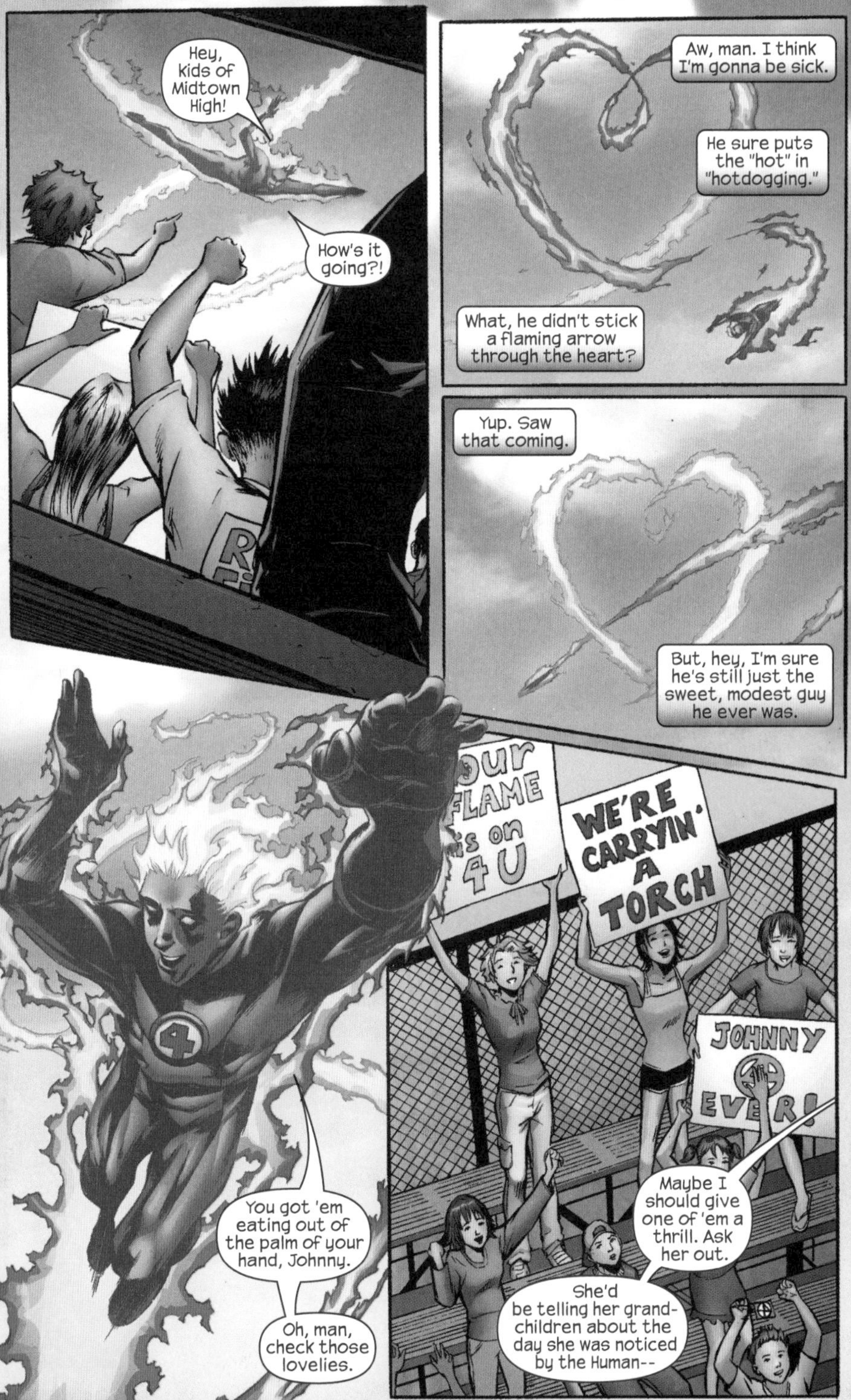
Hey, kids of Midtown High!
How's it going?!
Aw, man. I think I'm gonna be sick.
He sure puts the "hot" in "hotdogging."
What, he didn't stick a flaming arrow through the heart?
Yup. Saw that coming.
But, hey, I'm sure he's still just the sweet, modest guy he ever was.
FLAME is on 4U
WE'RE CARRYIN' A TORCH
JOHNNY 4 EVER!
You got 'em eating out of the palm of your hand, Johnny.
Oh, man, check those lovelies.
Maybe I should give one of 'em a thrill. Ask her out.
She'd be telling her grand-children about the day she was noticed by the Human--

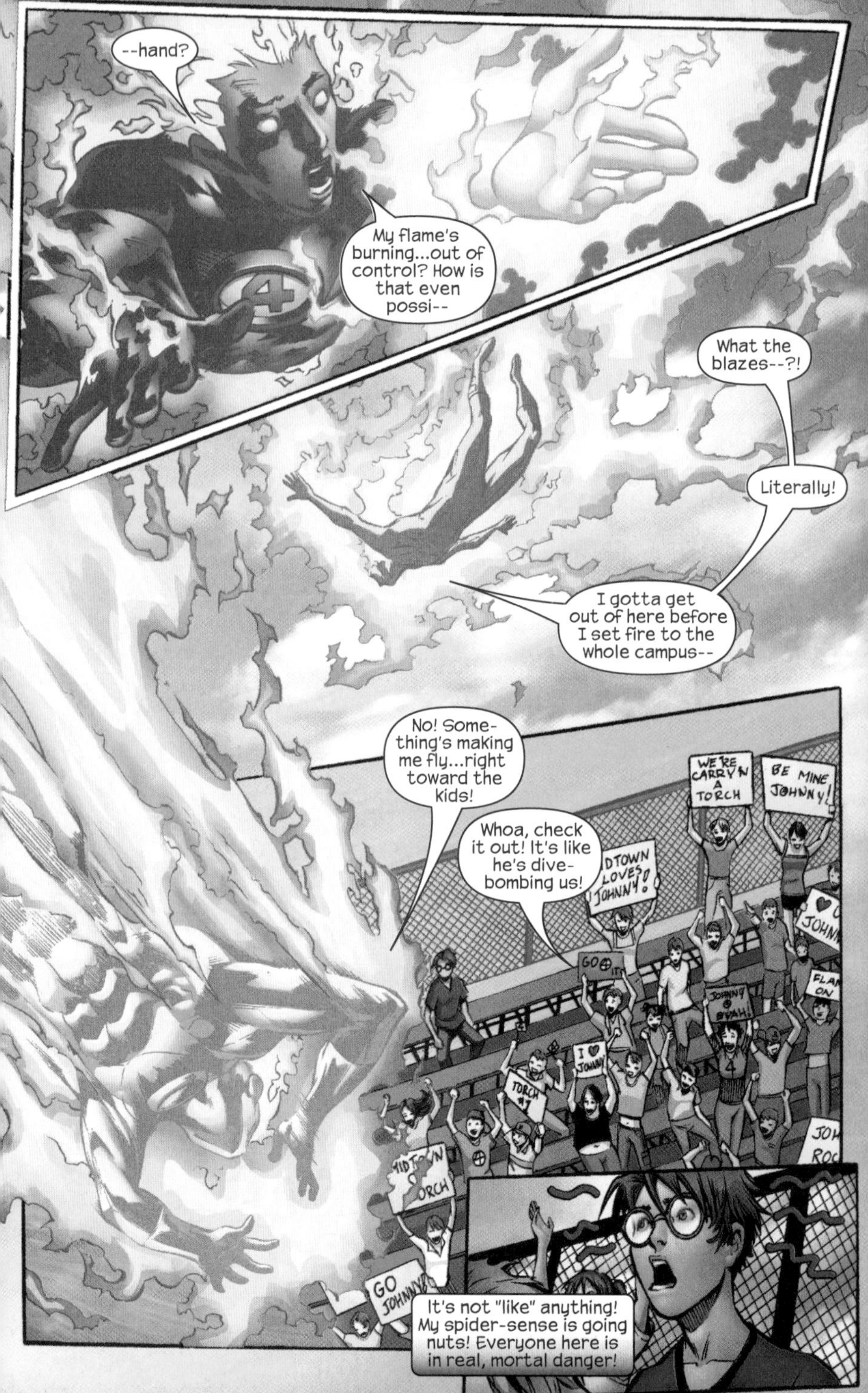
--hand?
My flame's burning...out of control? How is that even possi--
What the blazes--?!
Literally!
I gotta get out of here before I set fire to the whole campus--
No! Some-thing's making me fly...right toward the kids!
Whoa, check it out! It's like he's dive-bombing us!
WE'RE CARRY'N A TORCH
BE MINE JOHNNY!
TORCH #1
GO JOHNNY
It's not "like" anything! My spider-sense is going nuts! Everyone here is in real, mortal danger!

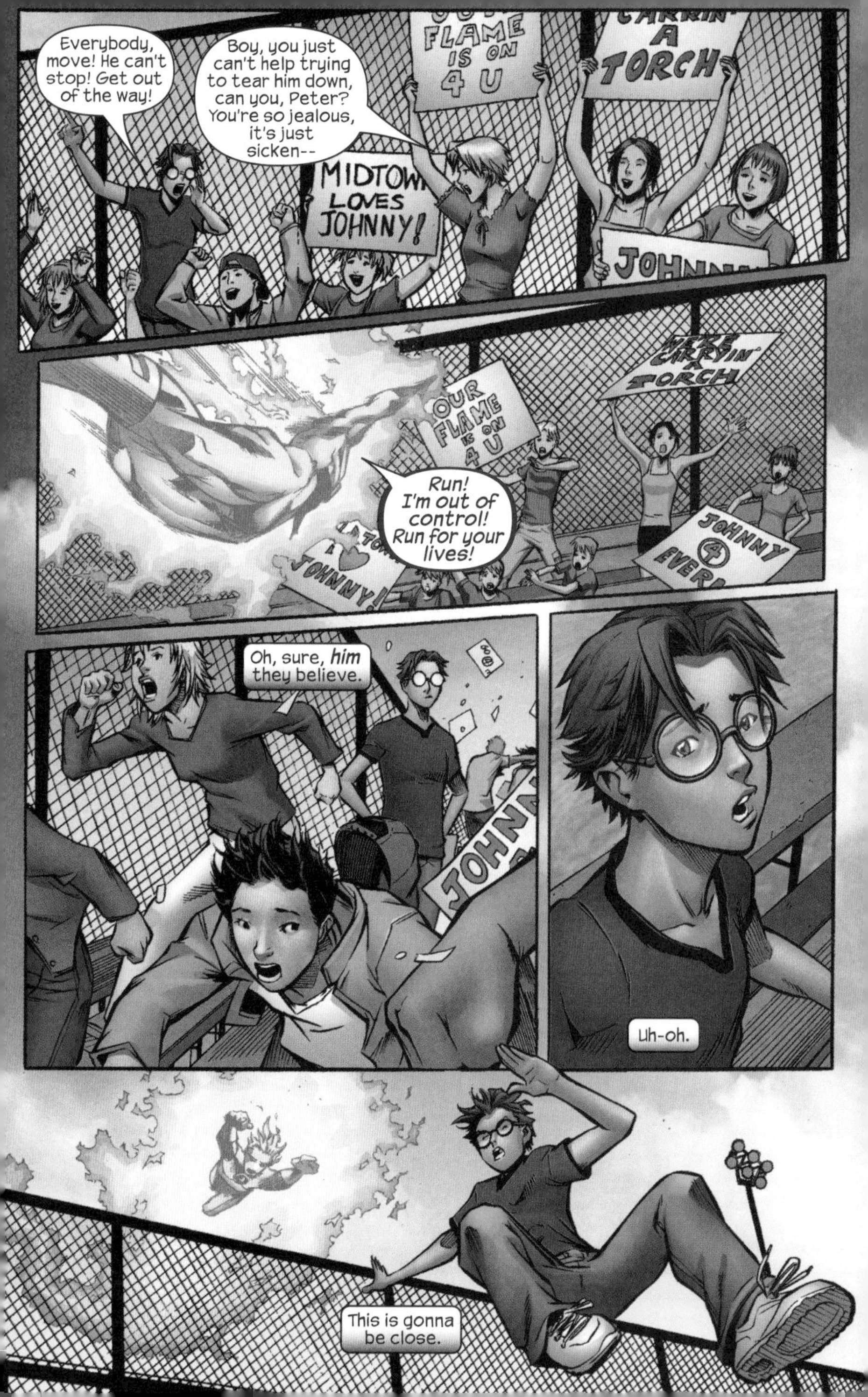
Everybody, move! He can't stop! Get out of the way!
Boy, you just can't help trying to tear him down, can you, Peter? You're so jealous, it's just sicken--
FLAME IS ON 4 U
A TORCH
MIDTOWN LOVES JOHNNY!
WE'RE CARRYIN' A TORCH
OUR FLAME IS ON 4 U
Run! I'm out of control! Run for your lives!
JOHNNY!
Oh, sure, him they believe.
Uh-oh.
This is gonna be close.

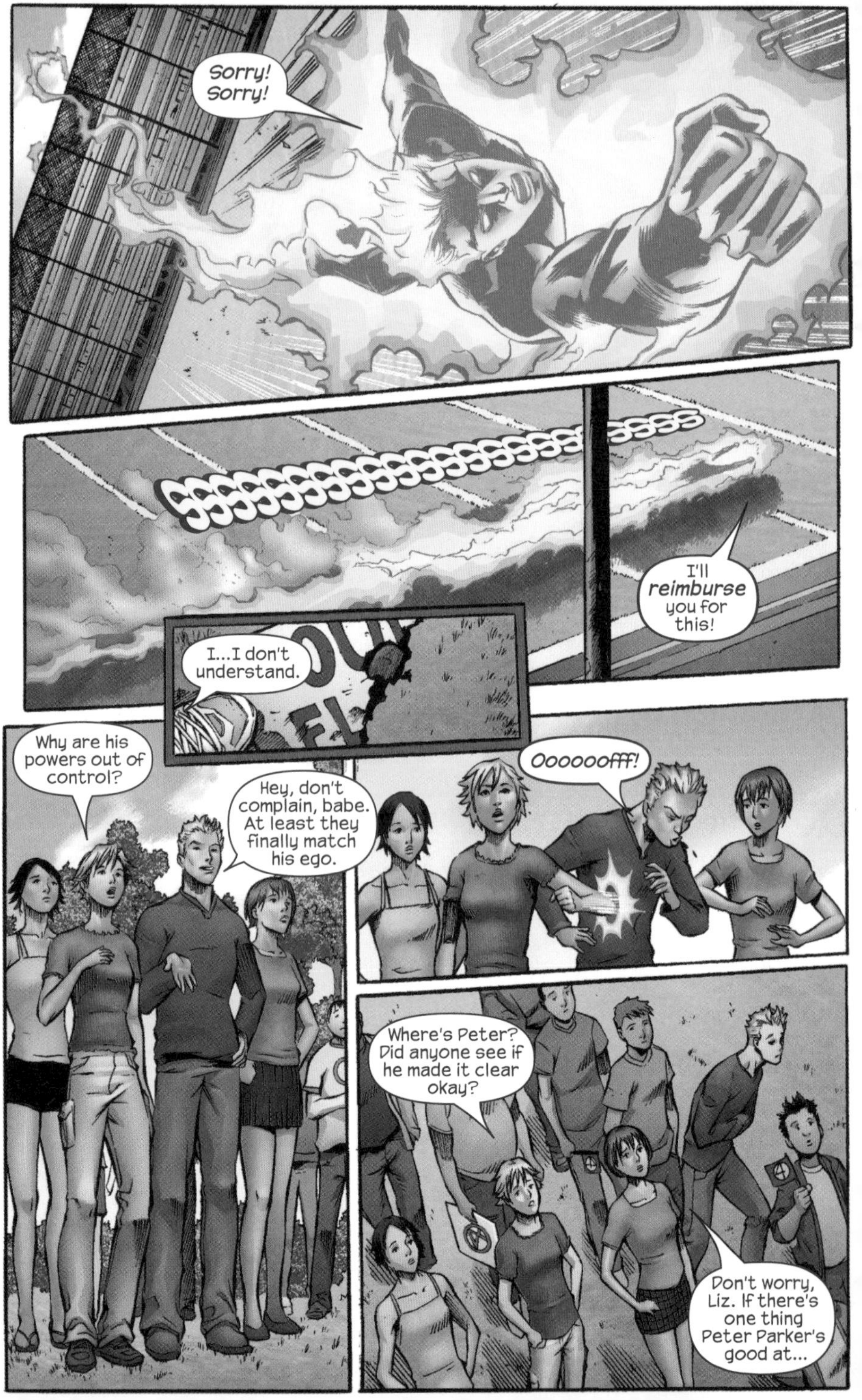
Sorry! Sorry!
SSSSSSSSSSSSSSSSSSSSSSSSS
I'll *reimburse* you for this!
I...I don't understand.
Why are his powers out of control?
Hey, don't complain, babe. At least they finally match his ego.
Ooooooffff!
Where's Peter? Did anyone see if he made it clear okay?
Don't worry, Liz. If there's one thing Peter Parker's good at...

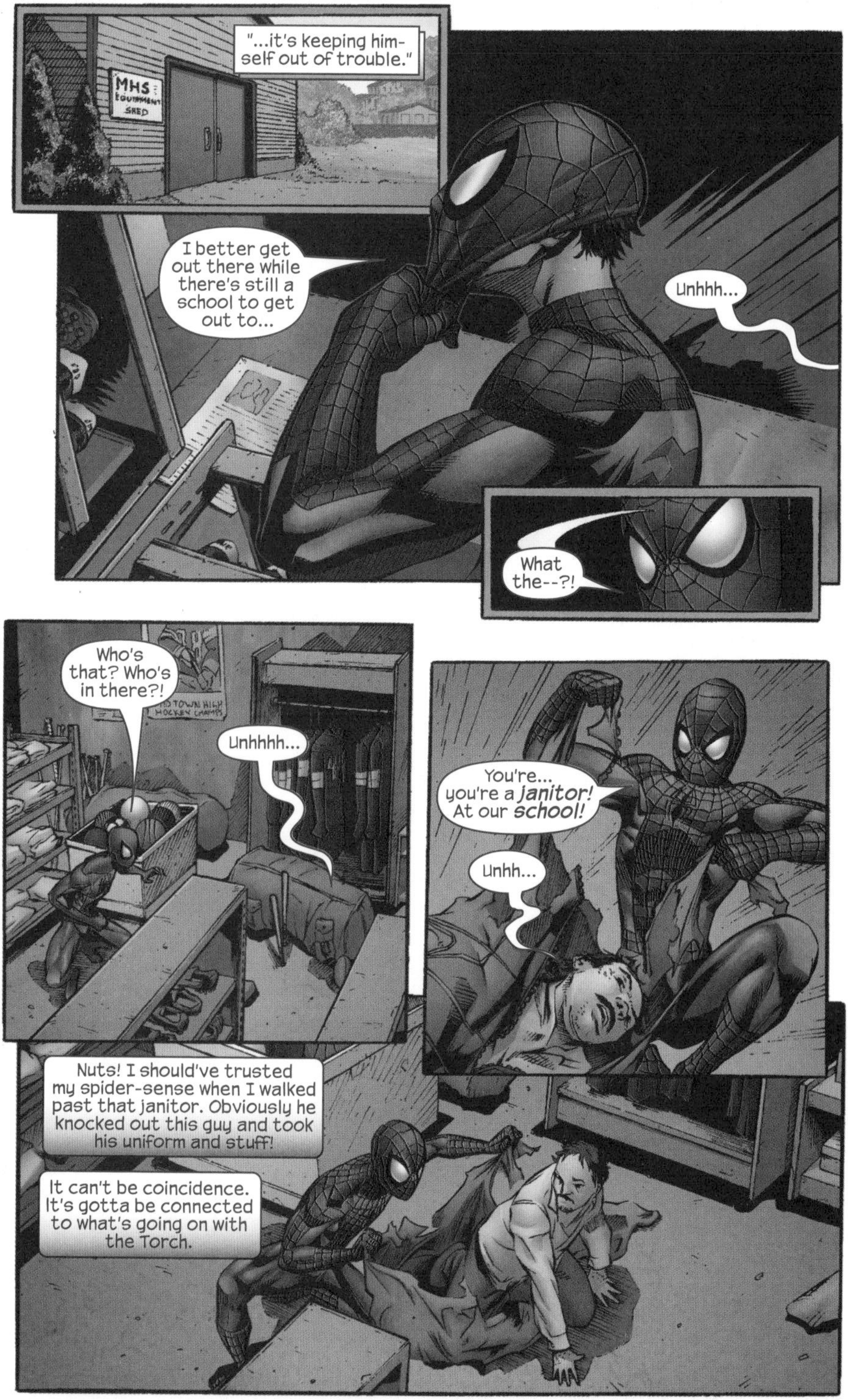
"...it's keeping him-self out of trouble."
MHS EQUIPMENT SHED
I better get out there while there's still a school to get out to...
Unhhh...
What the--?!
Who's that? Who's in there?!
Unhhhh...
You're... you're a *janitor!* At our *school!*
Unhh...
Nuts! I should've trusted my spider-sense when I walked past that janitor. Obviously he knocked out this guy and took his uniform and stuff!
It can't be coincidence. It's gotta be connected to what's going on with the Torch.

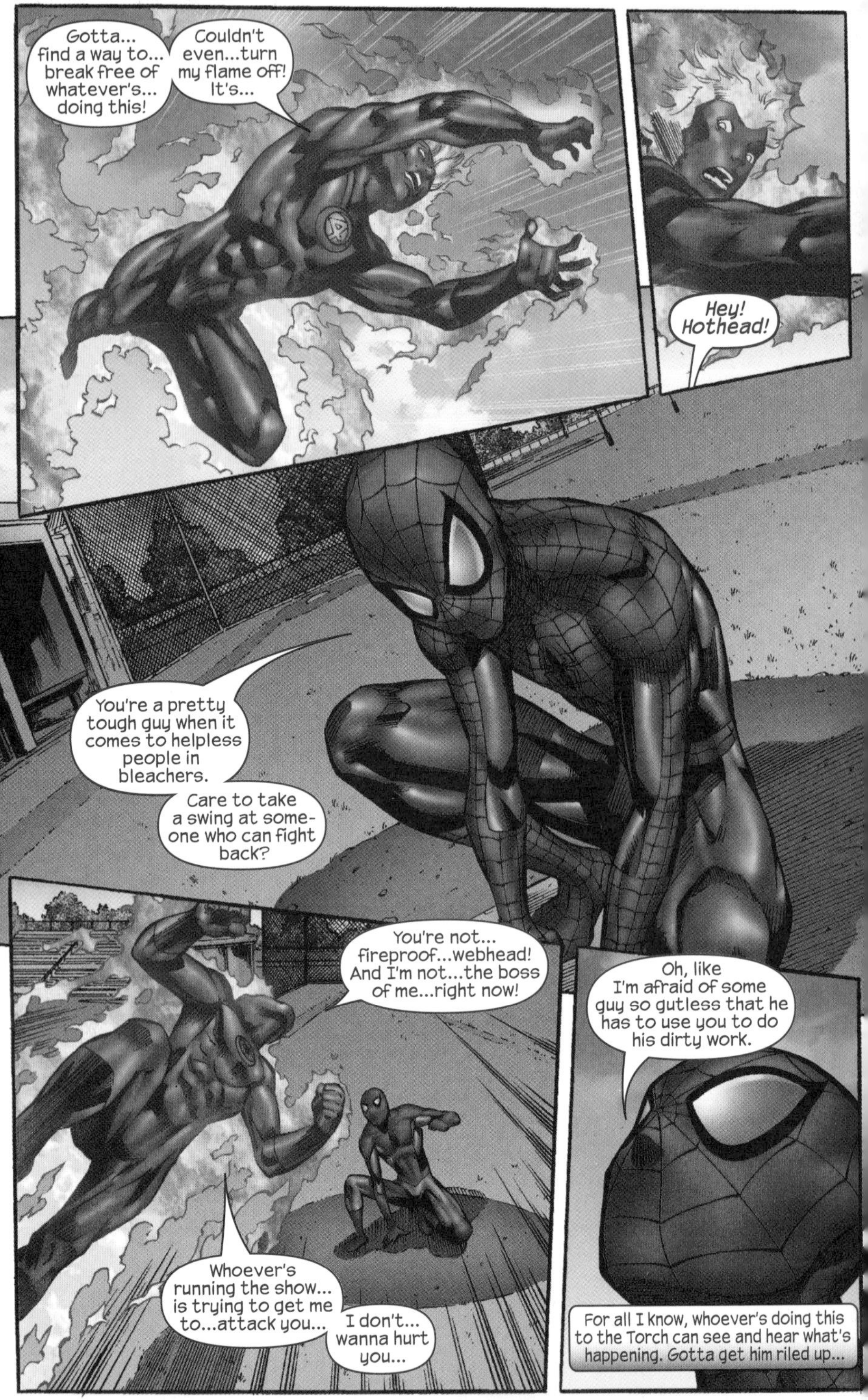
Gotta... find a way to... break free of whatever's... doing this!
Couldn't even...turn my flame off! It's...
Hey! Hothead!
You're a pretty tough guy when it comes to helpless people in bleachers.
Care to take a swing at some-one who can fight back?
You're not... fireproof...webhead! And I'm not...the boss of me...right now!
Whoever's running the show... is trying to get me to...attack you...
I don't... wanna hurt you...
Oh, like I'm afraid of some guy so gutless that he has to use you to do his dirty work.
For all I know, whoever's doing this to the Torch can see and hear what's happening. Gotta get him riled up...

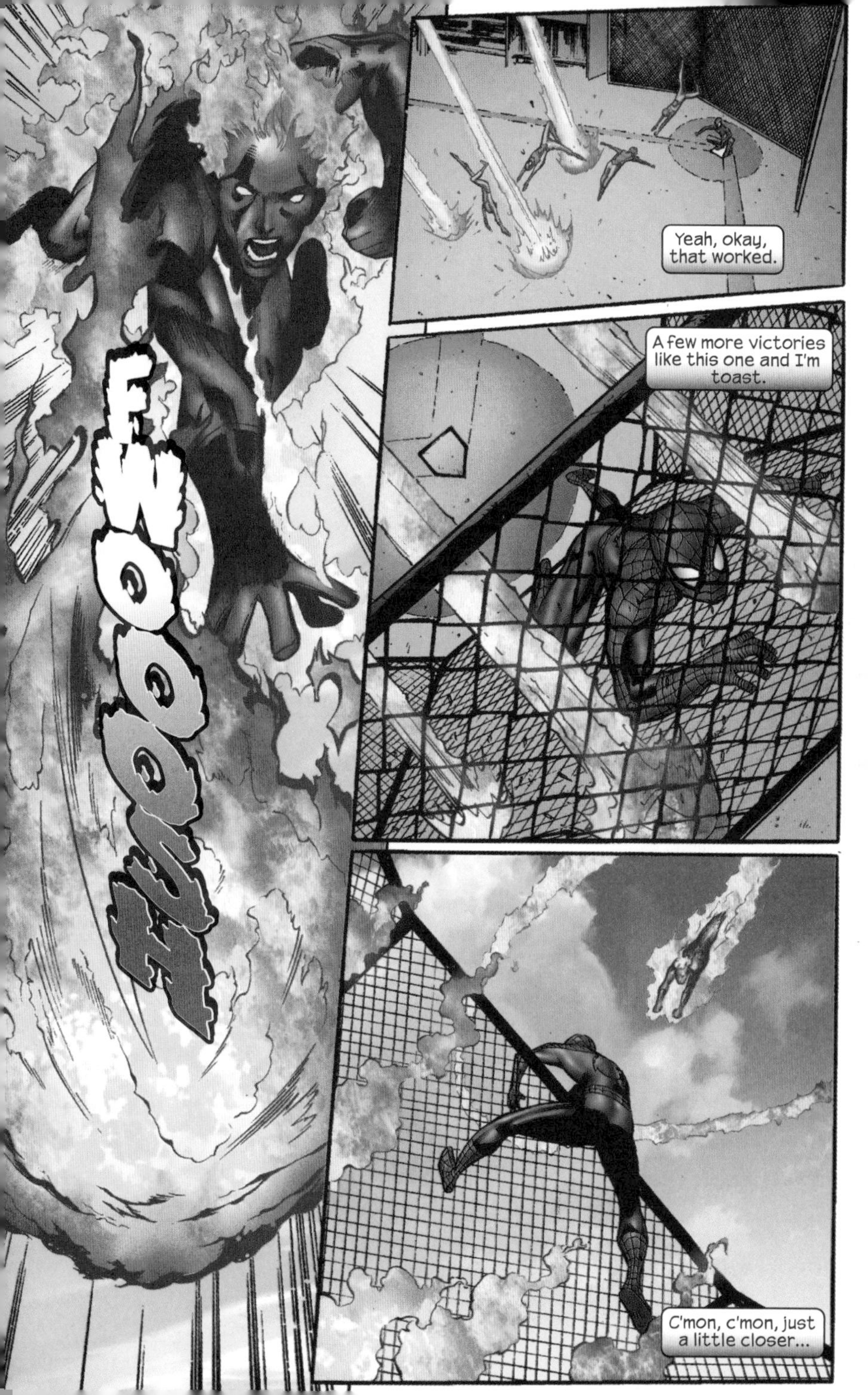
Yeah, okay, that worked.
A few more victories like this one and I'm toast.
FWOOOOSH
C'mon, c'mon, just a little closer...

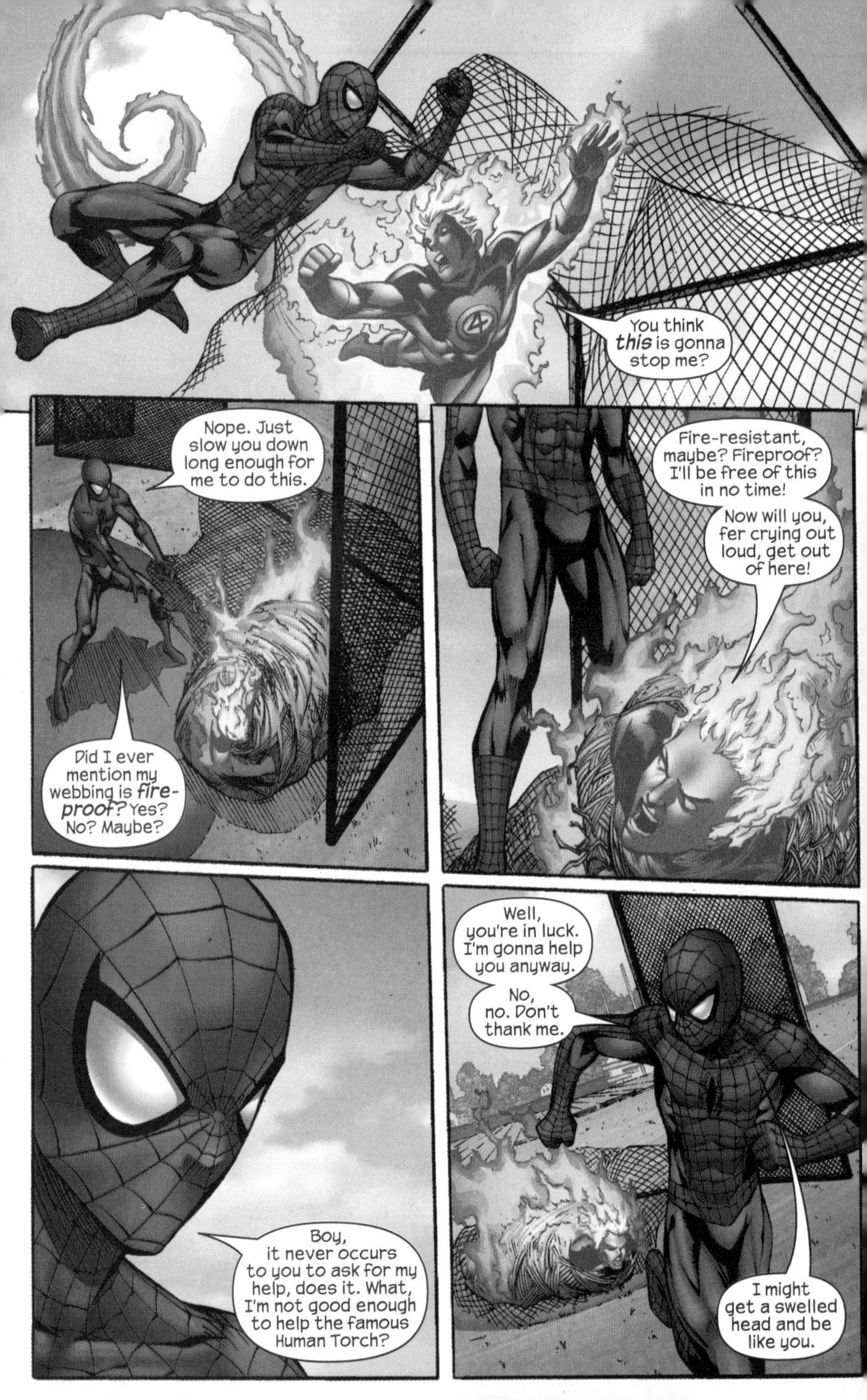

You think *this* is gonna stop me?
Nope. Just slow you down long enough for me to do this.
Did I ever mention my webbing is *fire-proof?* Yes? No? Maybe?
Fire-resistant, maybe? Fireproof? I'll be free of this in no time!
Now will you, fer crying out loud, get out of here!
Boy, it never occurs to you to ask for my help, does it. What, I'm not good enough to help the famous Human Torch?
Well, you're in luck. I'm gonna help you anyway.
No, no. Don't thank me.
I might get a swelled head and be like you.

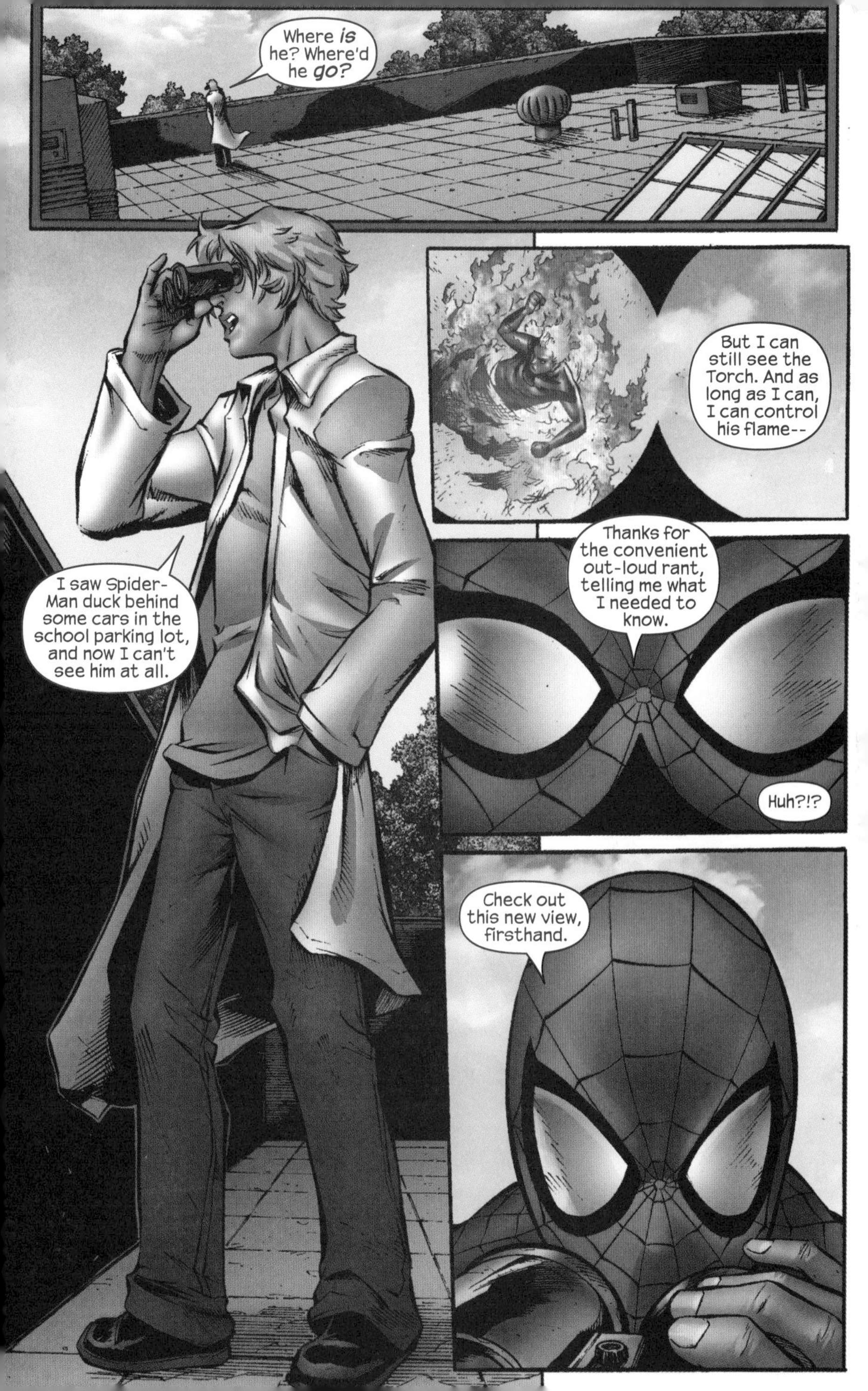
Where *is* he? Where'd he *go?*
I saw Spider-Man duck behind some cars in the school parking lot, and now I can't see him at all.
But I can still see the Torch. And as long as I can, I can control his flame--
Thanks for the convenient out-loud rant, telling me what I needed to know.
Huh?!?
Check out this new view, firsthand.

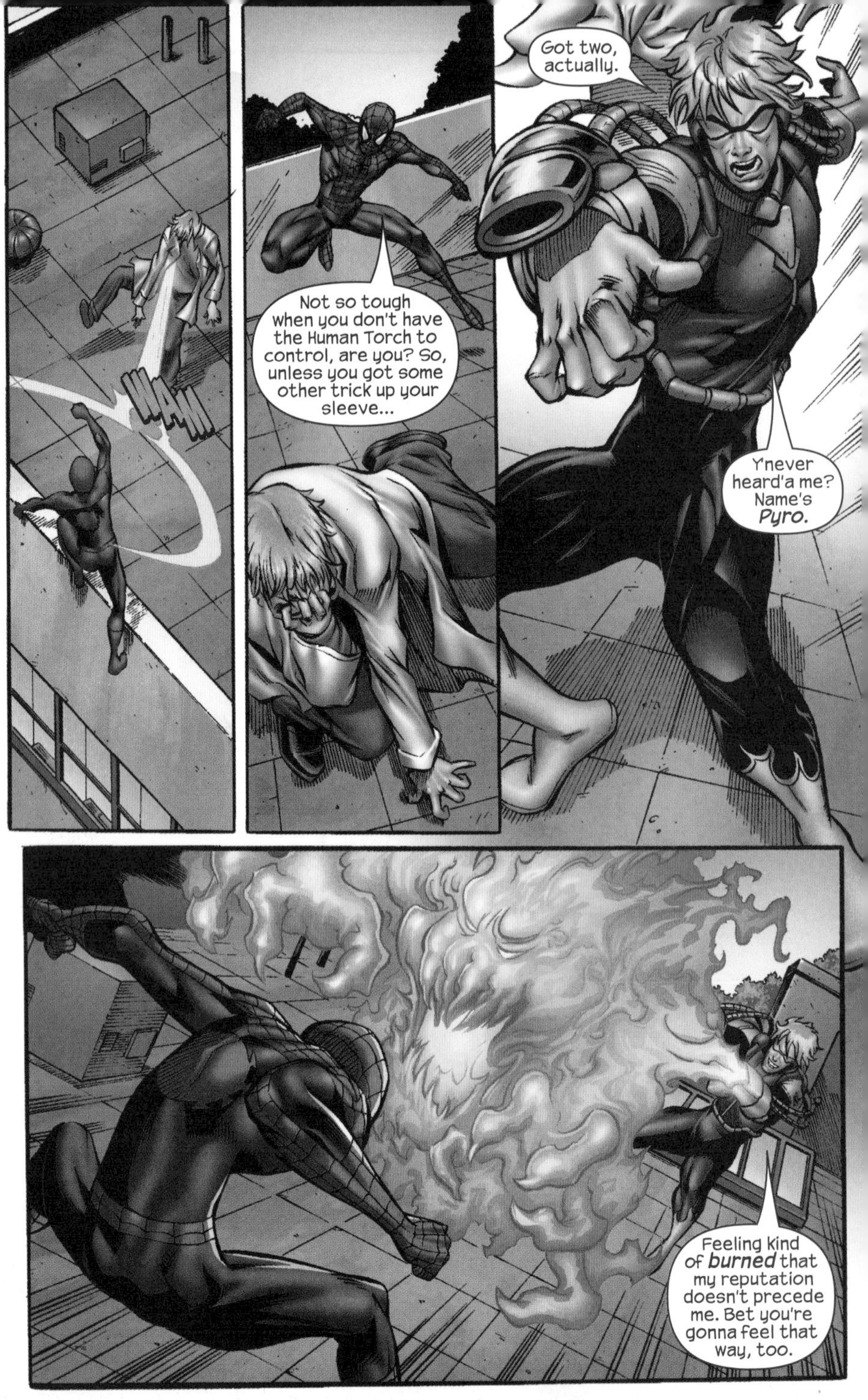
WAM
Not so tough when you don't have the Human Torch to control, are you? So, unless you got some other trick up your sleeve...
Got two, actually.
Y'never heard'a me? Name's *Pyro.*
Feeling kind of ***burned*** that my reputation doesn't precede me. Bet you're gonna feel that way, too.

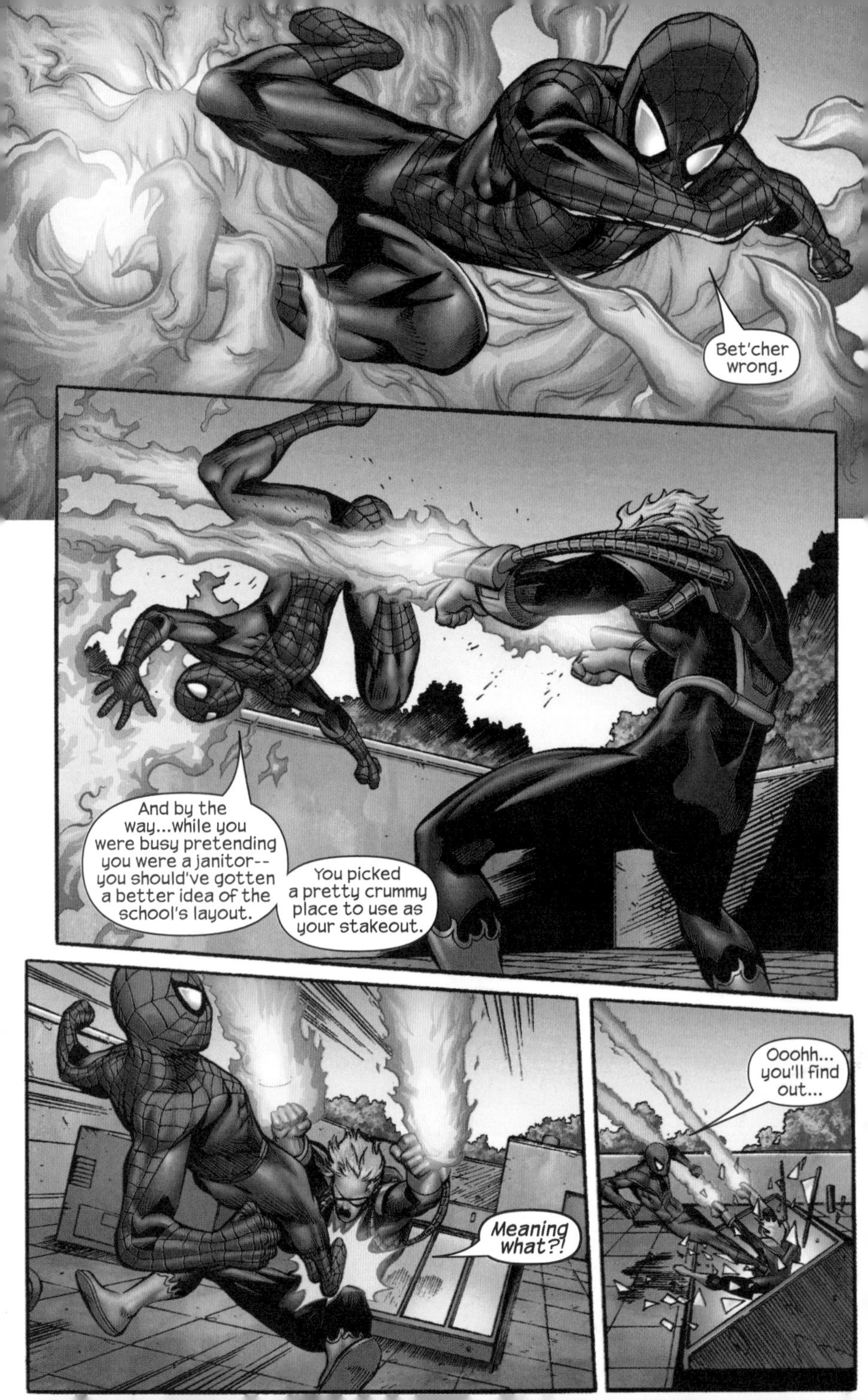
Bet'cher wrong.
And by the way...while you were busy pretending you were a janitor-- you should've gotten a better idea of the school's layout.
You picked a pretty crummy place to use as your stakeout.
Meaning what?!
Ooohh... you'll find out...

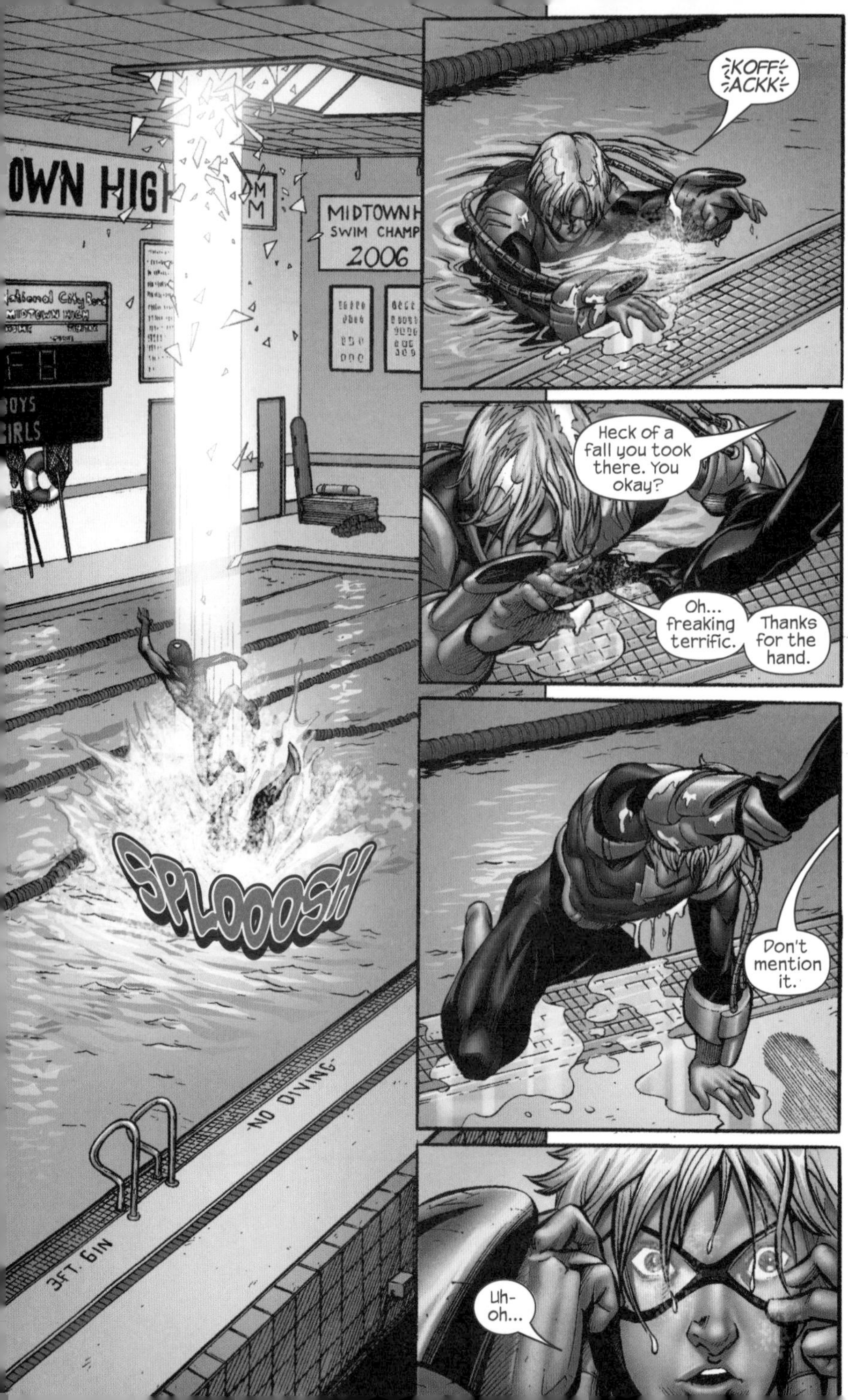
OWN HIGH
MIDTOWN H
SWIM CHAMP
2006
MIDTOWN HIGH
OYS
IRLS
SPLOOOSH
NO DIVING
3FT. 6IN
KOFF ACKK
Heck of a fall you took there. You okay?
Oh... freaking terrific.
Thanks for the hand.
Don't mention it.
Uh-oh...

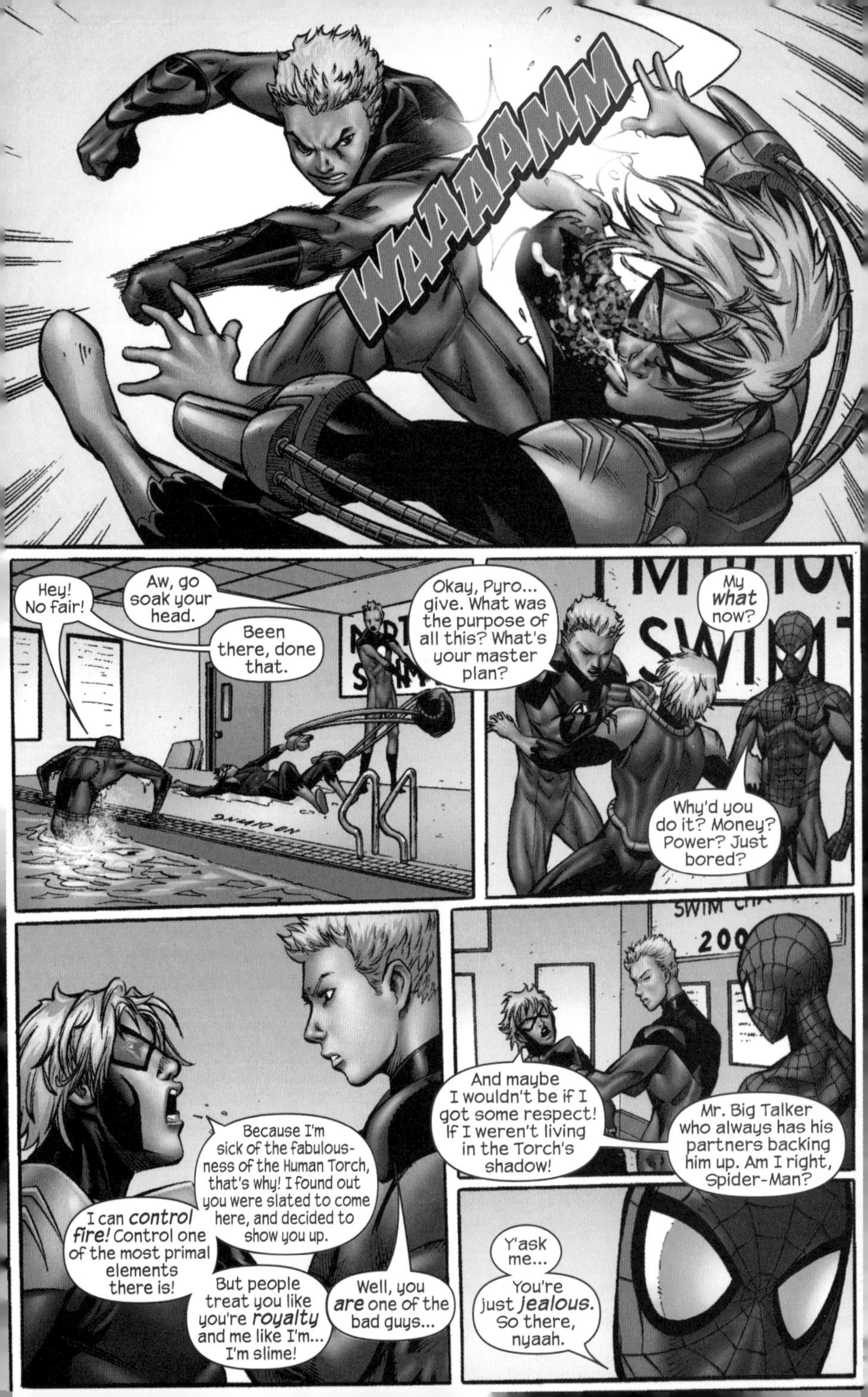
WHAAAMM
Hey! No fair!
Aw, go soak your head.
Been there, done that.
Okay, Pyro... give. What was the purpose of all this? What's your master plan?
My what now?
Why'd you do it? Money? Power? Just bored?
NO DIVING
Because I'm sick of the fabulousness of the Human Torch, that's why! I found out you were slated to come here, and decided to show you up.
I can control fire! Control one of the most primal elements there is!
But people treat you like you're royalty and me like I'm... I'm slime!
Well, you are one of the bad guys...
And maybe I wouldn't be if I got some respect! If I weren't living in the Torch's shadow!
Mr. Big Talker who always has his partners backing him up. Am I right, Spider-Man?
Y'ask me...
You're just jealous. So there, nyaah.

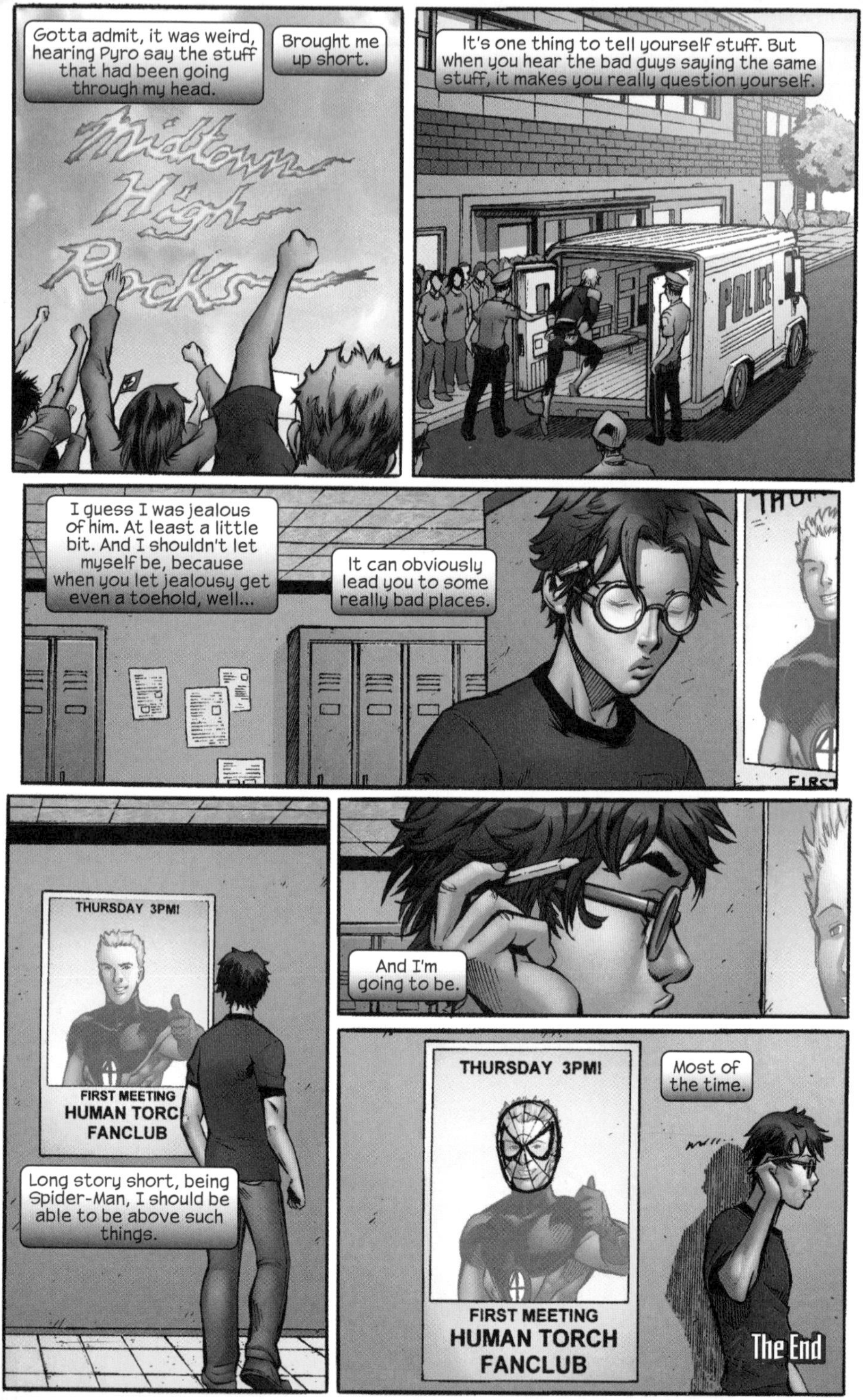
Gotta admit, it was weird, hearing Pyro say the stuff that had been going through my head.
Brought me up short.
Midtown High Rocks
It's one thing to tell yourself stuff. But when you hear the bad guys saying the same stuff, it makes you really question yourself.
POLICE
I guess I was jealous of him. At least a little bit. And I shouldn't let myself be, because when you let jealousy get even a toehold, well...
It can obviously lead you to some really bad places.
THURSDAY 3PM!
FIRST MEETING
HUMAN TORCH
FANCLUB
Long story short, being Spider-Man, I should be able to be above such things.
And I'm going to be.
THURSDAY 3PM!
FIRST MEETING
HUMAN TORCH
FANCLUB
Most of the time.
The End

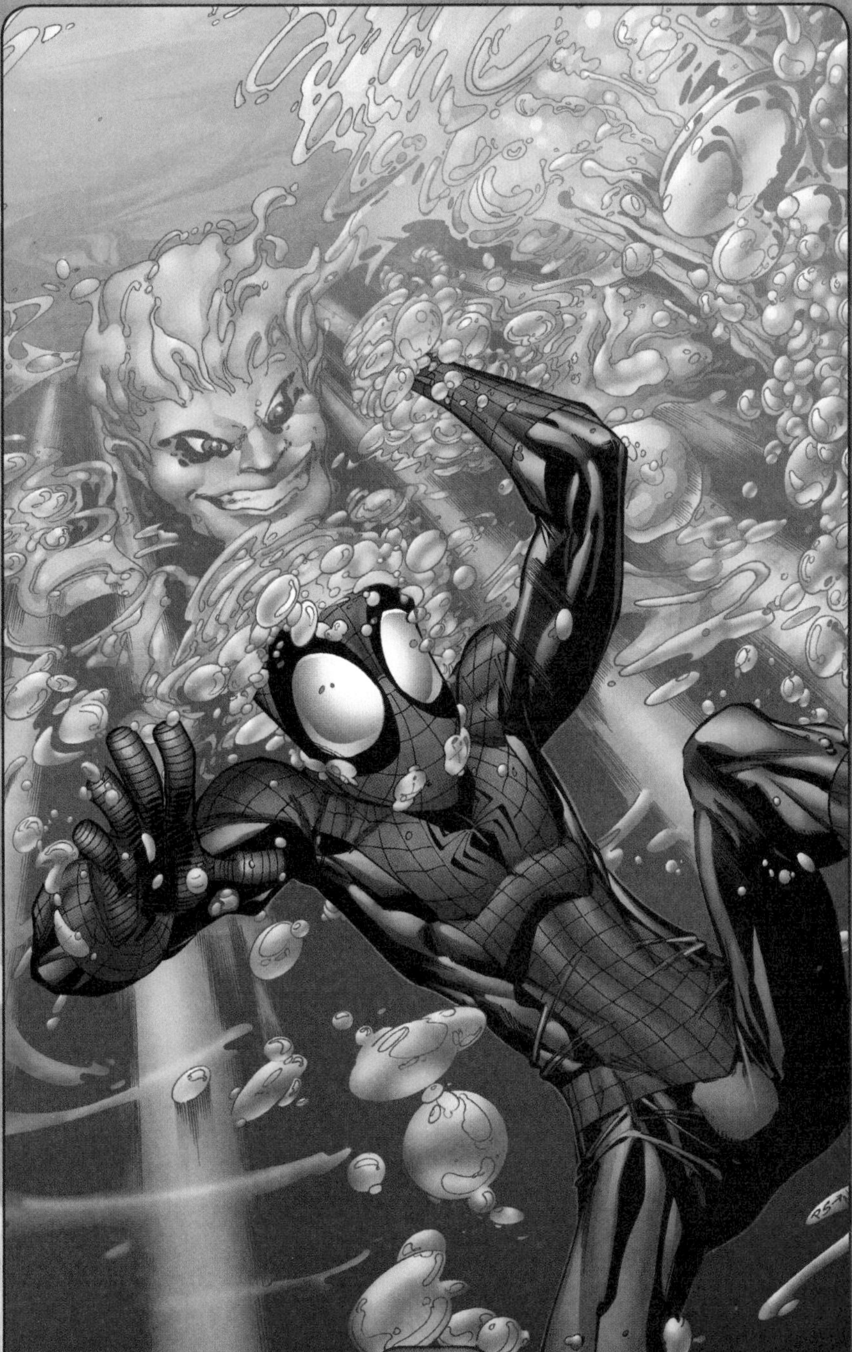

#32

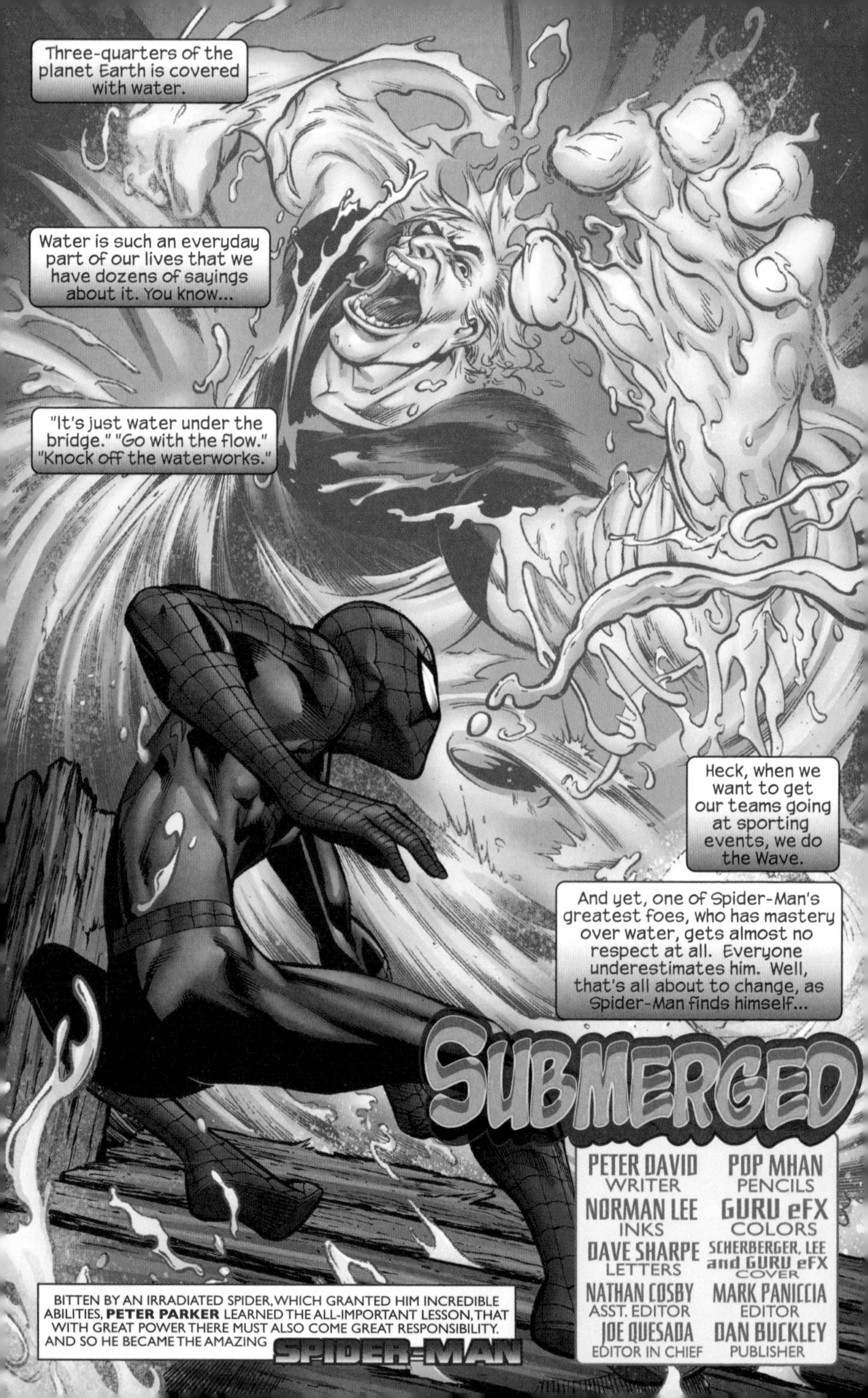

Three-quarters of the planet Earth is covered with water.
Water is such an everyday part of our lives that we have dozens of sayings about it. You know...
"It's just water under the bridge." "Go with the flow." "Knock off the waterworks."
Heck, when we want to get our teams going at sporting events, we do the Wave.
And yet, one of Spider-Man's greatest foes, who has mastery over water, gets almost no respect at all. Everyone underestimates him. Well, that's all about to change, as Spider-Man finds himself...
SUBMERGED
PETER DAVID WRITER
POP MHAN PENCILS
NORMAN LEE INKS
GURU eFX COLORS
DAVE SHARPE LETTERS
SCHERBERGER, LEE and GURU eFX COVER
NATHAN COSBY ASST. EDITOR
MARK PANICCIA EDITOR
JOE QUESADA EDITOR IN CHIEF
DAN BUCKLEY PUBLISHER
BITTEN BY AN IRRADIATED SPIDER, WHICH GRANTED HIM INCREDIBLE ABILITIES, PETER PARKER LEARNED THE ALL-IMPORTANT LESSON, THAT WITH GREAT POWER THERE MUST ALSO COME GREAT RESPONSIBILITY. AND SO HE BECAME THE AMAZING
SPIDER-MAN

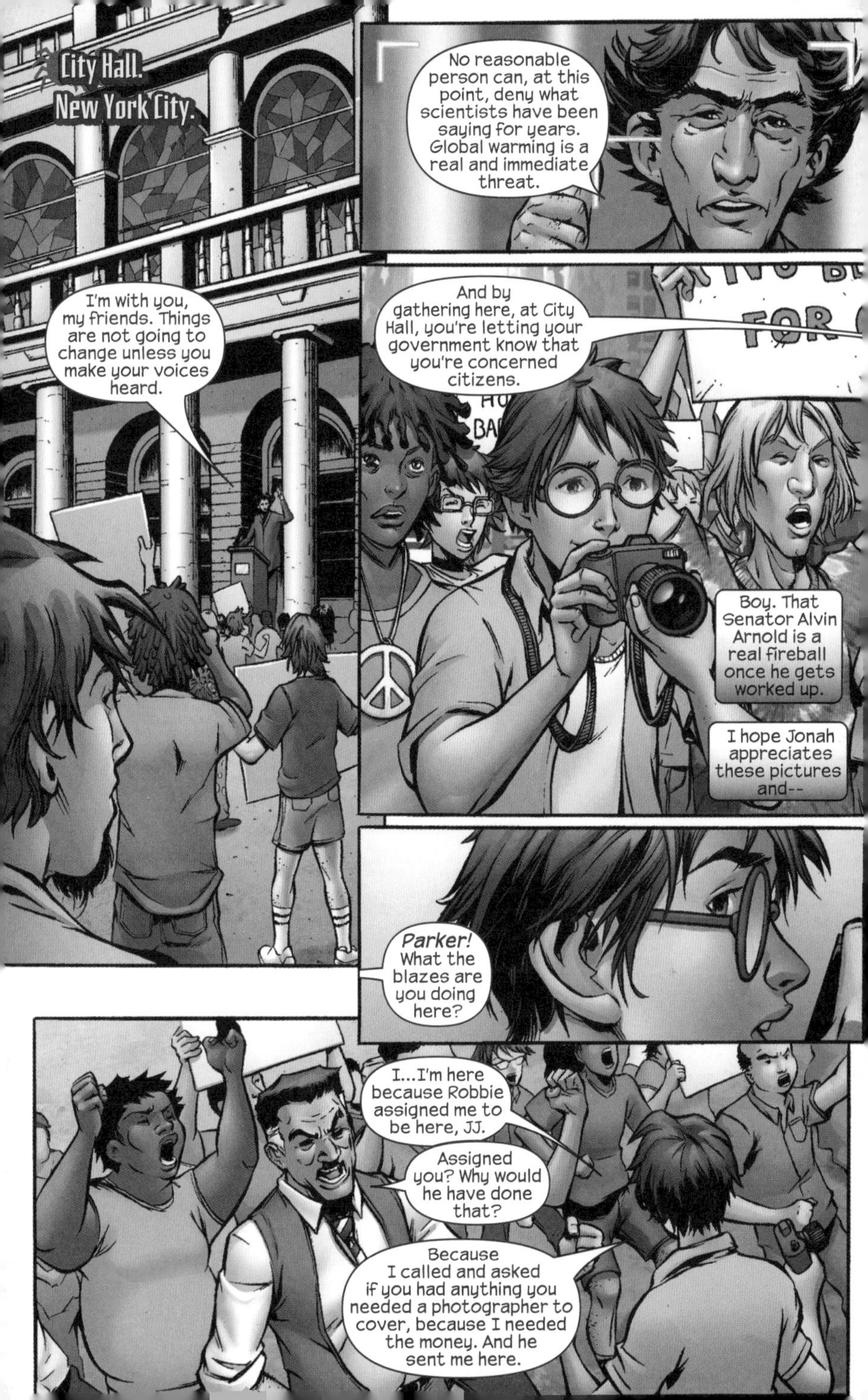
City Hall.
New York City.
I'm with you, my friends. Things are not going to change unless you make your voices heard.
No reasonable person can, at this point, deny what scientists have been saying for years. Global warming is a real and immediate threat.
And by gathering here, at City Hall, you're letting your government know that you're concerned citizens.
Boy. That Senator Alvin Arnold is a real fireball once he gets worked up.
I hope Jonah appreciates these pictures and--
Parker! What the blazes are you doing here?
I...I'm here because Robbie assigned me to be here, JJ.
Assigned you? Why would he have done that?
Because I called and asked if you had anything you needed a photographer to cover, because I needed the money. And he sent me here.

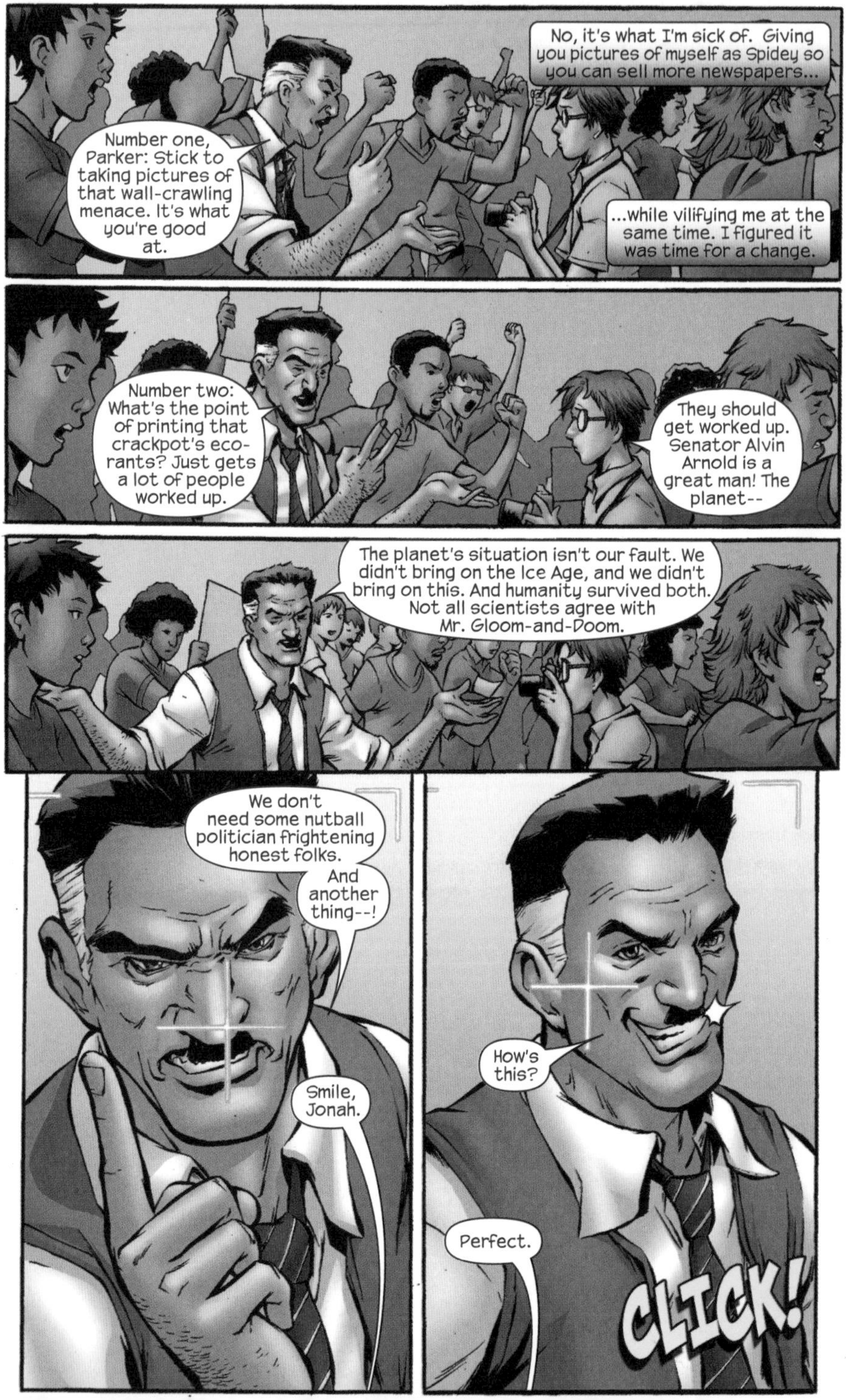
No, it's what I'm sick of. Giving you pictures of myself as Spidey so you can sell more newspapers...
Number one, Parker: Stick to taking pictures of that wall-crawling menace. It's what you're good at.
...while vilifying me at the same time. I figured it was time for a change.
Number two: What's the point of printing that crackpot's eco-rants? Just gets a lot of people worked up.
They should get worked up. Senator Alvin Arnold is a great man! The planet--
The planet's situation isn't our fault. We didn't bring on the Ice Age, and we didn't bring on this. And humanity survived both. Not all scientists agree with Mr. Gloom-and-Doom.
We don't need some nutball politician frightening honest folks.
And another thing--!
Smile, Jonah.
How's this?
Perfect.
CLICK!

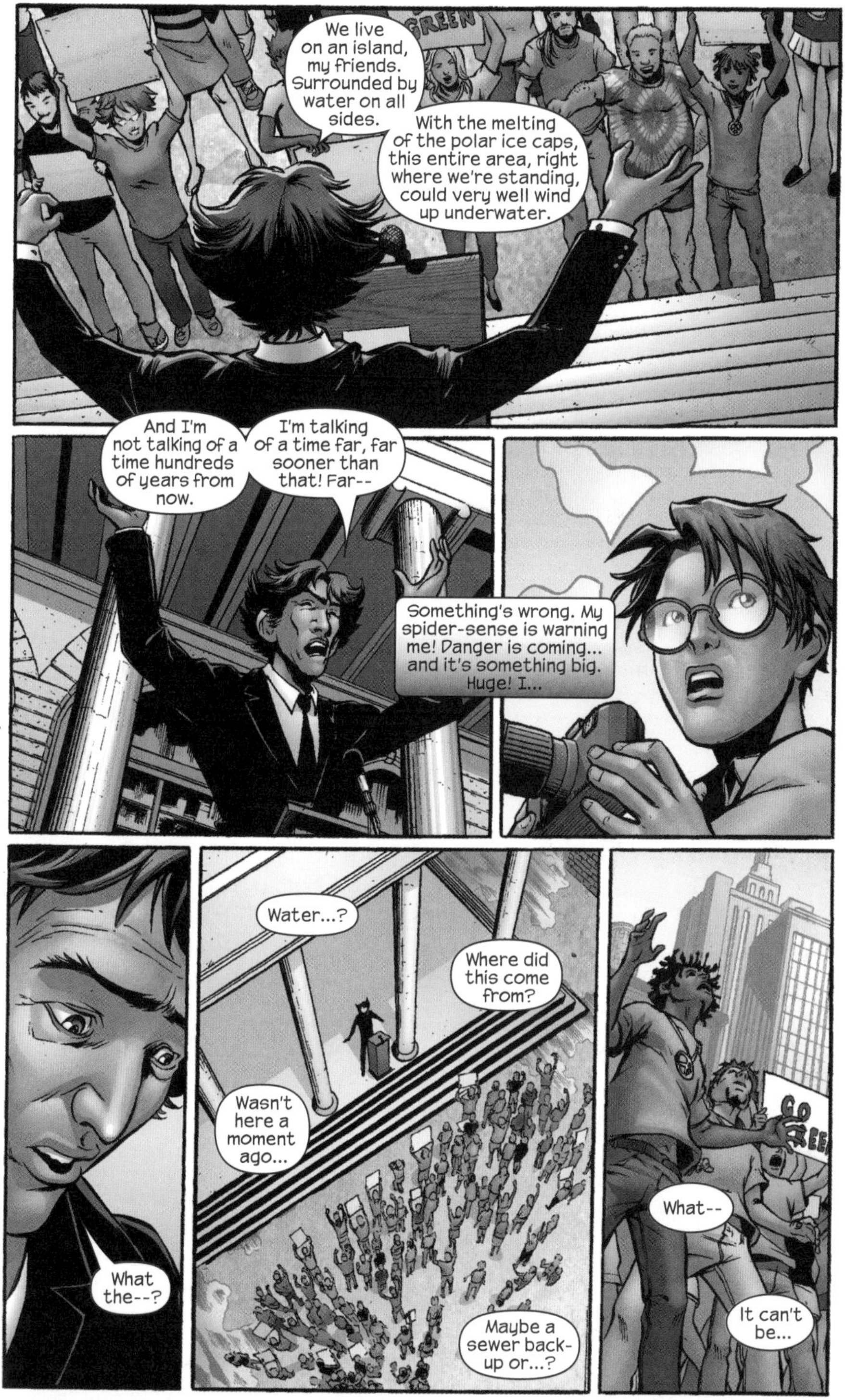

We live on an island, my friends. Surrounded by water on all sides.
With the melting of the polar ice caps, this entire area, right where we're standing, could very well wind up underwater.
GREEN
And I'm not talking of a time hundreds of years from now.
I'm talking of a time far, far sooner than that! Far--
Something's wrong. My spider-sense is warning me! Danger is coming... and it's something big. Huge! I...
What the--?
Water...?
Where did this come from?
Wasn't here a moment ago...
Maybe a sewer back-up or...?
What--
It can't be...

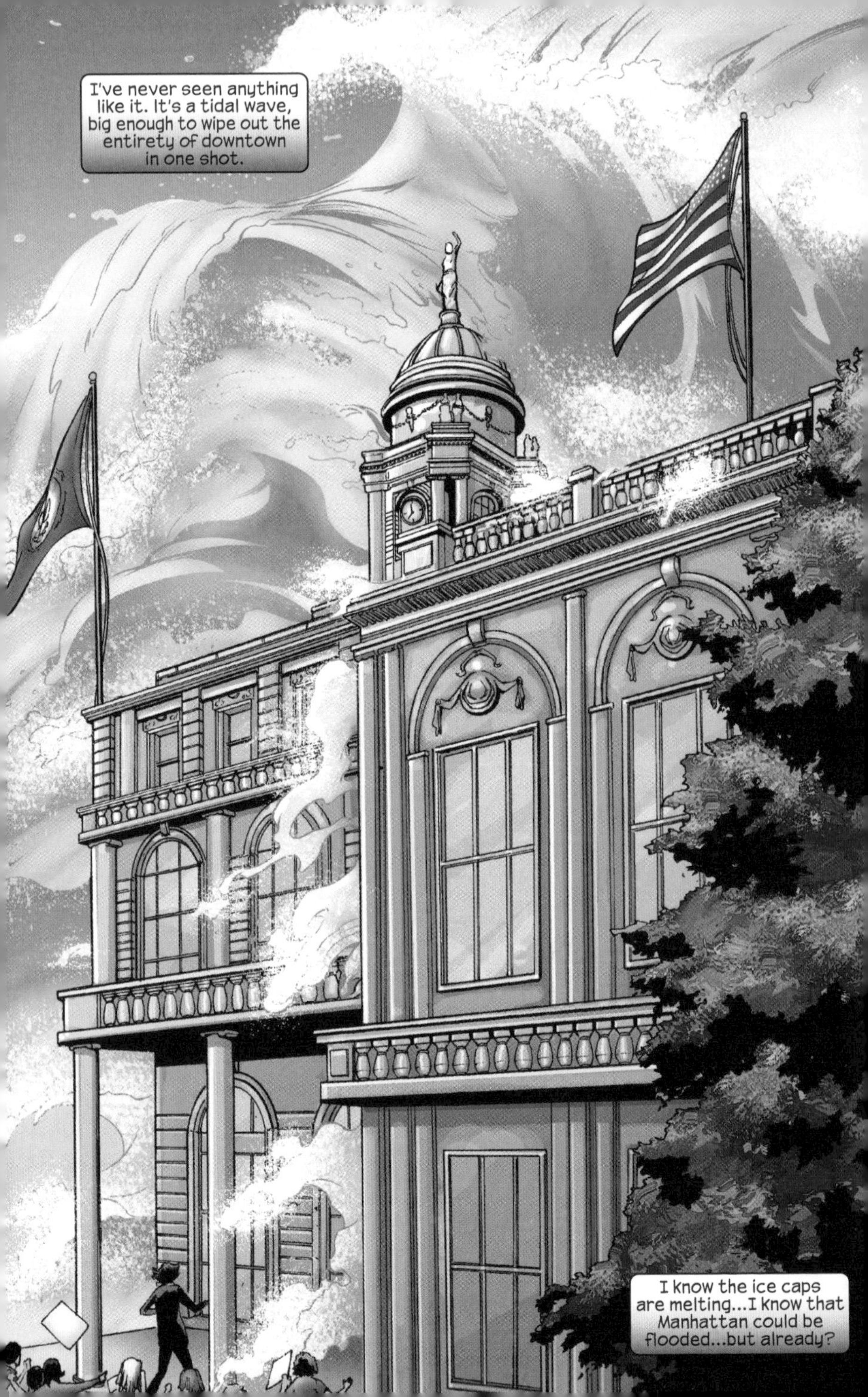
I've never seen anything like it. It's a tidal wave, big enough to wipe out the entirety of downtown in one shot.
I know the ice caps are melting...I know that Manhattan could be flooded...but already?

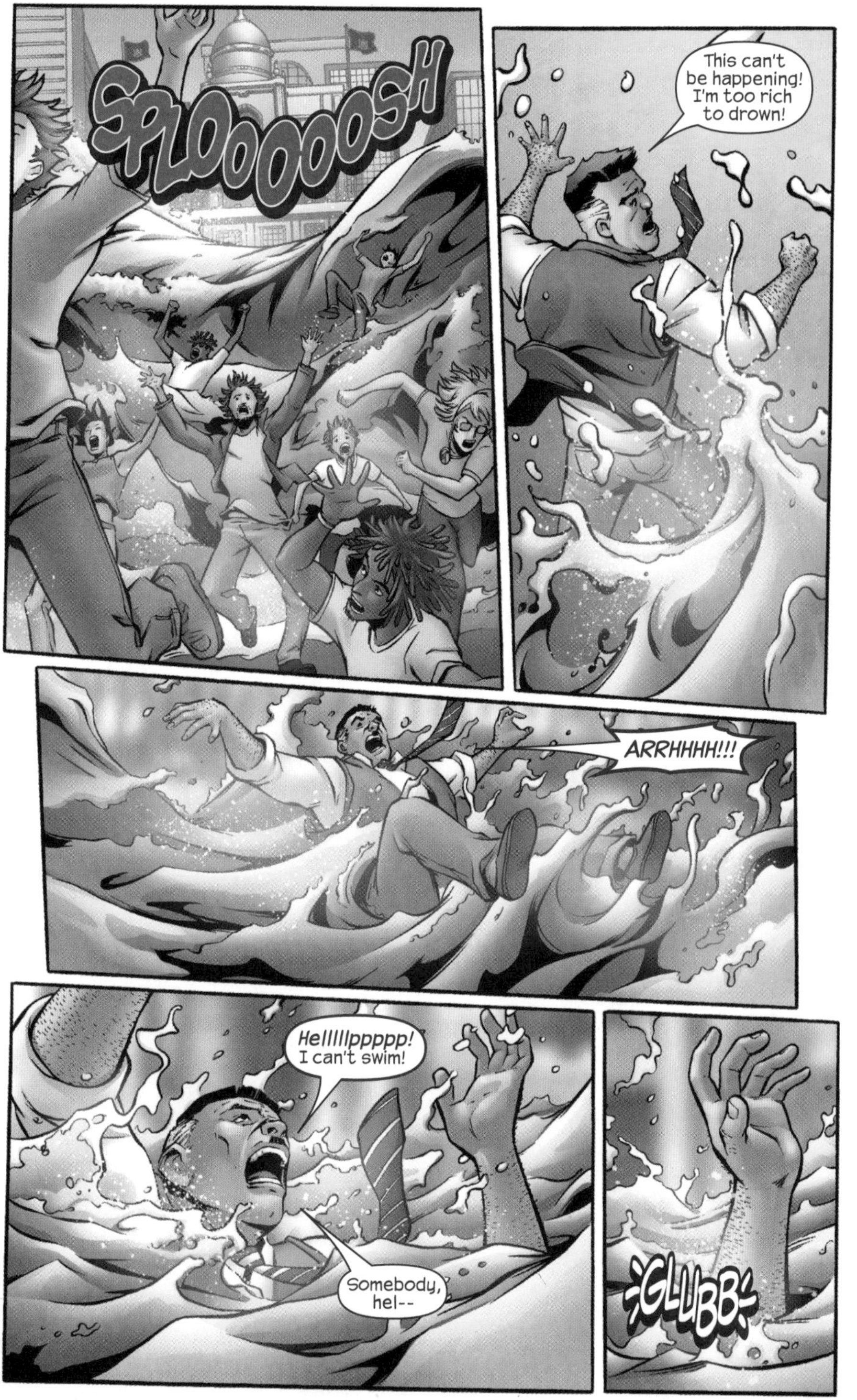
SPLOOOOOOSH
This can't be happening! I'm too rich to drown!
ARRHHHH!!!
Hellllllppppp! I can't swim!
Somebody, hel--
GLUBB

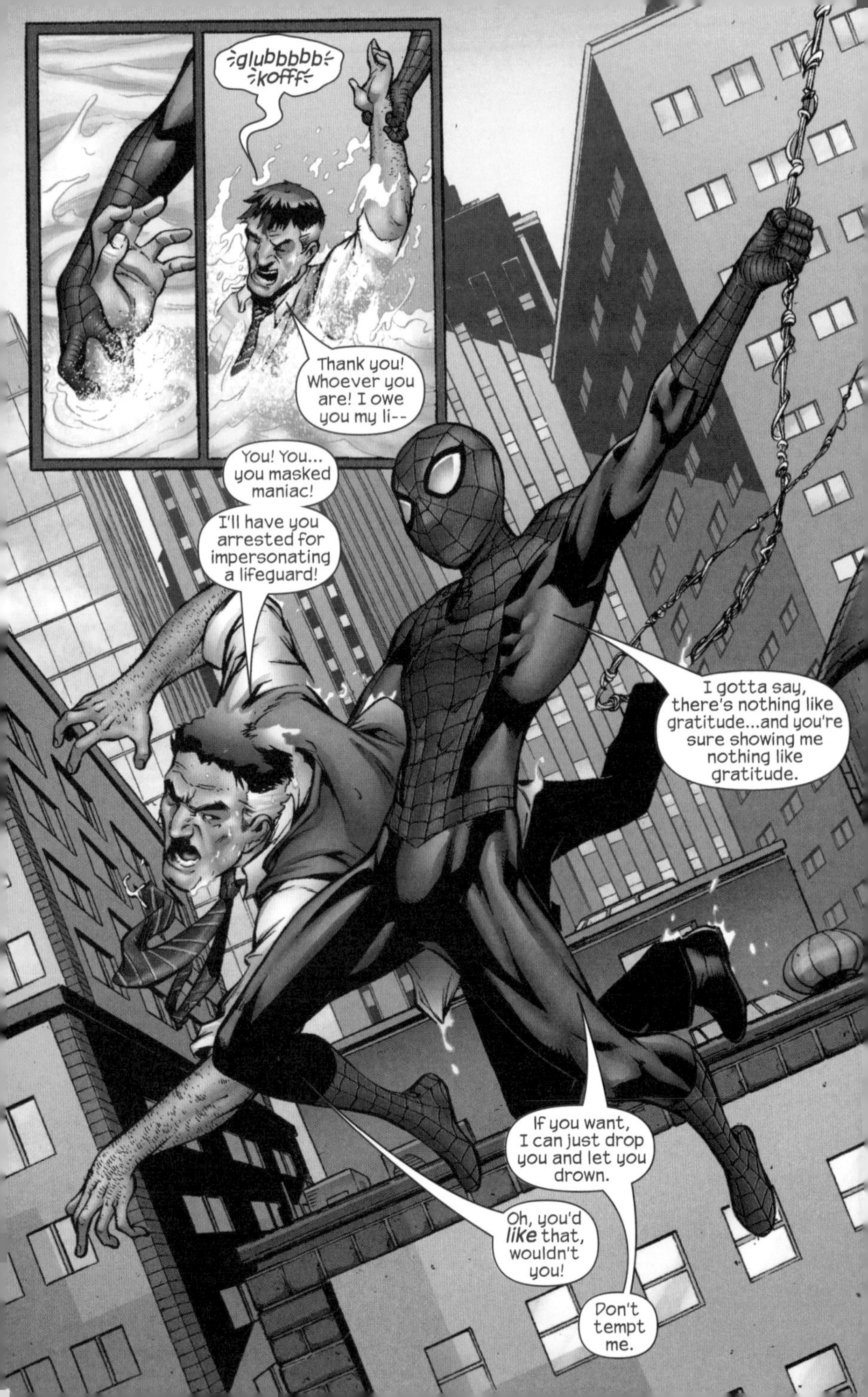
glubbbbb koffff
Thank you! Whoever you are! I owe you my li--
You! You... you masked maniac!
I'll have you arrested for impersonating a lifeguard!
I gotta say, there's nothing like gratitude...and you're sure showing me nothing like gratitude.
If you want, I can just drop you and let you drown.
Oh, you'd *like* that, wouldn't you!
Don't tempt me.

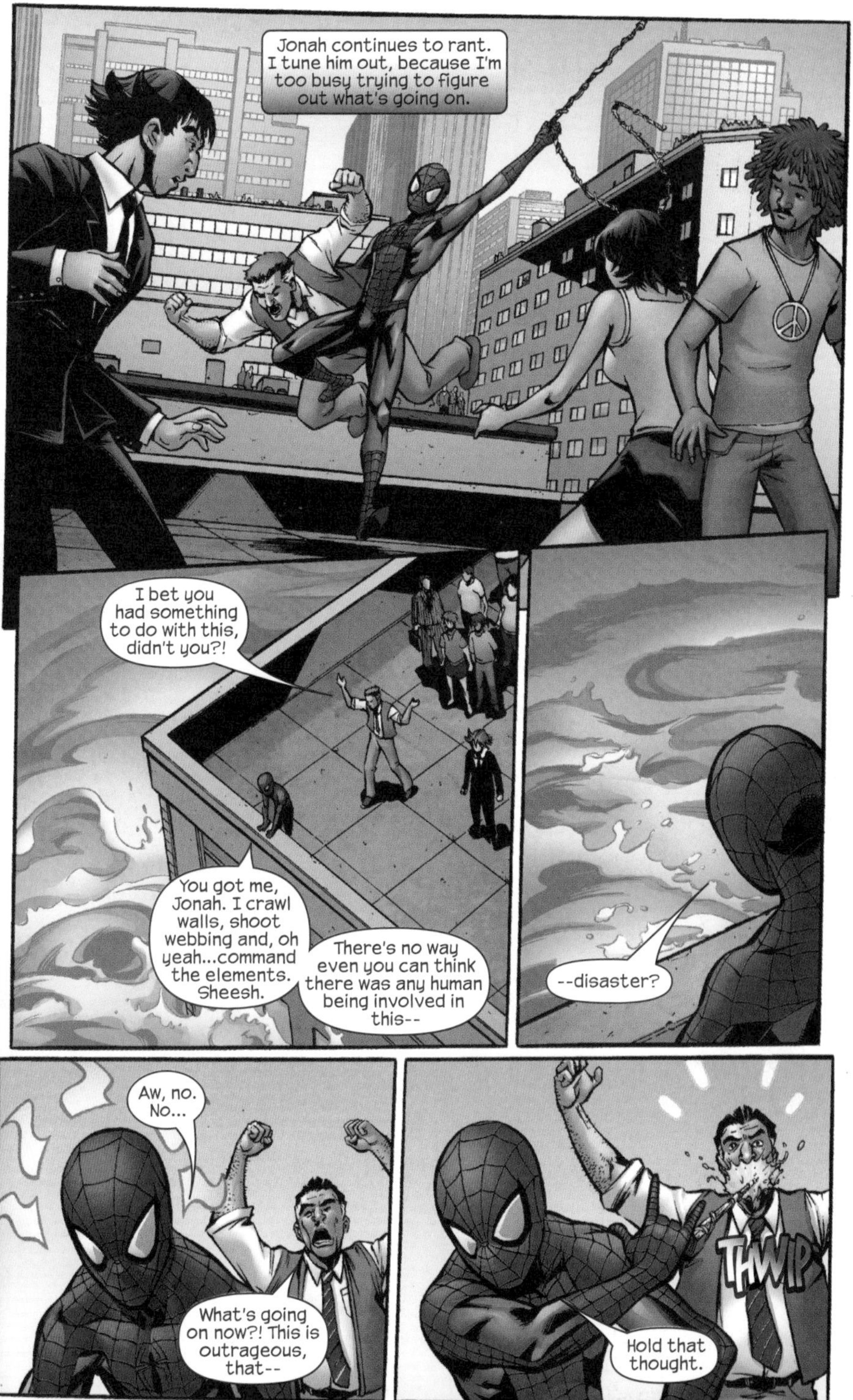
Jonah continues to rant. I tune him out, because I'm too busy trying to figure out what's going on.
I bet you had something to do with this, didn't you?!
You got me, Jonah. I crawl walls, shoot webbing and, oh yeah...command the elements. Sheesh.
There's no way even you can think there was any human being involved in this--
--disaster?
Aw, no. No...
What's going on now?! This is outrageous, that--
THWIP
Hold that thought.

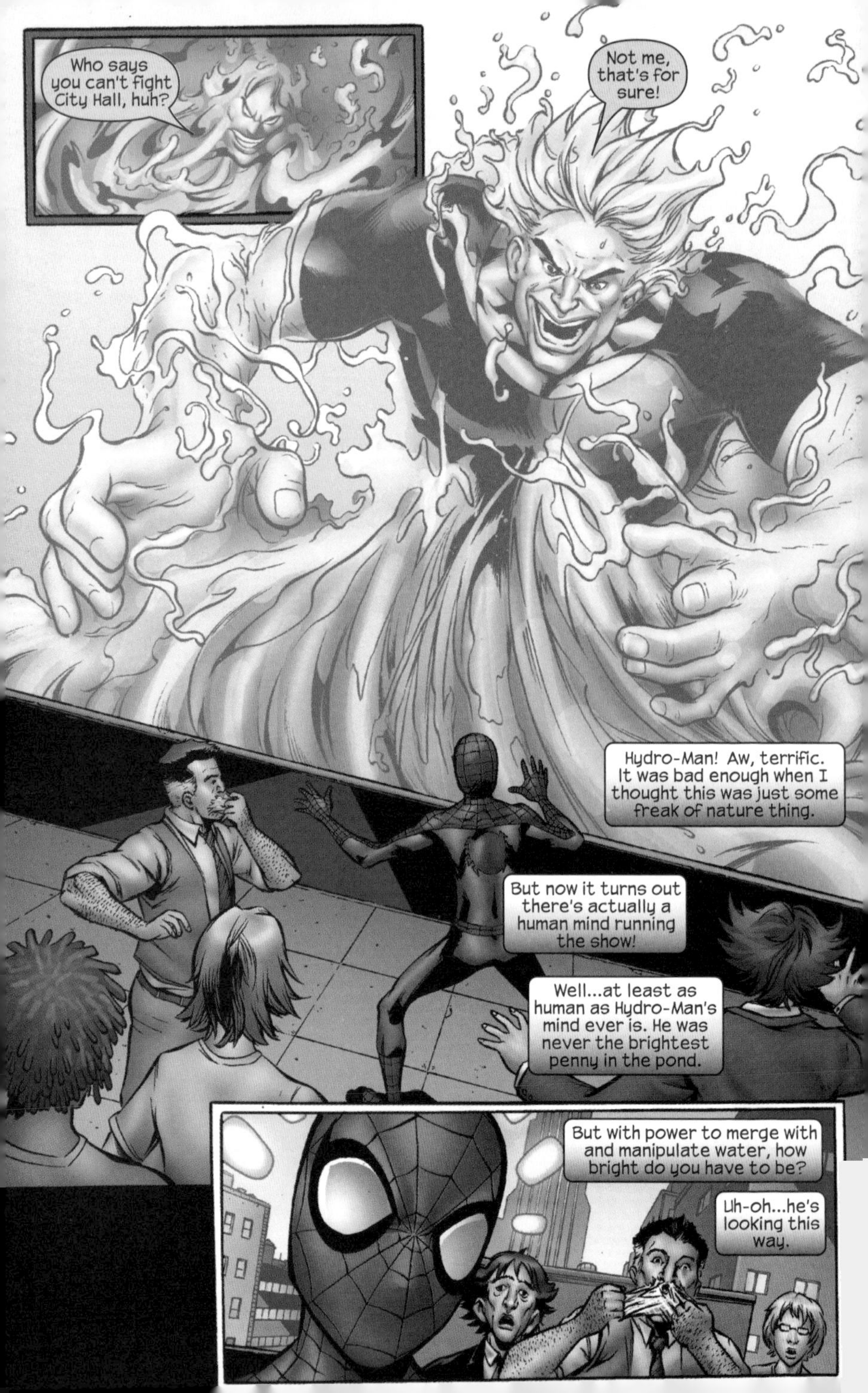
Who says you can't fight City Hall, huh?
Not me, that's for sure!
Hydro-Man! Aw, terrific. It was bad enough when I thought this was just some freak of nature thing.
But now it turns out there's actually a human mind running the show!
Well...at least as human as Hydro-Man's mind ever is. He was never the brightest penny in the pond.
But with power to merge with and manipulate water, how bright do you have to be?
Uh-oh...he's looking this way.

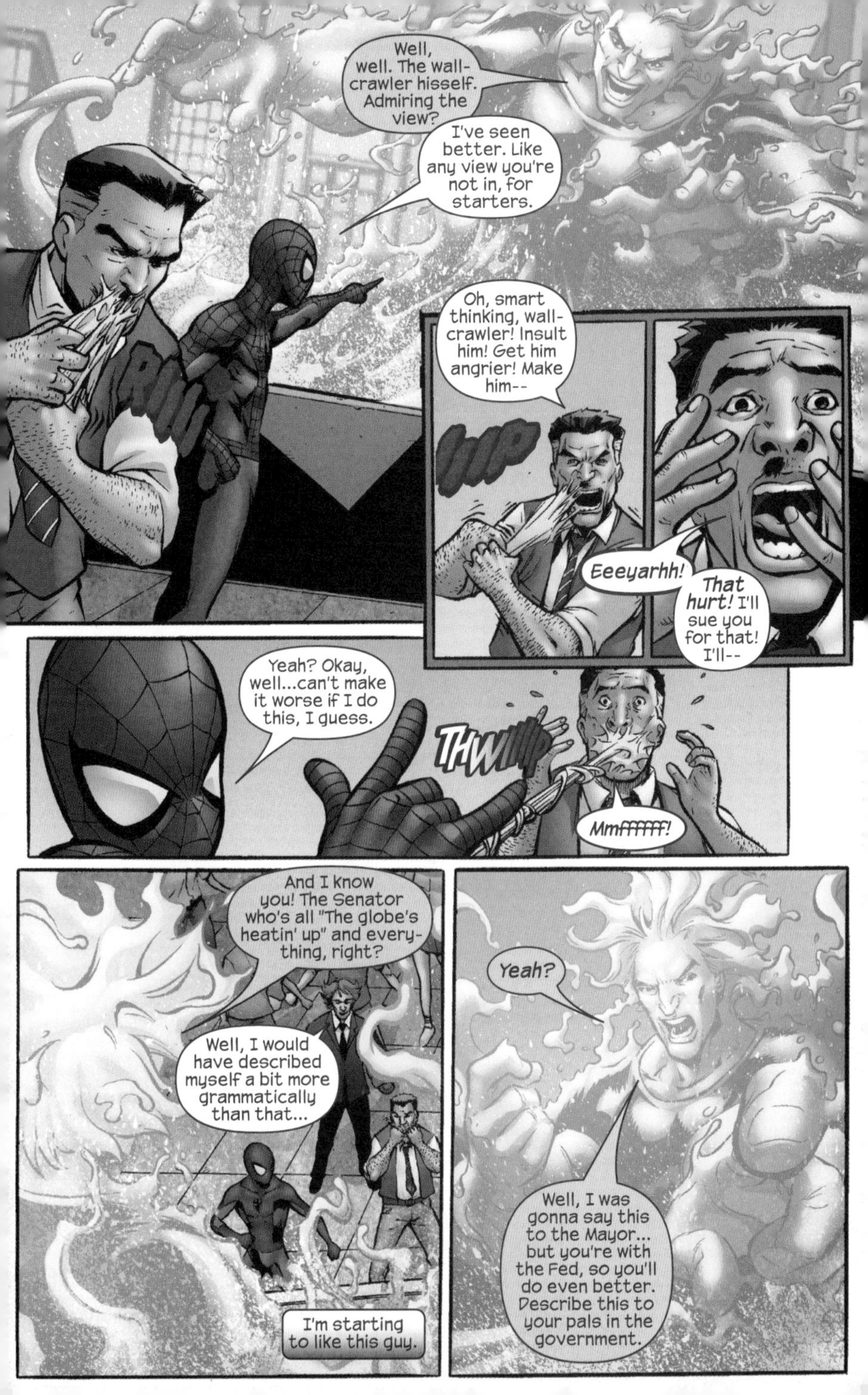

Well, well. The wall-crawler hisself. Admiring the view?
I've seen better. Like any view you're not in, for starters.
RIIIP
Oh, smart thinking, wall-crawler! Insult him! Get him angrier! Make him--
RIIIP
Eeeyarhh!
That hurt! I'll sue you for that! I'll--
Yeah? Okay, well...can't make it worse if I do this, I guess.
THWIIIP
Mmffffff!
And I know you! The Senator who's all "The globe's heatin' up" and every-thing, right?
Well, I would have described myself a bit more grammatically than that...
I'm starting to like this guy.
Yeah?
Well, I was gonna say this to the Mayor... but you're with the Fed, so you'll do even better. Describe this to your pals in the government.

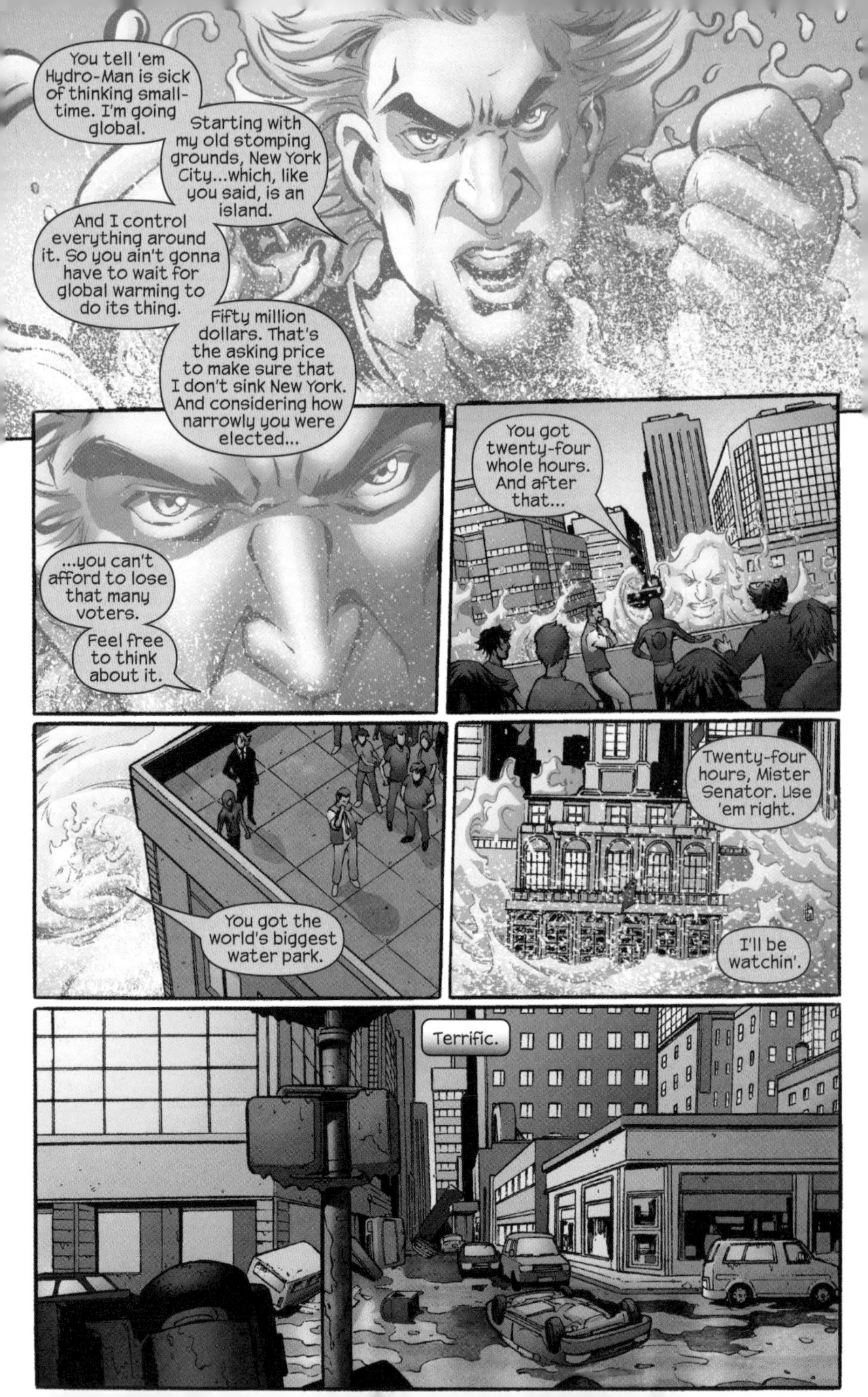

You tell 'em Hydro-Man is sick of thinking small-time. I'm going global.
Starting with my old stomping grounds, New York City...which, like you said, is an island.
And I control everything around it. So you ain't gonna have to wait for global warming to do its thing.
Fifty million dollars. That's the asking price to make sure that I don't sink New York. And considering how narrowly you were elected...
...you can't afford to lose that many voters.
Feel free to think about it.
You got twenty-four whole hours. And after that...
You got the world's biggest water park.
Twenty-four hours, Mister Senator. Use 'em right.
I'll be watchin'.
Terrific.

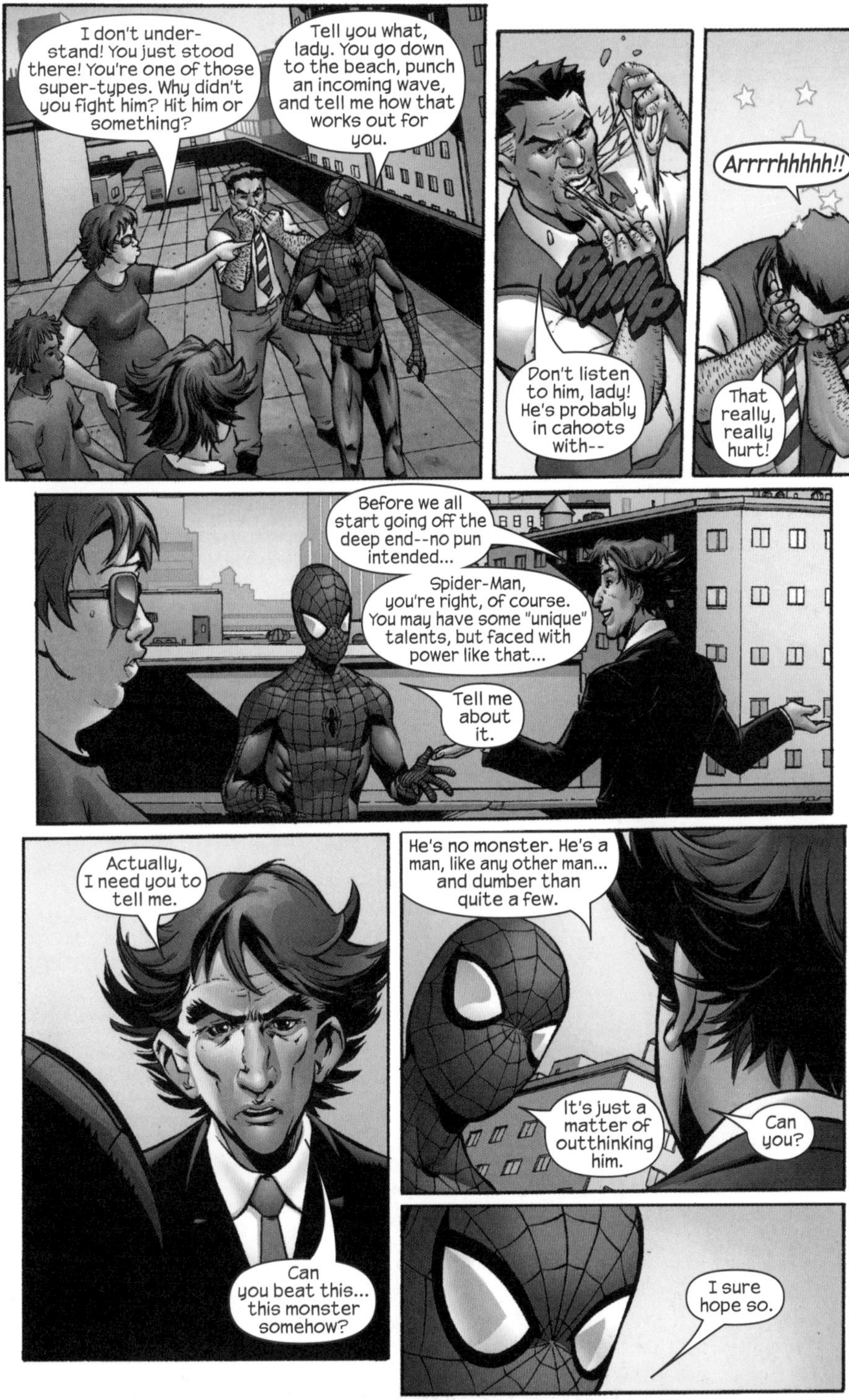
I don't under-stand! You just stood there! You're one of those super-types. Why didn't you fight him? Hit him or something?
Tell you what, lady. You go down to the beach, punch an incoming wave, and tell me how that works out for you.
RIIIIP
Don't listen to him, lady! He's probably in cahoots with--
Arrrrhhhhh!!
That really, really hurt!
Before we all start going off the deep end--no pun intended...
Spider-Man, you're right, of course. You may have some "unique" talents, but faced with power like that...
Tell me about it.
Actually, I need you to tell me.
Can you beat this... this monster somehow?
He's no monster. He's a man, like any other man... and dumber than quite a few.
It's just a matter of outthinking him.
Can you?
I sure hope so.

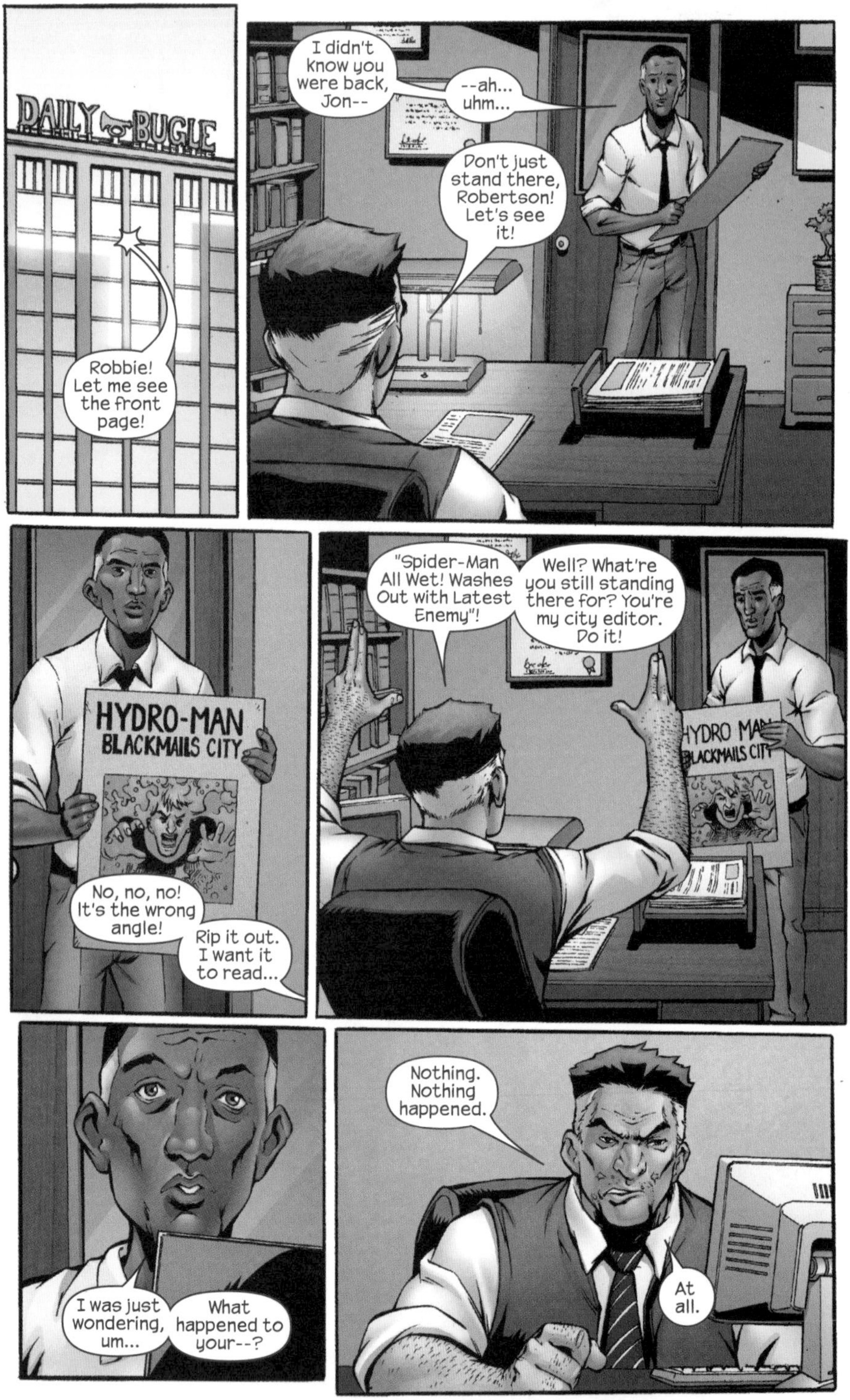

DAILY BUGLE
Robbie! Let me see the front page!
I didn't know you were back, Jon--
--ah... uhm...
Don't just stand there, Robertson! Let's see it!
HYDRO-MAN BLACKMAILS CITY
No, no, no! It's the wrong angle!
Rip it out. I want it to read...
"Spider-Man All Wet! Washes Out with Latest Enemy"!
Well? What're you still standing there for? You're my city editor. Do it!
I was just wondering, um...
What happened to your--?
Nothing. Nothing happened.
At all.

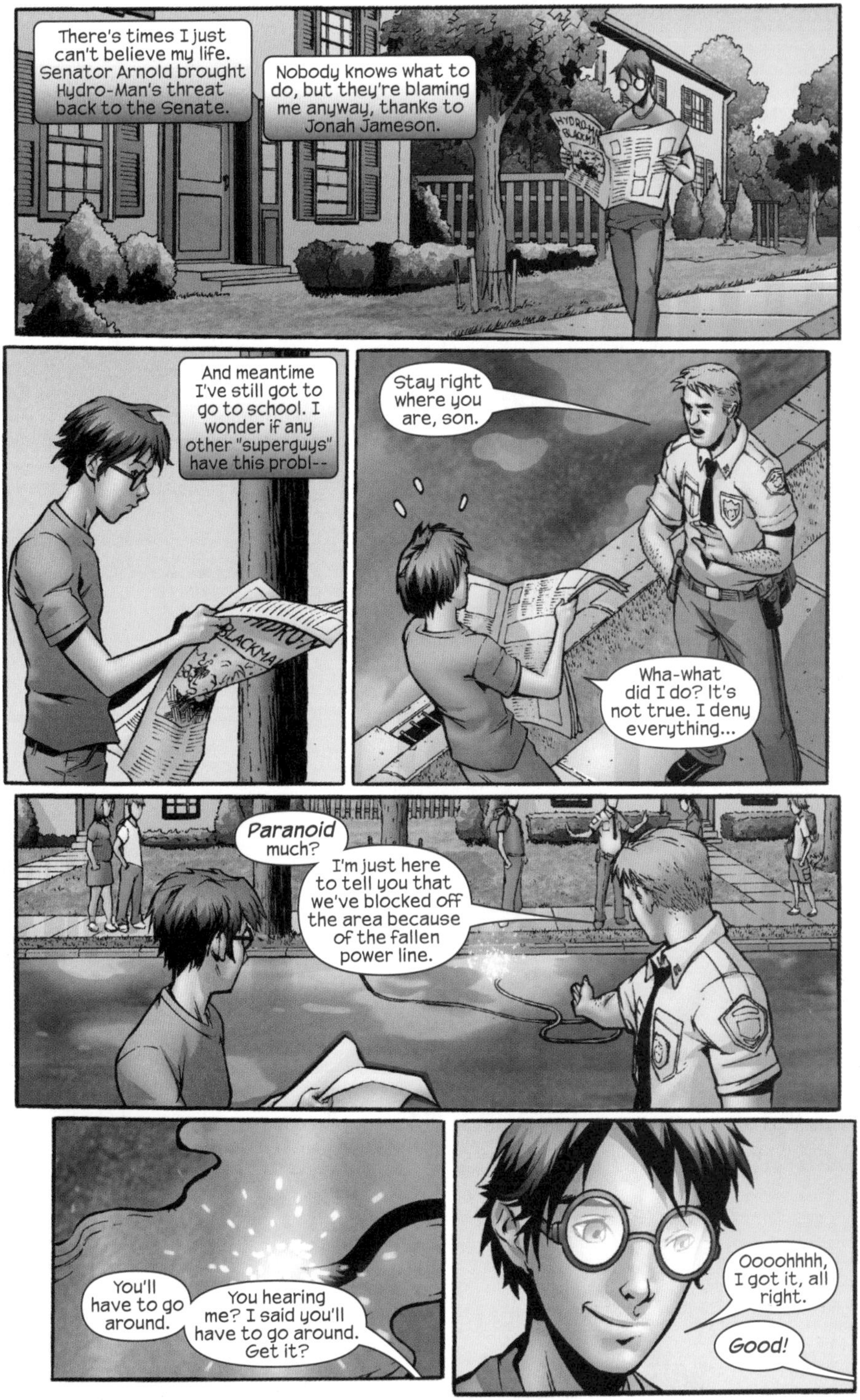
There's times I just can't believe my life. Senator Arnold brought Hydro-Man's threat back to the Senate.
Nobody knows what to do, but they're blaming me anyway, thanks to Jonah Jameson.
And meantime I've still got to go to school. I wonder if any other "superguys" have this probl--
Stay right where you are, son.
Wha-what did I do? It's not true. I deny everything...
Paranoid much?
I'm just here to tell you that we've blocked off the area because of the fallen power line.
You'll have to go around.
You hearing me? I said you'll have to go around. Get it?
Oooohhhh, I got it, all right.
Good!

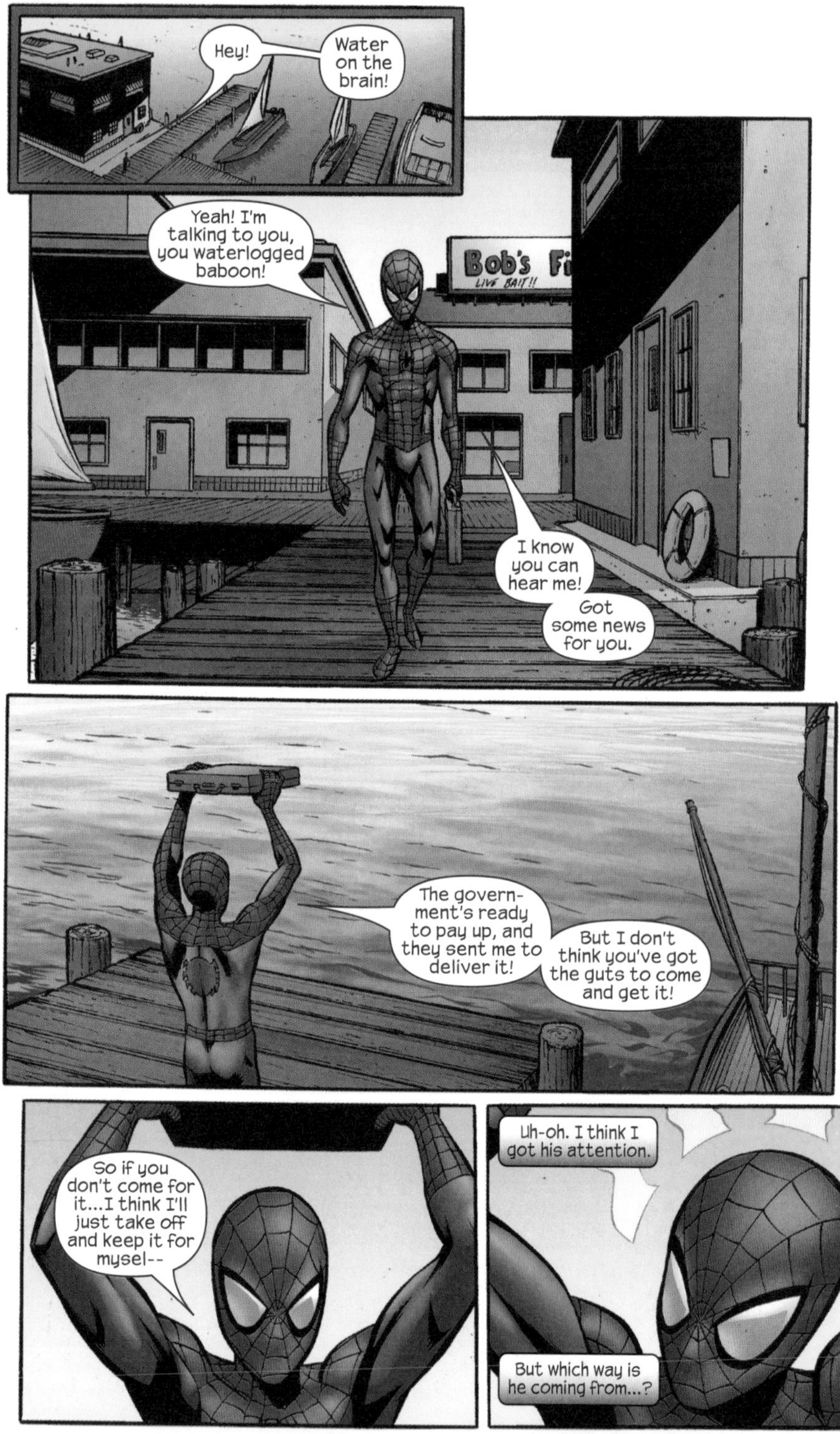
Hey!
Water on the brain!
Yeah! I'm talking to you, you waterlogged baboon!
Bob's Fi
LIVE BAIT!!
I know you can hear me!
Got some news for you.
The government's ready to pay up, and they sent me to deliver it!
But I don't think you've got the guts to come and get it!
So if you don't come for it...I think I'll just take off and keep it for mysel--
Uh-oh. I think I got his attention.
But which way is he coming from...?

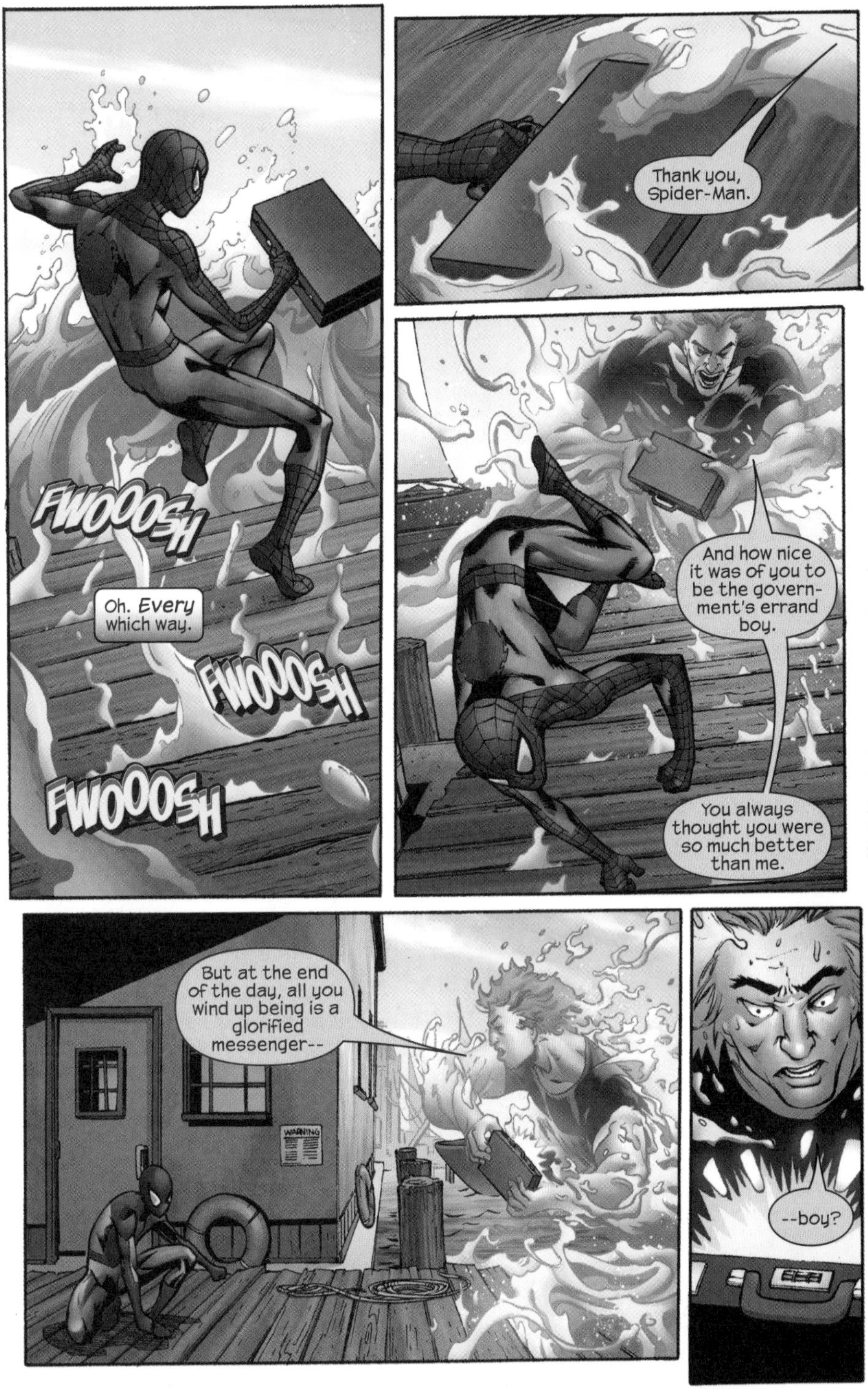
FWOOOSH
Oh. Every which way.
FWOOOSH
FWOOOSH
Thank you, Spider-Man.
And how nice it was of you to be the government's errand boy.
You always thought you were so much better than me.
But at the end of the day, all you wind up being is a glorified messenger--
WARNING
--boy?

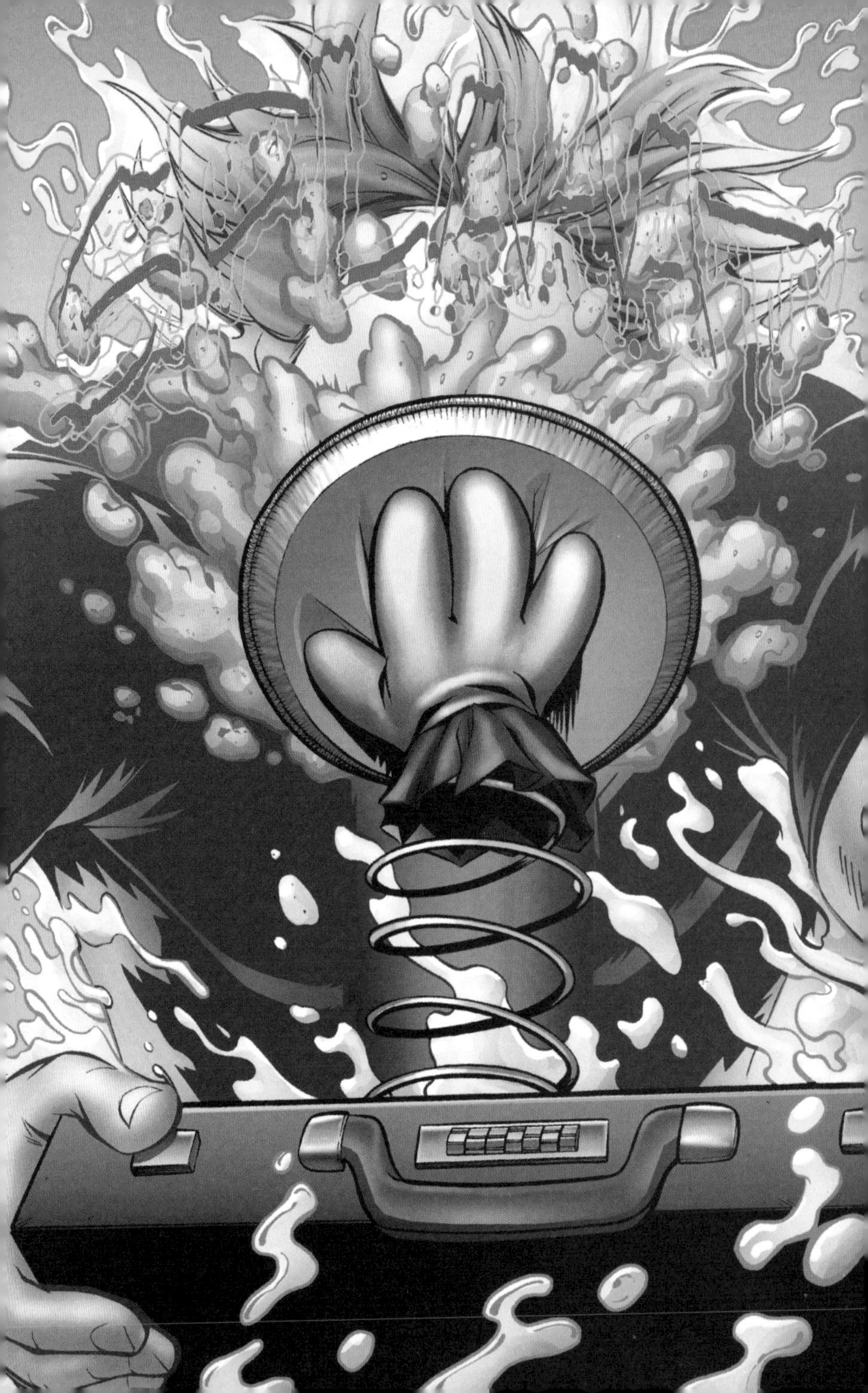

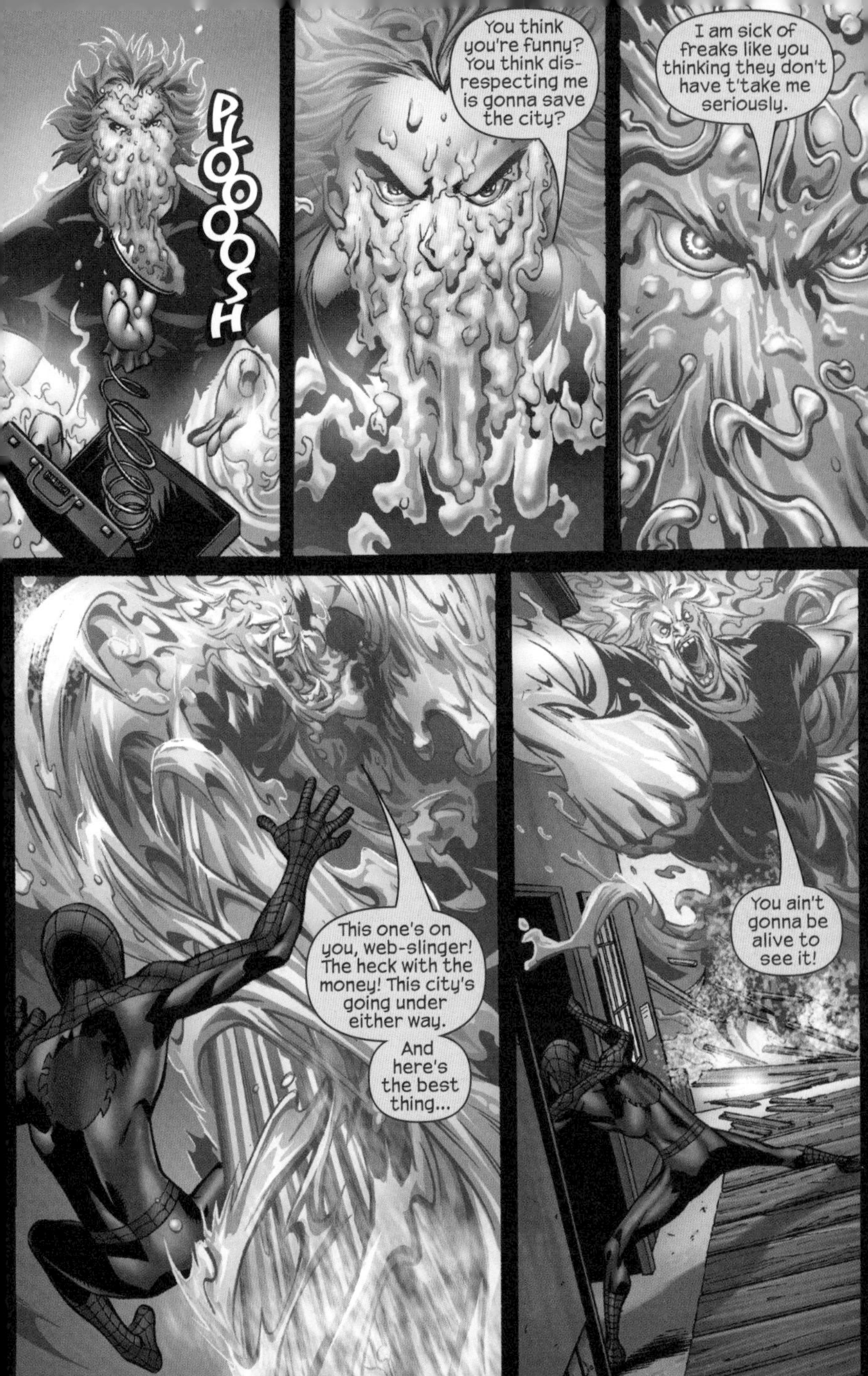
PLOOOOSH
You think you're funny? You think dis-respecting me is gonna save the city?
I am sick of freaks like you thinking they don't have t'take me seriously.
This one's on you, web-slinger! The heck with the money! This city's going under either way.
And here's the best thing...
You ain't gonna be alive to see it!

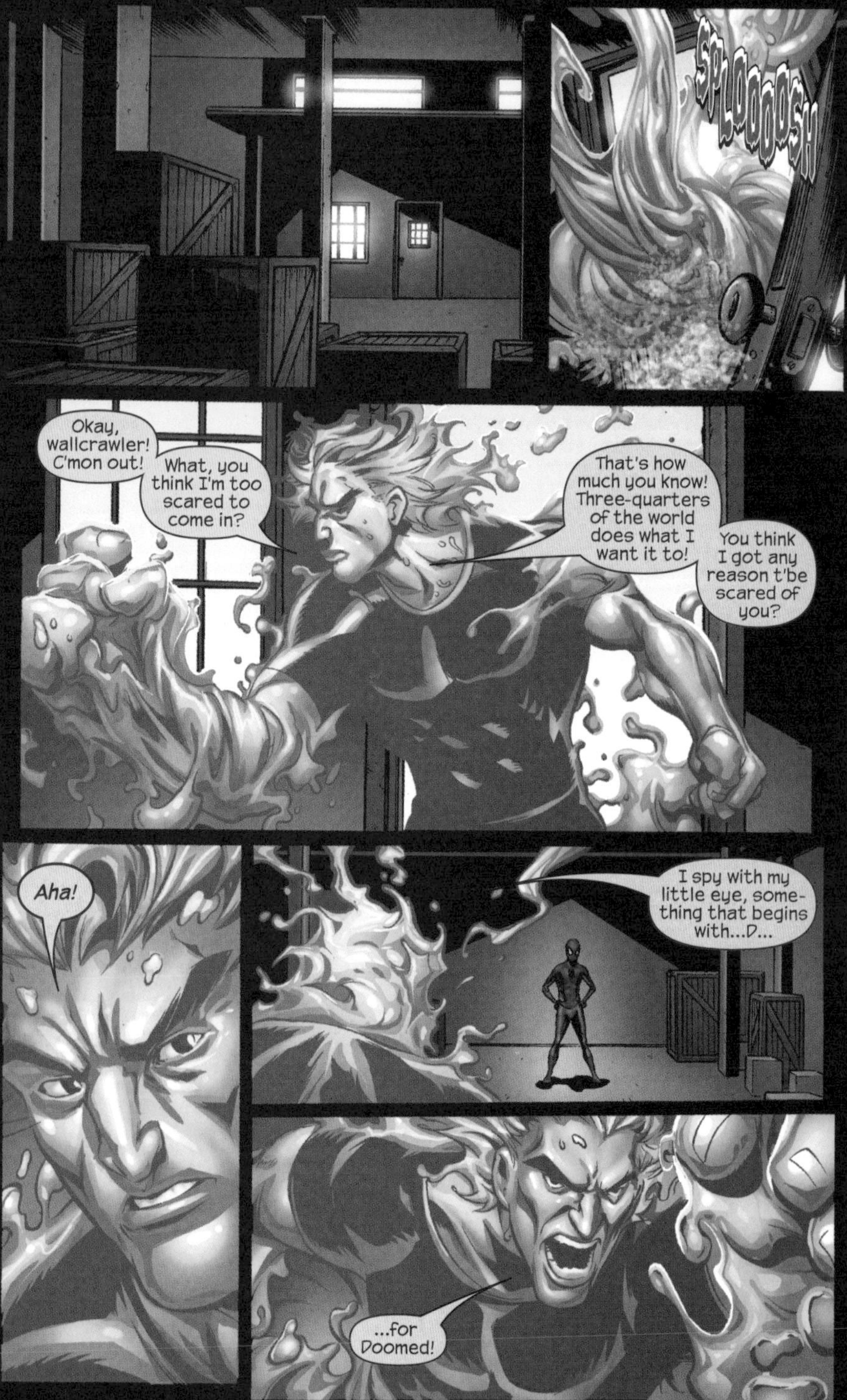
SPLOOOOSH
Okay, wallcrawler! C'mon out!
What, you think I'm too scared to come in?
That's how much you know! Three-quarters of the world does what I want it to!
You think I got any reason t'be scared of you?
Aha!
I spy with my little eye, something that begins with...D...
...for Doomed!

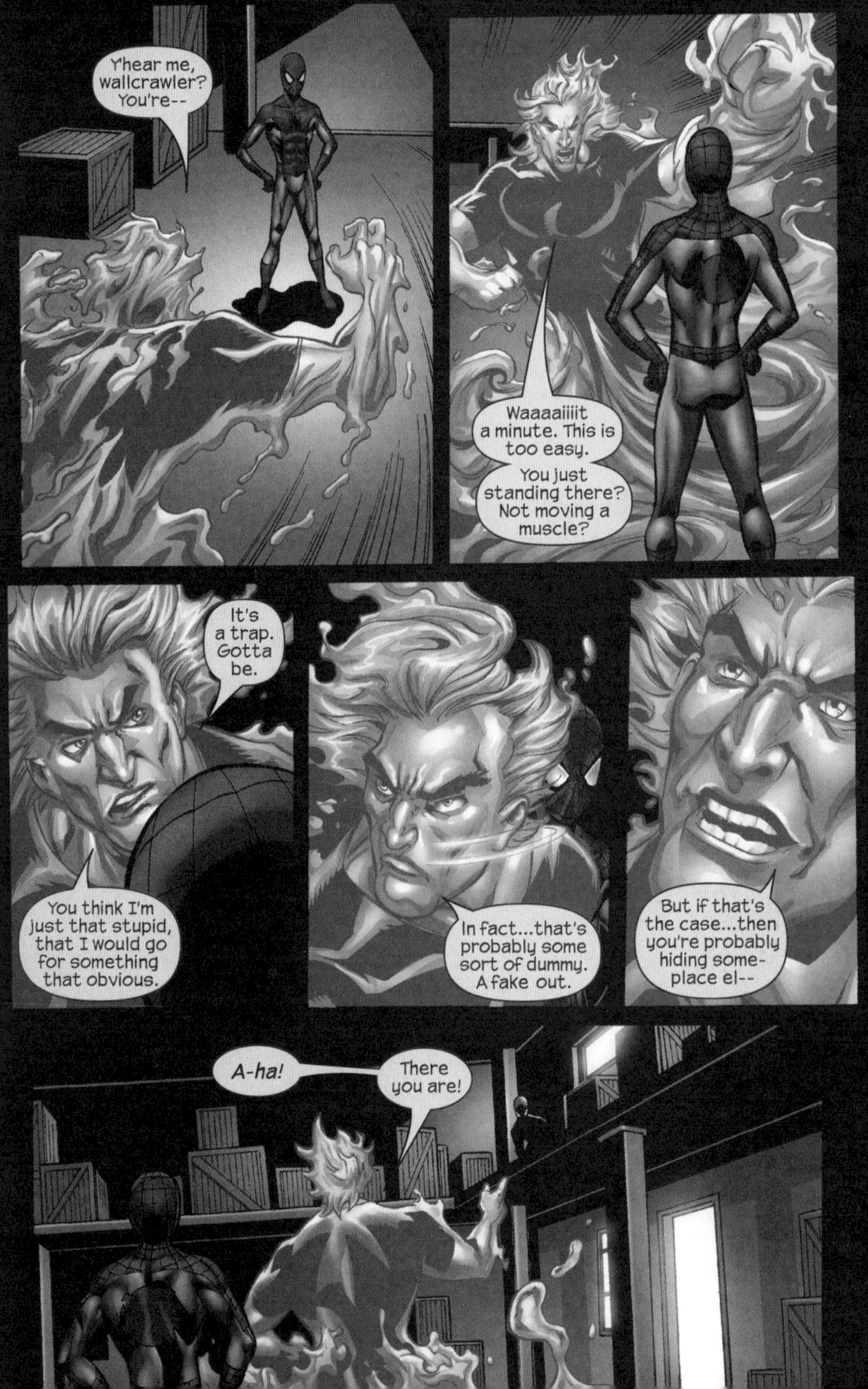
Y'hear me, wallcrawler? You're--
Waaaaiiiit a minute. This is too easy.
You just standing there? Not moving a muscle?
It's a trap. Gotta be.
You think I'm just that stupid, that I would go for something that obvious.
In fact...that's probably some sort of dummy. A fake out.
But if that's the case...then you're probably hiding some-place el--
A-ha!
There you are!

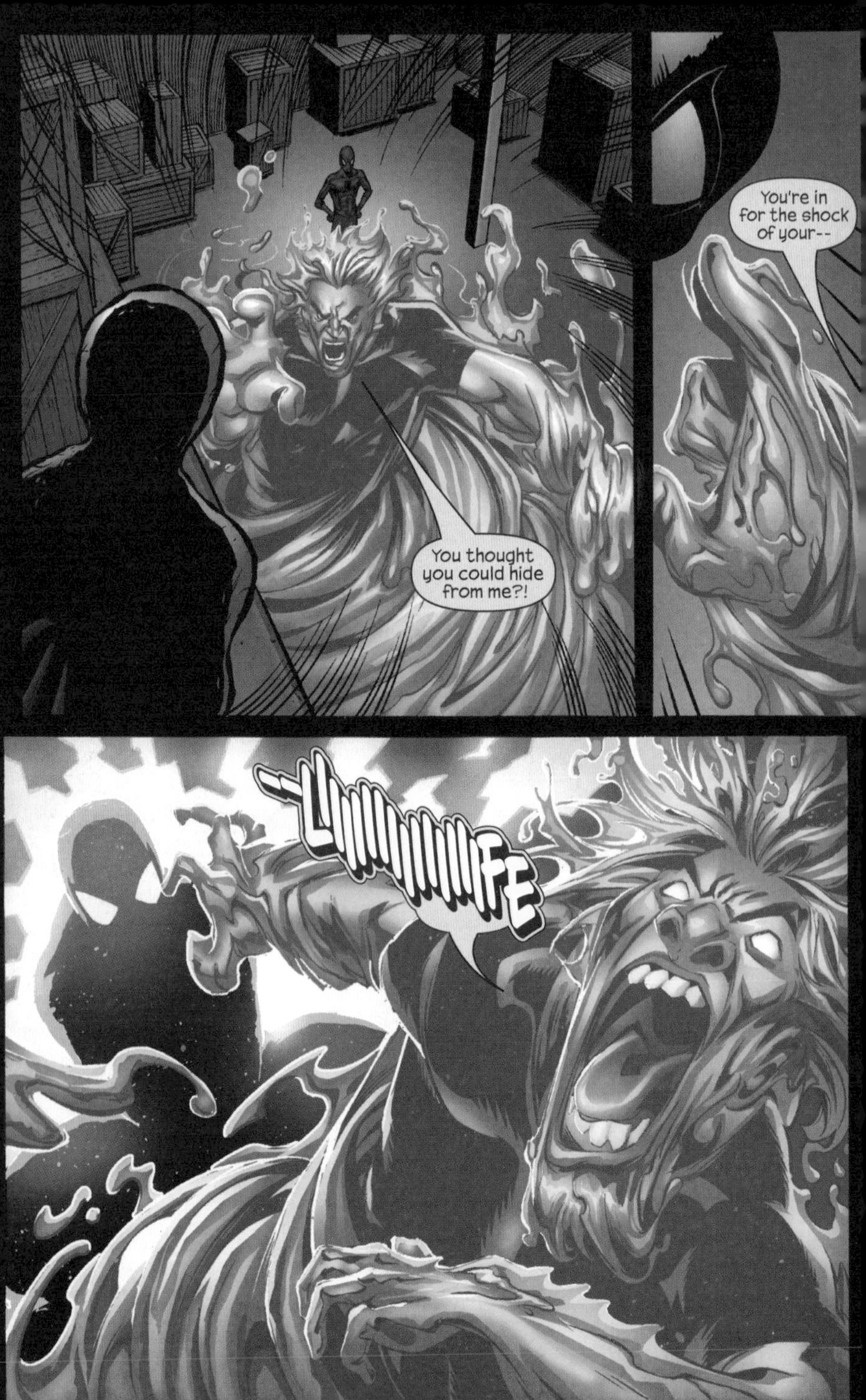
You thought you could hide from me?!
You're in for the shock of your--
--LIIIIIIIIIFE

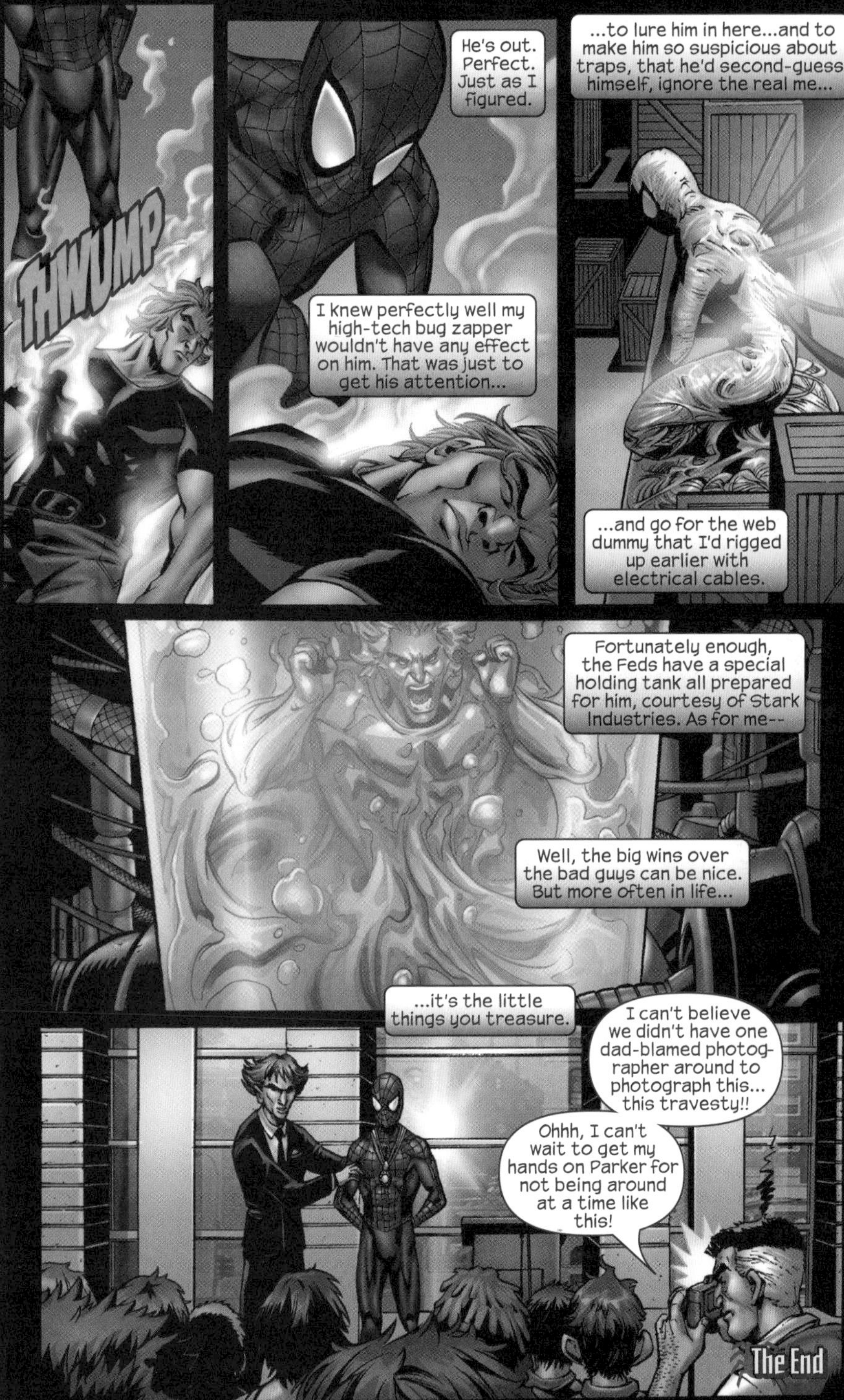
THWUMP
He's out. Perfect. Just as I figured.
I knew perfectly well my high-tech bug zapper wouldn't have any effect on him. That was just to get his attention...
...to lure him in here...and to make him so suspicious about traps, that he'd second-guess himself, ignore the real me...
...and go for the web dummy that I'd rigged up earlier with electrical cables.
Fortunately enough, the Feds have a special holding tank all prepared for him, courtesy of Stark Industries. As for me--
Well, the big wins over the bad guys can be nice. But more often in life...
...it's the little things you treasure.
I can't believe we didn't have one dad-blamed photographer around to photograph this... this travesty!!
Ohhh, I can't wait to get my hands on Parker for not being around at a time like this!
The End

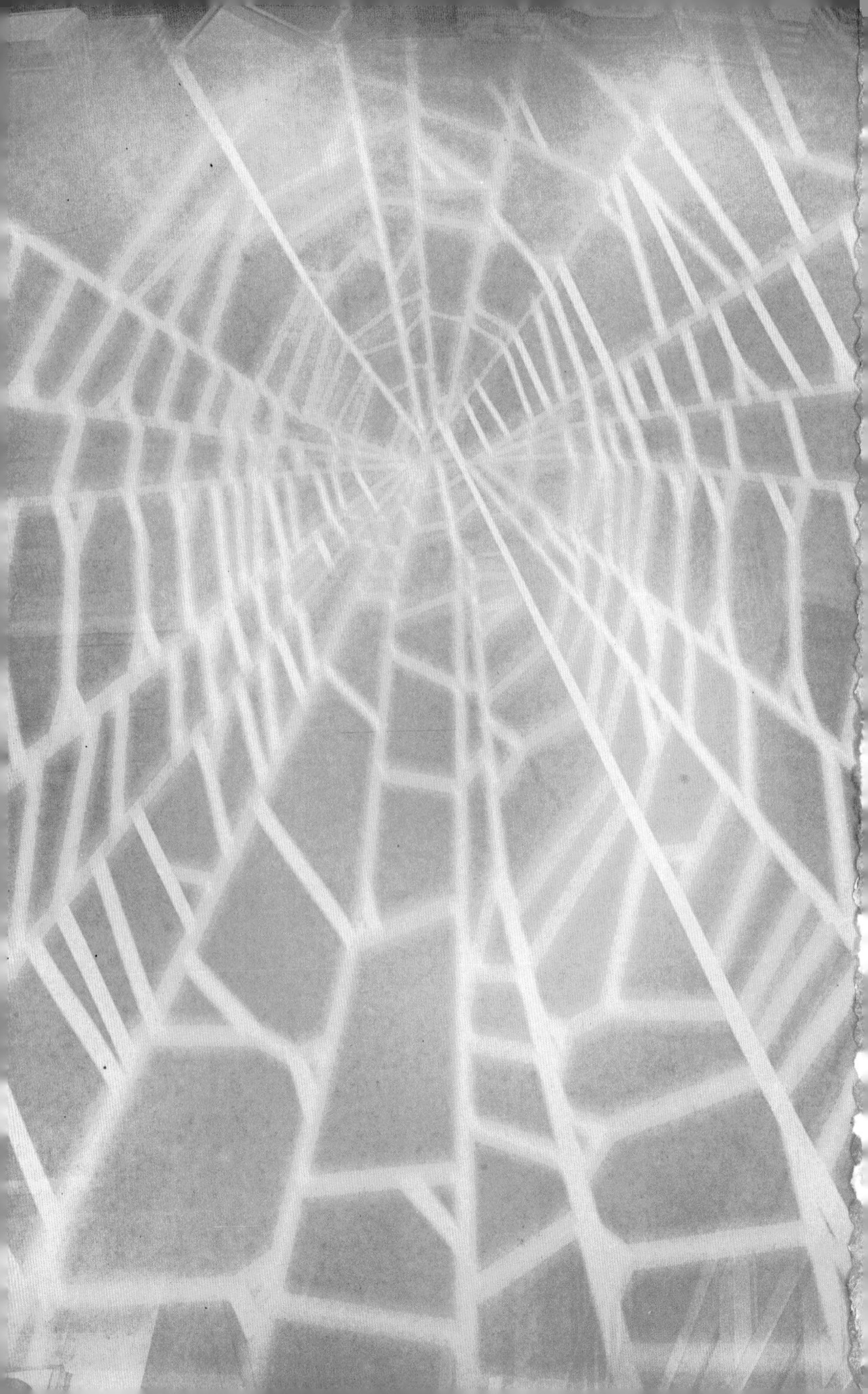